THE MAGPIE

MARRISSE WHITTAKER

BLOODHOUND
— BOOKS —

Print ISBN 978-1-913942-52-6

Bob Whittaker – Love of my life

1

RED SKY IN THE MORNING, SHEPHERDS' WARNING

It was a crazy day right from the start, the day that Billie Wilde discovered she had been erased from history. Snuffed out. Not even a single fragrant posy to mark her premature burial place.

At first light that morning, the sky had been indigo-bruised, streaked with vivid crimson gashes as bright as freshly spilled blood. *Red sky in the morning, shepherds' warning.* The rhyme had momentarily skipped through Billie's head as fragmented memories of the night before slashed through her addled brain.

She winced, trying to focus on the already heavy traffic at this early hour. Had she really been strutting to 'Murder on the Dancefloor' in that sleazy bar that Kate, her new housemate, had dragged her to? She only remembered having downed one cocktail. She shuddered to think what on earth was in the brightly coloured concoction.

'You okay?' Kate sounded chirpy enough, although she had stayed back when Billie had staggered off in search of a taxi. She had only arrived home about an hour ago, just in time to shower and hitch a ride with Billie.

'Brain-dead and I'm blaming you. I hope to God I didn't bump into anyone I know on the way home.'

'Lightweight.' Kate giggled. 'You need to get out more and I don't just mean dreary dinner parties. After you left, we had a wild time.' Kate clicked on her mobile phone. The sound of children singing an a cappella version of the ancient magpie counting nursery rhyme filled the car. It sounded hauntingly beautiful.

'My bad girls are singing this in a schools' choir competition. They almost sound angelic.' She laughed. 'No one would guess that they're all devils, excluded from mainstream education. That's why I chose this. Magpies, they're thieves and killers, my dad always says.'

'Looked like there were a few of them in that bar last night. I'm amazed I didn't recognise anyone I've arrested.'

It was her first day back on her job heading up the local Murder Investigation Team after enforced time out, yet if trouble loomed, she knew that she would risk being sent to the doghouse yet again. Absolutely nothing would stand in the way of her taking out the scum who preyed on vulnerable souls.

'I used to sing this rhyme to my baby sis to get her to sleep – One for sorrow...' Kate's half sung words spilled out like an uncanny prediction, as a black Mini sporting white go-faster stripes stole a reckless, lightning path across the lane ahead. It skidded with a sickening crash into the side of a soft-topped Mazda, pecking the head clean off the nearside passenger.

A bolt of raw adrenaline shot through Billie's veins. She slammed on the brakes and flung open her car door to a cacophony of screeching tyres and car horns. The smell and taste of damp rubber and exhaust fumes caught her breath as vehicles all around screamed to a halt. Billie vaulted over the bonnet of a still moving car, sprinted to the Mazda and swung open the driver's door. The woman inside was screaming, hysterical.

'It's okay.' Billie reached for her ID. 'Police.' The woman driver turned to her passenger and let out an even more distraught wail. Billie braced herself and glanced across.

'We had a date today at Scotswood Old People's Home.' The woman sobbed. 'What the hell am I supposed to do now? I can't bloody juggle or tap dance!'

Billie breathed a sigh of relief. She reached over and unclipped the seat belt, hauling out a decapitated ventriloquist's dummy. She held it high for the surrounding motorists to see. The dummy's head had landed in the foot well. Billie grabbed the grinning face by its flame-orange hair, stuffing it back onto the red-and-white-football-strip-clad body.

'There gans another Makem supporter off his nut!' one nearby wag shouted.

'Looks like another manager's got the chop!' another side-splitter joined in.

Billie rolled her eyes. In this part of the world, few incidents, no matter how horrific, passed by without an opportunity for banter between arch-rival football supporters of clubs Sunderland, the Makems and Newcastle, the Magpies. She tried to hide a grin at the absurdity of the situation, relieved that no real harm appeared to have been done.

The feeling lasted only seconds, as a harrowing wail alerted Billie now to the Mini driver, who had staggered from his car. Billie dropped the dummy and raced to him.

'Are you okay?' Billie's voice was calm. 'No bleeding?' Her eyes swept his body, looking for any injuries. He was wearing a woolly Newcastle United hat, pulled down low, matching scarf pulled high and astonishingly thick jam-jar specs. Billie decided to leave it to the hard-pressed traffic team to work out if his garb had affected his ability to drive in a straight line. She much preferred heading up the Murder Squad.

The man suddenly retched. Last night's vindaloo landed slap on Billie's new suede boots. *Happy Monday*, she silently greeted the start to the week. The agitated man pulled up his scarf once more, wiping his mouth as he pointed over her shoulder.

'*That's* what made me lose control!'

Billie glanced behind her. The huge shadow of the Angel of the North, Antony Gormley's magnificent sculpture, 66 feet tall and 177 feet wide, loomed on a hill above the road.

'Calm down.' Billie's voice was firm. She didn't fancy more projectile vomit heading her way. 'It's only the Angel.' The man shook his head, his voice muffled through shock or the thickness of his scarf, Billie wasn't sure which.

'No. That's the work of the Devil!' He pointed up again, as a shard of morning light pierced the dawn sky, catching the shape of something high up, fastened to the sculpture. It looked like a small rag doll; arms outstretched. Billie felt her heart hit the floor. She prayed that she was mistaken, but she'd seen enough in her police career to have her suspicions that the man was right. The body of a child appeared to be hanging up there in a horrible parody of the angel.

'Stay right here,' she commanded. She could already hear sirens, hopefully heading in their direction. Kate jogged up alongside her.

'I can give you a hand. I've got my emergency first-aid certificate,' Kate offered.

'Follow me,' Billie whispered. She leaped over the barrier dividing the two carriageways and wove between cars heading at speed in the opposite direction. Kate was hot on her heels. They scrambled up the slippery grass and shrub-covered slope leading to the foot of the iconic Angel of the North sculpture.

The child, for now it was horrifically clear that it was a flesh-

and-blood child, was hanging above them, attached with some sort of twine or wire. The ends of the dreadful bindings dangled down, presenting a sick distortion of a puppet, suspended by strings. The child's painfully thin arms and legs swung slowly, tugged by the cold dawn breeze, her strawberry-blonde curls a cloud of angel hair around her tiny shoulders. Billie grabbed her mobile and punched in a number.

'Ash. It's Billie. Major incident, Angel of the North. Kick arse. ASAP.'

'Right, boss–' Billie ended the call before her trusted wingman DS Ash Sanghera could ask for further details. Phone in hand, she wasted only a few seconds taking footage of the unreal scene above her head, before turning to Kate.

'Quick. We need to lower the wires.' Billie was already flinging herself onto the vast steel-and-copper legs of the Angel of the North, wedging her feet and hands on either side of the metal ribs and pulling hard. On her first attempt she slithered back down, falling onto the ground, the smooth metal of the structure making it almost impossible to maintain a grip. Kate now joined Billie, gaining traction with her rubber trainers. She half-leapt up towards the Angel's knee and caught hold of one of the strings. The child's body jerked down alarmingly to the left.

'Gently,' Billie instructed, edging her way up the leg of the structure once more. Her fingertips strained to reach the end of a wire hanging on the other side. Lunging upwards, she finally grabbed it. The child shot down at speed and bounced onto the hard ground at the Angel's feet.

'Oh my God!' Kate gasped; her gloved hand slapped to her mouth. Billie had immediately clocked that for this little babe, any sensation of pain on hitting the frosty earth was long gone. Small mercy. But she knew that she had to check for a pulse anyway. A gaping stab wound split open the child's chest. Billie was certain that there would be others, covered by the teddy-bear-print nightdress and copious amounts of blood on the body. Instead of happy bedtime stories and gentle slumbers this poor child had clearly endured a nightmare scenario.

Kate rushed forward and caught hold of the girl, trying to turn her into a recovery position. Billie grasped her arms firmly.

'Step back!' It was an order not a request. 'It's way too late for that.' In her search for any sign of life, Billie had noted that rigor mortis was already setting in around the tiny jaw. She guessed that the low temperatures and lack of muscle on the child's body would lead forensic pathologist, Josta King, to arrive at the conclusion that the little girl had been dead for at least three hours, probably a lot longer.

Billie was already in work mode, her mobile switched on and recording. The crime scene needed to be preserved. Had she not needed to be absolutely certain that the child was deceased, she would have liked to have left the body swinging there, despite the fact that any minute now, at full sunrise, the terrible scene would have been on open view far and wide. Sometimes, Billie reflected, one had to be cruel to be kind.

'We can't just leave her,' Kate cried, attempting to scoop the toddler up in her arms. Billie blocked her once more.

'Sit over there.' Billie waved towards a small mound of earth nearby, as she continued to record the surroundings. Kate staggered back.

'What are you *doing*?' Kate's panicked breathing created frosty clouds in the icy air. Billie took a close-up of the face of the tiny broken angel.

'This is the Golden Hour. The scene here is telling a major part of the story. I need to record every detail.'

As if she would ever forget. She talked silently in soothing tones, within her head, to the miniature shattered soul, as she continued her work. Billie vowed to herself that when she nabbed the person responsible, she would make sure that they would never forget that meeting, either.

'Oh my God, she's looking at me!' Kate screeched, hot tears now pouring down her face. 'She's looking at me!'

Billie tried to hide her impatience at Kate's reaction, reminding herself that her housemate was simply acting like any normal human, rather than a hardened murder detective.

'Calm down,' Billie softened her voice, 'this little babe is sleeping.' The child's blue eyes were indeed open and staring, but Billie knew better than to close them until the crime-scene team had finished their work. She carefully walked backwards, in Kate's footsteps, and put her arm around her friend's shoulders, musing that despite being built like a gladiator she was as soft as a marshmallow in spirit. She had certainly been a good shoulder for Billie herself to cry on in recent times.

'Shush, now. Turn around. Look at the car crash instead.' *What a choice*, Billie mused. She could see the first traffic police car weaving amongst the stationary vehicles to the collision location below.

'I'll sing her a lullaby,' Kate whispered tearfully. Billie mentally rolled her eyes as she pulled her invisible cloak of armour back around her. She needed focus, not waves of emotion. Returning to her recording, she hoped that her whole team were speeding flat out in their direction.

It was as Kate sang the first line of the magpie counting rhyme that she had earlier played in the car, that the terrible tableau before Billie started to fragment and dissolve. She blinked, tightening her hand around her mobile. A wave of nausea passed through her body as a feeling rose from deep inside, a physical power that left her breathless. Instead of the tragic scene at her feet, another view waved and merged with the murdered child, then sprang to life in her mind's eye.

'*No!*' Billie silently gave a low childlike cry. A sense of dread forced into her body like a punch to the stomach. Sharp fragmented pictures from a child's perspective. An adult hand holding a kitchen knife. Fear, screaming, a struggle, other children crying, a table being kicked over. The adult looming over her...

Billie gasped in panic. It was by no means the first time that similar terrifying moving pictures had burst from nowhere and overwhelmed her mind, but the sensations of utter terror got stronger every time. She blinked hard, struggling to reclaim her equilibrium.

'Hey, boss. Stop hanging around and get on with the job!'

Billie turned, the panic attack immediately evaporating. Her trusted wingman, Ash Sanghera, nodded to the little wrecked angel's former bindings hanging either side of Billie whilst slinging out one of his sub-Christmas-cracker-level jokes as he was flanked by Crime Scene Manager, Charlie Holden. They looked like a child's vision of two friendly storybook snowmen, clad in protective white overalls. Charlie with eternally rosy cheeks and Ash all round cappuccino-skinned face and big, brown, laughter-crinkled eyes.

'Brought the cavalry,' Ash added, indicating an incongruous parade of flashing lights, coming to a halt on the roadside behind the Angel of the North.

'Forget the ambulance and secure the perimeter. Move that lot back.' Billie could see a crowd gathering at the edge of the entrance to the attraction, where the sad streamers of death, yellow-and-black crime-scene tape, were hastily being strung. 'I'm guessing this is going to be all across the internet any minute.'

'Done,' replied Ash. He thumbed two uniformed constables in the direction of the expanding crowd. His mobile alert pinged. He glanced at it. 'Sorry, boss. Pictures are online already.' Billie sighed. Given the location it was hardly shocking news.

'Let's crack on.' Billie focused again on the child. Ash joined her; his jovial manner wiped out the instant he viewed the doll-like figure. Billie reflected that even battle-hardened MIT detectives invariably found themselves silenced at first sight of a murdered child.

'She's just a baby,' said Ash, his voice breaking, no doubt at the thought of his own three precious daughters. He wiped his hand over his face and turned away. 'What sort of monster does this?'

For a split second, panic swept over Billie again, a vision of the same kitchen, turbulence, a knife being raised. Screaming all around. The sound of a hard punch, a thud, then darkness. Ash muttered the question once again. Billie shivered in horror. Could the killer be someone just like her, someone who seemed to be totally losing their mind?

2

OVER MY DEAD BODY

Billie stabbed with her knife, splitting open the flesh of a large sausage. The fried egg she was aiming for oozed bright yellow yolk over her huge breakfast roll. The comfort food waft of grease and cremated meat caught on the wind.

'Gore?' Ash didn't wait for confirmation as he squirted the red unctuous portion of tomato ketchup from a miniscule sachet, onto Billie's breakfast. She smeared it over the mess with her white plastic knife and tucked in. It was a scene that had been undertaken so many times before that it needed no polite table conversation.

Ash took a mammoth bite of his own bacon version, devoured as they leaned on the bonnet of a police car at the side of the road watching the crime-scene team at work. A white tent had now been assembled over the area where the tiny victim lay. Behind them, a large crew, directed by Billie, were well underway with door-to-door enquiries.

'Make sure HOLMES flags up any mountain climbers, roofers...' Billie took another bite.

'Astronauts?' Ash chimed in. 'Somebody must have a head for heights to climb up there in the dark, and some strength too.'

'Manual labourer possibly, or weightlifter... check for joint offenders too.' Billie's mind was already racing, trying to narrow down the range of suspects. 'We should have an ID soon,' Billie added, 'pre-schoolers don't just go missing without anyone giving a damn.'

Her voice was muffled with food, desperately hoping that the stodge would calm down the headache beating against the back of her skull like a hammer, now the early adrenaline surge of this morning's situation had dissipated.

'You're looking a bit fragile.' Ash nudged Billie. 'Late night swinging from the chandeliers with your fabulous fiancé, Mrs Silver?'

Guilt washed over Billie. She had told her fiancé, David, that she was having an early night, in order to get out of yet another tetchy encounter with his mother about wedding arrangements. She had been pulling on her PJs when Kate had instead coaxed her out, claiming that her workmates had found a great place and were heading there later.

Billie couldn't remember anything great about it. Instead, she vaguely recalled the sticky postage-stamp dance floor, where she had indulged in a session of ill-choreographed pre-wedding dancing that would have put her dad to shame. She quickly changed the subject.

'You can forget the Mrs Silver malarkey. I'm not swapping my name.'

'Wilde for evermore. That figures.' Ash chuckled. 'Still not got your wedding dress? Way you're going you'll have to borrow a white scene-of-crime suit.'

'Not a bad idea.' Billie feigned a grin. Fresh and unwelcome shards of memory from the night before started stabbing through her mind. The Dive Bar, buried deep in the dark bowels of the city, wasn't the sort of place a senior detective should have been frequenting, even in dress-down mode and definitely not the night before her return from a period of suspension. She must have stuck out like a sore thumb.

She did recall the barman, with the pitted skin of a clapped-out dartboard and the charisma of an empty bag of crisps, scratching his greasy head of hair in bemusement at Kate's cocktail request. Right now, it felt like he had substituted some sort of poison for out-of-stock ingredients, cocktails clearly not being top of the hit parade amongst his raddled regulars.

She also had a vague memory of her feet feeling glued to the drink-sodden carpet for a beat, as she had waved goodbye to anyone who cared to notice. Then she had set off unsteadily down one of the pitch-black rat runs in search of a taxi rank. Had someone else left at the same time, asking if she was okay?

Billie shook her head, astonished that she truly couldn't remember. Flushed with embarrassment, she thanked her lucky stars that she hadn't run into any shady souls scuttling around that murky location in the dead of night. After the recent enquiry into her behaviour at work, it really would have been more than her job was worth to have gotten into a messy situation that could have brought her character into question – yet again.

'Came in early this morning to catch up on some expenses and there was a guy looking worse than this breakfast bap.' Ash waved the half-eaten bacon and ketchup-splattered sandwich in her face. 'Seems he was lured into a serious assault by some woman of the night. Can you imagine it? He was probably hoping for a bit of hanky-panky behind the wife's back, then wham, bam, thank you, Sam.' Ash chuckled, tucking in again. 'Surprised he came forward to report it, but The Grass is looking into it. Like a dog with a bone that one.'

Billie felt her hackles rise at the mention of the name. DC Jo Green, nicknamed The Grass is Green, or The Grass for short, had made a formal complaint about Billie's last, allegedly heavy-handed arrest technique, on a man who had raped and killed a frail disabled grandmother. Billie's blood ran cold at the recollection of the murder, not to mention the damning report filed by the junior police detective.

'She's practically printing out *"Wanted"* posters.' Ash continued tucking in. 'Trying to find any witnesses at a place called The Dive Bar. Ever come across it?'

'Not that I recall.' Billie shook her head. Part of that was true. The smell of bacon suddenly turned her stomach.

'Victim's story was that he was simply playing the Good Samaritan. Said there was this great-looking girl in the bar, pie-eyed, doing a raunchy dance routine. He followed her out, claims it was to make sure she made it to a taxi safely, then he was jumped. Reckons it was a group of grifters working together. Pretty lady playing the carrot on a stick to lure the sucker. The Grass is convinced that if she finds the gal, she'll nab the gang and get a gold star off the Chief. Been a few similar incidents recently. He's just made a big press announcement about clearing up the mean streets. She's off on the hunt for CCTV footage.'

Billie's heart jumped into her mouth. If The Grass was wading through CCTV, she could well be at risk of playing a walk-on part in a GBH investigation. That was the last thing she needed, today of all days.

'I overheard his description of the perp,' Ash continued, 'tall, legs all the way up to her armpits, long curly red hair – hey.' Ash nudged Billie. 'You weren't hanging around any dark alleyways last night?' He laughed as Billie slapped his hand, sending the last of his bacon sandwich spiralling to the ground.

'My sides have just split.' Billie rolled her eyes and forced a grin, mortified at the truth of the matter, as well as the thought of the conversation required to set the story straight. 'Guilty, my dear friend The Grass, of dodgy dancing in a dump, inebriated somehow, on just one drink. But not guilty of GBH, despite your earlier claims of my predilections in that direction, to a police disciplinary panel, no less.'

Billie cringed. Her relationship with the junior detective hadn't been a bed of roses even before she'd had to fight against The Grass's misconduct claim. What if she were to jump at the chance to prove that Billie was in the wrong for a second time? She really couldn't stomach the thought of having that nasty little telltale thorn in her side yet again.

A uniformed police constable burst between them, red-faced and shocked at the effort needed to move at pace along the mean streets on two legs rather than four wheels for a change.

'Think we've got an ID, ma'am. Looks like the little one was Gracie-May McGill. House is just a couple of streets away. One of the neighbours saw the footage on the internet so she's in a bit of a state, but she's certain her ID's spot on. Victim was playing in her backyard with her own kids only yesterday.'

'Let's go.' Billie nodded the policeman back in the direction he'd come from. 'Any contact with the parents?' she interrogated, gathering speed as she did so.

'No one at home,' the police constable replied. 'Foster parents. Kiddie had only been with them a couple of weeks. Seems the foster mum went off to Benidorm for the weekend on a hen do leaving Dad to look after her.'

'Did a good job of that then.' Ash shook his head in exasperation.

Billie wasn't quite so shocked. She had worked as a young PC in the family law division and knew that the whole care system was at breaking point. She had come across some amazing foster parents, dedicated to the kids they cared for, but sadly there were also some terrible specimens out there, simply in the job for the money.

'Seems that he wanted the neighbour to babysit her last

14

night.' The officer struggled to talk and keep up with Billie's quickening pace. 'He'd made plans to watch the game at his local. She turned him down. Had her hands full with her own brood.'

'So, he just left her alone?' Ash's voice rose in anger. Billie had heard a lot worse. So many children's lives ruined these days, in so many ways. Desperately vulnerable kids emptied out of the frying pan of a dangerous and dysfunctional family into the fire of spectacularly unsuitable care placements.

'Looks like it. Seems that the pub had a lock-in, an all-nighter. Celebrating after the Toon won the match.' The officer made it sound like a half-reasonable excuse, football in this area accepted as a religion, the pursuit of which regularly took precedence.

As they turned the corner the crumbling Victorian brickwork of The Bird in The Hand loomed ahead of them. A motley bunch of men in black-and-white football strips would have put a band of vampires to shame, as they squinted in horror at the brittle morning sunlight.

'Is he in there?' Billie felt her chest rise in fury. The policeman nodded.

'Seems it was a bit of a reunion with some of his old rock-climbing mates.' Billie and Ash exchanged glances. 'He's had a few, ma'am. You'll be lucky to get much sense out of him.'

'Don't be too sure of that,' Billie quietly threatened. Ash caught Billie's arm.

'Boss, let me deal with this, round them all up and bring them in for questioning – by the book.' Billie pulled away.

'Are you questioning my authority?' Billie's voice was suddenly clipped and defensive.

'Look, you're the boss and you always will be as far as I'm concerned. You know you're the best, but it's your first day back.' Ash paused before delivering the killer blow. 'We all know the score, boss, and the team admire you for doing what you did. But at the end of the day, you very nearly killed the last guy.'

Billie stood deflated as Ash moved towards the pub, grudgingly accepting that he was right. One of these days, in her crusade to prove that she was well and truly capable of being in such a senior position at her ripe young age, she'd go totally over the top. If she didn't cool it a little, she ran the risk getting locked up herself.

Her mobile rang. Sandy, the chief of police's eternally upbeat personal assistant, sounded way too cheery for a Monday morning.

'Hi Billie. Welcome back. It's been quiet without you. Just to let you know the Chief wants to see you here at base immediately.' Billy rolled her eyes.

'I can tell you're rolling your eyes.' Sandy laughed.

'I'm in the middle of a murder enquiry.' Billie sighed, knowing this was going to be another argument lost.

'He's well aware of that. The way he's going absolutely ballistic, anyone would think you'd committed the crime.'

Billie ran her fingers through her long copper hair. If there had been CCTV retrieved from inside The Dive Bar her 'Murder on the Dancefloor' routine would no doubt make The Grass's day. She couldn't remember any doppelgangers hanging around the bar, regardless of the fact that the victim's suspicions were way off the mark. Was she about to be suspended again, pending another misconduct investigation, on her very first morning back at work?

Billie's office wasn't big enough to swing a corpse. Just as well. The chief constable had murder in his eyes as he swept in and slammed the door behind him. A cloud of expensive scent, all part of the senior police officer's silver fox persona, settled on top of the layer of dust that had accumulated during the month Billie had been away.

'Forgive me, I was under the impression that serious crime investigation appointments are my job?'

'Apologies, Chief. I happened to be the first officer at the scene and–' The chief constable cut across Billie's explanation.

'Decided that you would take it upon yourself to be SIO?'

'I'm perfectly capable of doing a good job, sir.' Billie tried to look at the middle ground rather than the Chief.

'I had Jo Green earmarked for promotion to deputy on the next homicide...' Billie felt a surge of fury at the mention of the name.

'Ash Sanghera's by far the better qualified officer, sir.' Billie was tersely polite in her reply. Humiliation washed over her yet again, as she recalled the whole demeaning misconduct investigation.

'Indeed. He's ready to step up to your job.'

'What?' Billie forgot politeness for a second. 'I was cleared of any professional misconduct. My self-defence claim was upheld!' She distractedly rubbed the long scar tracing an ugly zigzag down her arm.

'For God's sake, Billie. You don't have to remind me of that. But you push your luck. Very nearly ended up on a slab alongside that old dear. It can't happen again!' The Chief softened his voice. 'You know how proud you made your father.'

Billie closed her eyes. She needed to be focused on the case, not recent tragic events involving family. The Chief sounded a note of tender exasperation.

'You're still supposed to be on bereavement leave.' Billie gritted her teeth.

'I feel fine to work, sir.' Her voice was clipped. 'I feel it is what my father would expect me to do.' She decided to rally, play the Chief at his own game by using her dearly loved and newly dead father to argue her corner. 'As a former chief constable himself, he will doubtless be cheering me back to work from that big crime scene in the sky.' The Chief sighed heavily.

'I was about to make a public announcement on your return. I'm furious that you've mucked it up.'

'Sir?'

'Your promotion to Assistant Chief Constable, Billie. You've got the job!' The chief constable grinned. Billie looked back in horror.

'No... I'm not sure...' Billie damned herself for being talked into applying for the job by her family and fiancé. How come she could be such a people pleaser at home? It was like a tale of two different personalities. After an enforced month away from work she was more certain than ever that her passion was for the MIT, grabbing murderers by the scruff of their necks on the ground. There was not a hope in hell that she would take a job that involved policing from some lofty perch.

The Chief swept away proper procedure and pulled Billie into a huge bear hug. Sure, he was allowed. He was her godfather as well as her boss. Billie couldn't help fearing that nepotism had played a part. The sensation followed her everywhere like a bad smell, despite her many spectacular self-motivated achievements. The girl born with the silver spoon. It didn't sit right with her.

'Stop being coy, Billie. You know you deserve it. You were the best candidate for the job by a million miles! Amazing record, amazing work ethic and by far the best pedigree. You'll be the youngest ACC in the country! Yes, you've sometimes gone too far in the line of duty, but your new responsibility will be Communication and Digital Solutions. You'll be off the streets and–'

'No way!' Billie pulled back. 'I made a mistake. I want to stay in MIT. The homicide this morning–' The chief constable held his hand up grimly.

'Is not your problem. Think you can concentrate on a murdered kid, when you are walking up the aisle any minute?'

'I'm expecting to wrap this case up pretty sharpish, sir,' Billie persisted. 'We already have key suspects in for questioning. If you'll just let me get on.' Billie reached for the door handle. The Chief finally dropped his arms in exasperation.

'You're definitely your father's daughter, Billie Wilde.' He thought for a beat. Billie held her breath. 'Okay. God-daughter privileges. I'll allow one last case on the ground. But Green's on your team. She's a steadying influence.'

'A matter of opinion, sir.' Billie could see that she wasn't going to win.

'And another condition. You need to finish the counselling course. You're aware that it's a condition of your return to work.' Billie's heart sank. She thought that she had got away with that one. 'Sandy has checked. You've completed exactly half a session.' He raised his eyebrows. Billie refused to respond. 'She's booked you in for 3pm this afternoon.'

'I don't need it.' No way did she want to cross swords with the damn counsellor again. The chief constable put his finger to her lips as he blocked the doorway.

'That's the deal, young lady.' Billie knew that tone. He was going to brook no argument this time. 'I'm determined to get you up the aisle physically and mentally in one piece; promoted out of harm's way. It's my parting gift to your dad.' He swung the door open. Billie bolted out. The idea of a future overseeing IT instead of murder was like a knife through her heart. In her head, she screamed out her response loud and clear.

'*Over my dead body.*'

3

KEEP YOUR ENEMIES CLOSE

The big screen on the wall showed Billie holding up the headless ventriloquist dummy during the car crash madness earlier that morning.

'Taken another scalp already, boss? Welcome back!' one of her team shouted. The others chuckled and gave her a round of applause. Billie felt the tension in her shoulders release. She was back in her comfort zone.

'Good to see you've been cracking on with some work. Briefing in ten minutes. Online searches and CCTV thrown up anything more than my *Britain's Got Talent* audition?'

It never failed to amaze Billie that members of the public would rather reach for their mobile phones than run to help in such situations. Still, the content could turn out to be useful.

DS Beduwa Mensah did a quick spin, moving at pace across the floor in her shiny silver wheelchair, waving Billie over to her PC screen. Her beaded braids jangled in the movement. She went by the nickname Boo, short for Boudicca. No doubt she would have made a great warrior queen. Injured in the line of duty, she still knew how to kick arse as incident office manager.

Billie often expected blades to be protruding from her ever-spinning wheels.

'Bit of grainy CCTV just came in. Working on it now, but it could be tasty.' Boo opened a file. A short and blurred shot momentarily filled the screen. Billie caught her breath. A tiny figure in a nightdress, holding a soft toy in one hand, was led through the picture by a tall figure. Billie blinked. Tears pricked the back of her eyes. She blinked again, willing them away. 'He's wearing an NUC football hoodie,' Boo added.

'That narrows it down to around 50,000 people then.' Billie sighed. On match nights, practically eighty per cent of the locals would have been parading around in similar kit. Ash entered, fresh from bringing the football group in for inquiries. Billie waved him over.

'This guy look anything like Daddy of the Year down in the cells?' she asked. Ash squinted at the footage as Boo played it again.

'Sorry, boss. Dad looks like he's just eaten twenty of him for breakfast. Big lad. Not a hope in hell he could have scaled the Angel. His cronies likewise. Last time that shambolic crew were rock climbing Fred Flintstone was in diapers.'

'That's just the lock-in lot. Maybe there were younger, fitter climbing chums who left earlier.'

'We're checking, boss.' Billie knew her trusted wingman would have the vital early enquiry teams hard at work and Boo would be keeping them on their toes as far as logging incoming evidence was concerned. For a split second Billie imagined that she was alone in a room with the hooded monster. She blinked hard to sweep away the shockingly violent scene that swept across her mind's eye.

'Been a couple of comments online about everyone's favourite foster daddy. His name has done the rounds pretty quickly.' Boo clicked on her keyboard and brought up the files.

'These two young ladies were both former placements with him and his wife.'

Billie looked the two scrawny women up and down. Key examples of the neglected, used and abused products of the care system. By the needle track marks on their arms and emaciated bodies they were both on target for early graves.

'Both commented separately that he was a bit of a perv. Liked to catch them half dressed, brushed up close, that sort of thing.'

'We'll need full statements,' Billie ordered, knowing it could mean something or nothing. She'd met plenty of kids in care who would insist that their own mothers were paedos if they thought there was a couple of quid in it. Still, some of the mothers she'd encountered in the line of duty were... no, she didn't want to go there.

'Seems he potentially has thirty minutes missing out of his alibi,' Ash added, 'but I don't think he was scaling the Angel. Half-time. Game was sagging a bit and there were a couple of girls working out of the dosshouse above the pub. They look about a hundred, probably nearer sixteen. By all accounts he didn't get much further than a handshake before he clapped out to kip on the bed. Girl saw to someone else, came back and had to slap him awake, on account of the queue waiting outside.' Ash couldn't help himself. 'At least the Toon scored, even if he didn't.' He mimed a drum roll and symbols. Billie set off towards the door.

'Can't wait to be introduced to this charmer.' She swung the door open, colliding with Jo Green – The Grass – knocking the armful of files she had been carrying, across the floor.

If Harry Potter had been separated at birth from his almost identical twin sister, then Jo Green was that child. Even today she wasn't much taller than one. Spiky, short dark hair that had clearly never been on speaking terms with a brush could have shamed a prize-winning hedgehog. She pushed her round specs up on her nose, crouching down to retrieve the scattered files.

'Ma'am.' The Grass's dark, wide eyes looked huge behind her lenses. 'Might I trouble you for a moment?' She stretched across the floor to reach a folder that had landed at Billie's curry flecked feet.

'Why change a habit of a lifetime, Green?' Billie was in no mood for forgiveness.

Grass retrieved the file and added it to the huge stack now wobbling between her childlike arms. She stood and looked up at Billie.

'I'm helping to clear up a few cases for other departments,' The Grass began.

That didn't surprise Billie. No one wanted a Grass in their division. But any distraction from discovering her drunk and disorderly dance routine last night got the thumbs up as far as she was concerned.

'I believe that you were in a traffic incident this morning. The driver of the Mini went AWOL. False number plates. Might you be able to give a description–'

'Jeez, I'm in the middle of a child murder investigation!' Billie exploded, pushing Grass to one side. The folders scattered once more across the floor. A particularly chunky file burst open.

Photos of a man whom Billie immediately recognised from The Dive Bar the night before, fell at her feet like a flush of cards. His face was seriously beaten. Stills of a second man, also sporting extensive injuries, knocked heads with the first. Horror gripped Billie's heart. She could see why an investigation was underway. At that moment, the chief constable suddenly emerged from his palatial office and clocked the scattered pictures.

'Looks a bit nasty. Lucky we're not talking homicide with

that one,' he kicked the victim from the night before with the toe of his glossy black boot, 'maybe you should focus on this case after all, Green. Go over any CCTV with a fine-tooth comb and trawl through everyone who was at that bar–'

'No!' Billie crouched down and scooped up the photos, bundling them quickly back into Grass's file. 'I need her on my case, sir!'

It was difficult to know whether The Grass, Ash or the Chief had the most startled reaction.

'Dump that lot,' Billie instructed The Grass, who had managed to retrieve her pile. 'All hands on deck for witness interviews. We want a speedy resolution to this crime, sir!'

The Chief smiled, showing a row of expensively-white teeth. They had probably cost more than an entire row of terraced houses in the local area.

'That's my girl,' he patted Billie's shoulder, 'that's my girl.'

Ash waited for Billie to catch up, struggling to regain her composure. The Grass kicked open a door further along the corridor and disappeared in with her files.

'You all right, boss?' Ash frowned, nodding towards The Grass dumping her load alongside a vast pile of other lost causes, looking as though all her Christmases had come at once.

'Yep.' Billie resisted the temptation to add '*call me Pinocchio and whittle me a longer nose*'. 'Don't look so surprised. First day back. Merciful new me.' She hoped her grin passed muster.

'Must be the stress of your wedding.' Ash shook his head, miming a screwdriver being driven into his ear as The Grass emerged again and practically scampered along the corridor ahead of them.

'Sounds like you're more anxious than me, Ash.' Billie forced herself to tease – anything to avoid running to the dusty rubber plant slumped in the corner and vomiting a heady mixture of mortification and dread into it. 'Best man's speech not going well then?'

Billie realised that the nicest thing about her coming nuptials was that she and her fiancé both adored Ash. Due to recent events, Ash, his wife and three gorgeous daughters, were the nearest thing she had left to a family.

Boo suddenly swung through the door, grating the last shards of paint from the bottom of the scuffed frame with the sharp metal edge of her wheelchair.

'Warrant to search Dad's house has just been granted and the autopsy is at 1pm.' She shaved another centimetre off the edge of the door as she swung back out, all systems go. The custody officer appeared at the end of the corridor.

'Sorry, ma'am. Same brief is representing the lot of them and he's insisting no contact whilst they are still under the influence.'

Billie rolled her eyes. She was well aware of the fact that nothing formal could be achieved but was still hoping to hover around the cells putting the frighteners on.

'Such an interview wouldn't be admissible in court, ma'am,' The Grass piped up. Billie bit her tongue. It was exactly this sort of input that regularly made her have fantasies of beating The Grass to death. But for the moment, it was time to keep her friends close and this particular enemy on total lockdown.

4

ONE FOR SORROW, TWO FOR JOY

'Without a doubt, murder by Teddy Bear.' Top forensic pathologist, Josta King, had seen it all, so Billie didn't doubt her words. They also offered some small comfort. Between them on the autopsy table, lay the body of little Gracie-May McGill. It wasn't the first time by a long chalk that Billie had been called on to investigate the unexplained death of a child, but looking at The Grass's ashen face, it may well have been hers.

The investigation had been respectful and thorough, sensitively talked through by Josta as she had made her incisions and cuts, carefully removed tiny organs, weighed and measured and closely observed. It still made for a harrowing ritual.

'No sign of sexual interference?' Billie tried desperately to glean some positivity from the heartbreaking scene.

'Thankfully, none. No sign of penetration or ejaculation fluid in, on or around the body.' The Grass coughed and then bit her lip hard. Billie doubted that it was just down to the overwhelming smell of formalin.

'That is not to say that no sexual interference has taken place in the past, short of penetration. There is clear evidence of abuse on earlier occasions, but the main stab wound to the chest and all seven stab wounds around the body inflicted during this event are all, thankfully, post-mortem. Suffocation was the modus operandi of death.'

The Grass finally slapped her hand over her mouth and Billie nodded her release from her position. She made a run for the door. Billie guessed that it would be a close thing if she made it to the ladies in time. Her own head was thumping. She shook it in utter despair. Every sinew in Billie's body was screaming out to spring into action and forcefully bring the perpetrator to justice.

'She has some old scars, a couple of bone breaks. Rather suspect. Nothing before today that looks as though it was inflicted in the past month, however. How long has she been in the current foster placement?' Josta continued to write notes and mark up samples as she spoke.

'Just a couple of weeks.' Billie started to feel hot and shaky. 'Hard to place the kid by all accounts.' The Grass had called in Gracie-May's notes from social services and read them out to Billie en route, in meticulous detail as only The Grass was want to do. It was a tragically sad history of a fragile life. 'Seems she'd been passed from pillar to post from birth. Couldn't settle anywhere.'

'One doesn't need to speculate why.' Josta looked up over her specs. 'Poor mite appears to have been abused on more than one occasion.'

'This was her tenth placement.' *At four years old*, Billie screamed silently to herself. What did you have to do to a child to make it that terrified to settle with *any* adult?

Tears pricked the back of Billie's eyes. She willed them away. It was utterly unprofessional to exhibit mawkish emotion during such examinations. Luckily, the door opened and The

Grass slunk back into the room. Billie vowed that hell would freeze over before she showed any weakness in front of her subordinate. It would probably lead to another Grass Special Report being filed by teatime.

'I will have to do some research on the knife used for the main chest wound,' Josta continued. 'My guess is that it was some sort of hunting knife. Are you still coming around for dinner tonight by the way? I may have the answer by then.'

'I'll bring takeaway pizza,' Billie replied. Though she relished the thought of getting an early heads-up on anything that could help with the investigation, Josta was renowned for using her vast array of kitchen knives to test out her theories on weapons of crime.

'If I recall rightly, when you last invited me for Sunday lunch, I was served up a slab of beef which had three vicious stab wounds inflicted upon it.'

'Helped you solve the crime did it not?' Josta chuckled. 'Six-inch bread knife blade was identified as the culprit if I recall.'

'Yep, sunk into the left ventricle to a depth of three inches, swung by a left-handed man, six feet tall.' Billie couldn't help grinning.

'There you go then,' Josta nodded to The Grass, eyes twinkling, 'you don't get an opportunity to make deductions like that with pizza.'

To Billie's relief, it looked as though Josta was nearly done.

'Nasty old injury there to the ankle. See that strange cut?' Josta pointed out a small set of cuts behind Gracie-May's left ankle bone. Together they made a rough shape resembling an M. 'I would say those were inflicted by a Stanley knife.' Billie bent closer.

'Could be a signature...' she murmured.

'Meet the killer himself!' Josta lifted an evidence bag, laid alongside others on the adjoining countertop. Inside of it, a blue teddy bear stared out, a startled sort of look in the one remaining glass eye. Pools of blood were soaked into the toy's fur, not completely covering the threadbare cuddle spots. It had clearly been a much-loved belonging. Billie caught her breath as though she had been winded.

'I picked Ted's blue cotton fibres out of her airways, nose and mouth. Then, strange this, he was located tucked inside of her nightdress, hence the saturation of post-mortem blood. Secured inside the elastic of her pants so that he didn't fall out.'

Billie felt the strange sensation that she had experienced earlier that morning. The autopsy suite seemed to fragment into a kaleidoscope effect of bodies, shapes and colours before it dissolved. Suddenly she was back inside another room, with a swirly red carpet. The smell of beer and dope. People laughing... a man threatening her... *why*?

'Are you all right?' Billie heard Josta's voice sounding extremely far away, a note of concern within it, unlike the cold, cruel laughter getting louder in her head. She felt panic, tears filling her eyes as she rushed towards an open fire where a blue teddy with one eye and threadbare patches was being held dangerously over the open flames.

'I told you what would happen if you didn't get to bed!' The rough male voice made Billie's stomach churn. She felt herself dart forward in temper and fear, hand towards the fire, determined to save her beloved Teddy. Then a sudden sharp agonising pain as a large heavy shoe stamped on her tiny bare foot.

'Ma'am? Are you okay?' The Grass's voice was the last thing she heard, before having the strange sensation of falling backwards and hearing her body crash to the hard-tiled floor of the autopsy suite with a sickening thud.

〜

You could have cut the atmosphere with a knife. The Grass slowed the car at a traffic light a beat before amber turned to red. *Of course, she would.*

'A fishing knife.' Billie was on her mobile talking to Ash as she read through the first draft autopsy notes. 'Also a Stanley knife. Cessation of life in situ, which confirms the CCTV footage. Got that tidied up yet? Josta thinks that some of the twine was fishing line. Rush forensics on that.'

'Sorry to interrupt, ma'am,' The Grass cut in, 'the hospital's just here to the left if–'

Billie shook her head forcefully, holding up her hand for The Grass to be silent.

'Any luck with our friends downstairs yet?' Billie listened for a beat as Ash filled her in.

'To be fair, he appears to be genuinely cut up, boss. Still a bit befuddled with the booze, but he's banging on the cell door insisting that he's never left a kid alone before. Claims he's been stressed. Having trouble with his marriage.'

'No shit?' Billie glanced sideways at The Grass, who quickly returned her own stare back on the road. 'Good luck to him with that. Even without a murder charge, he's facing child neglect for starters. That's before we check out the former placement's claims and the young hooker in the pub. Leave the breaking of that cheery news to me. I'll be there in ten.'

The lights stayed on red. The Grass chanced her luck, seemingly oblivious to the danger signs.

'It's just that it was a nasty bump to the head, ma'am–'

The elephant in the car. Billie was mortified that she had come around on the floor of the autopsy suite to find The Grass arranging her limbs in the recovery position.

'I just slipped. Wet floor.' Billie felt her face flush. 'Not a word of this to anyone,' she added, 'that's an order.' The Grass finally moved the car forward at a snail's pace. 'Put your foot down, Green. We've got a murder investigation on the go, in case you haven't noticed.'

'I'll need to fill in an accident form.'

Billie was at exploding point. It was the first time she had ever shown any weakness during a damn autopsy and of all the people to witness the crushingly embarrassing incident, it had to have been The Grass. Her mobile rang. Billie grabbed it. *Saved by the bell.*

'DSI Wilde?' It was Sandy, the Chief's PA. Billie's heart sank. It wasn't like Sandy to sound so formal. That meant that the Chief must be hovering close by. 'You're late for your, em, afternoon appointment.' Billie shot a glance at The Grass.

'Er, the autopsy has just finished and–'

Sandy cut in. 'The Chief is ordering you to go there immediately.' Billie looked at her watch. The shrink session was nearly due to be over anyway.

'Perhaps I can reschedule. I have to get back for an important interview,' Billie argued.

'The Chief is asking me to relay to you that unless you head there now, I am to schedule you onto the first available DCC training course. There is one starting the day after tomorrow.'

Billie sighed, knowing when she was beaten.

'Okay. Okay. On my way.' Billie ended the call. 'Drop me here. I have a meeting on behalf of the Chief.' Billie's voice was clipped as she thumbed The Grass to pull over to the side of the road, remembering that the shrink's office was only a block away. She would hoof it. She didn't want The Grass having the foggiest where she was heading.

'Would you like me to wait for you, ma'am?' Billie considered for less than a split second before deciding that she would rather eat her own spleen.

'I think your talents would be put to better use by assisting DS Sanghera with witness interviews.' Give the dog a bone. It almost sounded like a compliment. As she unclipped her belt and got out of the car, Billie turned. 'Remember.' She put her finger to her lips. 'Schtum.' The Grass blinked.

'Ma'am,' was all that she answered. Billie could feel her myopic eyes boring a hole into her back as she headed off around the nearest corner, hyperaware that The Grass of all people, was holding the Sword of Damocles over her head.

5

THREE FOR A GIRL AND FOUR FOR A BOY

'Hey, welcome back to Crazy Central,' Billie announced, as she flung the door open. The nameplate of Dr Max Strong jangled dangerously as it banged hard against the wall. The doctor swung around slowly on his chair, which had been facing the window. A gentle smile lit up his way-too-handsome face.

'Ah, DSI Wilde. How nice to see you. Better late than never.' His large brown eyes crinkled at the corners. Billie checked her watch.

'I've got five minutes, so let's make this quick.' Billie knew the expected drill from her first visit, even if she did detest it. She slumped into the deep, soft, egg-shaped seat opposite Max Strong, trying to ignore the fact that it felt like she was sinking back into the womb. She stifled a yawn.

'No rush. You're my last patient. You have my undivided attention for the rest of the day.'

'Nice work if you can get it.' Billie swung her feet up on the coffee table, just for irritation purposes. 'I, on the other hand have a few problems to iron out at work, so can you just fill in the damn shrink report and be done with it.'

Dr Strong looked down at the notes balanced on his knee, dark hair flopping over his forehead.

'Would you like to discuss your problems at work?' He looked straight up into Billie's eyes. She remembered that he'd been taught, most probably, a clever technique designed to make patients feel as though he was looking into their very souls. She decided to stare him out.

'Main issue I have with work, Doctor, is that *you* are keeping me from it. A murder enquiry, in fact, with several urgent interrogations pending. A fact that *you* of all people, should have sympathy with. So crack on with question number two.'

Max Strong was still looking straight at her. 'It doesn't quite work that way, Billie,' he answered, 'the report requires some measure of input from the participant. What's more, your chief contacted me this morning, to insist that your report should be extremely thorough.'

Billie rolled her eyes and sighed loudly, as she ran her fingers through her long red hair.

'So let's get back to your work situation, starting with the incident that originally brought you here.' He crossed his legs, looking like he was settled for the day. It struck Billie that he could be put to better use down the cop shop getting vital info out of the football mob. She finally lost patience, suddenly springing forward in her seat.

'Okay then. If we must! Serial murderer, killing frail old women. Assailant collared by me, finishing off the job. This old dear had been dragged out of her wheelchair, beaten and sexually assaulted in ways that would give someone like you nightmares for the rest of your life. However, I am not one hundred per cent bog sure that the poor old biddy *is* completely dead. Therefore, I use justifiable force to ensure me lad's merry work is curtailed with immediate effect.' Billie rubbed the long scar on her arm. It didn't go unnoticed by Max Strong.

'Temporary officer assisting arrest was of the opinion that I used too much force, despite him waving a damn machete like a tennis racket, so she kindly instigated a formal complaint procedure against me. That was investigated and was found not proven. Back on the job today. End of. Can you get all that in the little box you have there?' Billie added defiantly. Max Strong raised his eyebrows and smiled.

'Billie, I give a summary of my findings as far as your psychological health is concerned, not every nut and bolt of our conversation. The aim is to ensure that you're fit and well. I don't report every detail that you tell me. That is confidential. This is a safe space.' He sat for a second looking down then gazed straight into her eyes once more. 'I sense feelings of anger over that incident,' he said carefully.

'Wow,' Billie goaded, 'are there actually degrees in this stuff? An embryo might have jumped to that clever conclusion.'

'Does violence against male offenders excite you?' His response was unexpected. Billie sprang out of her chair, trying to swipe away a memory of her arrest of the old lady's murderer.

'What insane sort of question is that?' Billie was furious. She started to pace the room. 'No actually,' she snapped, 'I'm happy to kick the crap out of anyone who murders defenceless old ladies and tiny children. Men, women, gender neutral, I'm not that picky!'

Billie spun around, her heart beating rapidly. She stared out of the French windows overlooking the beautiful walled garden beyond. Suddenly a quick flash in her mind's eye, of a teddy bear about to be roasted on a fire, made her want to cry out. She caught her breath as the vision skipped like a moving picture across the carefully mown lawn, disintegrating as swiftly as it had formed. She struggled to regain her equilibrium, as a hint of fresh lemony cologne signalled that Max Strong had moved to her side.

'Must be tough working on the child murder all over today's news.' His voice was calm. Reassuring. Billie rallied.

'Details of which are highly confidential, Doctor.' Two could play the confidentiality game.

'One hell of a statement killing.' He glanced at Billie. She stayed silent, despite her agreement. Without even setting eyes on Gracie-May's foster dad, she knew that the murderer was of a different calibre than the sad specimen described by Ash, stuck down in the police cells.

'In my experience, such shocking child homicides are generally perpetrated by someone focused on revenge, using the crime as an instrument of retaliation.'

Billie reflected on his words but remained tight-lipped. Max Strong opened the French windows. A welcome breeze lifted Billie's hair; the smell of roses carried upon it.

'When you came for your first appointment, you didn't mention that your parents had just passed away.'

Billie bit her lip and concentrated on a pink rose bush in the garden. Roses had been her mother's favourite flowers. In fact, pink roses just like those had crowned her mother's coffin. Her father's casket had been topped by his ceremonial police cap, the design heralding his extremely senior status. A lot had happened in the past few weeks. Seemed her godfather had been spilling the beans.

'Nothing much to tell.' Billie attempted to sound nonchalant. 'On a clear sunny day, on the way back from a Sunday afternoon tootle to the seaside, with absolutely no other traffic on the road, the old folks managed to launch their Merc at great speed off a clifftop and smash it onto the rocks fifty feet below. Way to go.' Billie shrugged, hoping to cut off any further questions in that area too.

'Only weeks before your wedding,' Max Strong continued. Billie scratched her head, considering whether it must be

National Grass-Up Day. No wonder the Chief was keen on promoting Jo Green. Peas in a damn pod.

'With all of these recent events in your life, you're scoring pretty high on the stress scale.' Max Strong stepped out onto the beautiful stone patio.

'No shit, Sherlock.' Billie followed him, undoing the top button of her shirt. She desperately needed some fresh air.

Climbing plants and fruit trees traced delicate patterns across the red weathered bricks of the walled garden. Coloured petals, tugged free by the soft wind from their mother plants, tumbled across the grass like confetti.

'It's understandable that your emotions have been out of kilter.' Max smiled and bent down to click his fingers at a magpie hopping towards him on the grass. Billie felt a momentary measure of calm. This was the sort of life her family had wanted for her. Serene and safe and filled with birds and pretty roses. It was hers for the taking, had been from birth, so why did she fight so hard against it?

'Been sleeping okay?' Max turned to Billie whilst the bird flirted under his attention. Billie shrugged, refusing to drop her act of bravado to share the fact that, in truth, she hadn't slept for more than a couple of hours at a stretch lately. Not since that late afternoon when a uniformed PC had turned up to announce her parents' shockingly unexpected deaths. Night had fallen by the time the officer had left, just as the sun had set on Billie's bright life, it seemed, forever. Hence Kate's encouragement to get out and grab some fun the night before.

'Another patient of yours?' Billie nodded to the bird. 'You seem to attract aggressive types.' She recalled Kate's conversation in the car that morning. 'I understand that your little friend there is a thief and a killer.' Max Strong smiled as the bird hopped back and forth.

'Depends how you look at it,' he answered, turning to look at

Billie. 'The ideas that were drummed into your head as a child. In the UK we are brought up to believe the evil magpie myth, but I view them with awe. They are highly intelligent, beautiful and feisty,' he added, as the magpie approached her.

'Predators.' Billie couldn't help but be charmed by the bird almost standing at her feet now.

'I prefer to see it as a determination to do what they have to in order to survive. Do you know that they mate for life?' A sudden projected image of her walking down the aisle with David flashed through Billie's mind. She shivered, not sure why. It was as though someone had walked over her grave. 'The mate of this one was killed outside by a car yesterday. I brought it in here. Its fellow magpies gathered this morning in the garden for the funeral.'

'You're kidding me.' Billie laughed cynically.

'Known fact. In the East they are viewed as magical creatures.' Billie glanced at Max Strong. He wasn't joking. His eyes, as dark as brown velvet, locked on hers for a moment before he clicked his fingers again. The magpie hopped back towards him.

'You believe in clairvoyance?' Billie glanced across, gauging his reaction. He seemed open to the idea of magic. The sudden vision of the scene with the teddy bear just now and the similar ones earlier that day, weren't new and they were gathering momentum. Maybe it wouldn't hurt to gently interrogate a shrink on the subject, seeing as she was stuck here anyway?

'Is clairvoyance part of your current enquiries?' Max asked.

'Might be...' Billie moved nearer, looking around. There were no gardeners hiding behind trees to hear her nonsense.

'Can you tell me more?' His voice was low. 'Confidentially of course.' Billie felt his undivided attention as she approached, sitting down further along the patio, on the top step leading down to the cool green lawn.

'This is not about me. This can't go in your Big Brother report,' Billie warned.

'You have my word,' Max replied, also sitting down. Billie felt the space between them, like a piece of elastic. She edged a little closer.

'A witness has reported sort of fragments, of scenes, things that she may be tuning in to. Some of them may be premonitions?'

Max was suddenly alert. He moved a few inches nearer. Billie hesitated.

'Violent scenes. Always a child in them... from the child's perspective... that just erupt from nowhere...'

Billie's voice faded to a fearful silence as a sickening feeling started to make her stomach quiver. Talking about the subject was causing her to have another event.

She was back in the cold kitchen. Sticky dirt, maybe ancient dog food, glued onto the bare lino floor. The man's voice again, mocking her. She was frightened, shaking. The sensation of being swung up in the air, the hood of her jacket hooked over a lofty cupboard handle. The terrible fear of falling as the man cackled, flapping his arms like wings. A stabbing sensation in her throat as the metal zip of her jacket cut into her neck. She clenched her fists in pain...

'Billie?' The fresh lemony scent caught on the breeze and rescued her senses, the feeling of terror faded again as quickly as it had come. Max Strong was close beside her. He touched her arm. She jumped.

'Sorry, I...' Billie scrambled to her feet, staggering a little as she did so. Max raised himself up alongside her, worry etched across his features, as the startled magpie flapped its wings and skittered up onto the branch of a tree.

'I've got to go.' Billie headed back across the patio.

'Post-traumatic stress.' Max was nimbler on his feet, blocking her way back through the French windows, holding his hands up to show that he meant no harm.

'What?' Billie felt panic. She needed to get out.

'Post-traumatic stress,' Max said more gently now. His eyes bored into her own. 'Repressed memories of traumatic events. I think that's what you're suffering from.' Billie pushed Max to one side angrily, heading back indoors.

'Are you crazy?' she answered with force. 'I've never had a single moment of stress in my totally perfect childhood! It's been ballet, ponies and tennis courts all the way! I'm the girl born with the silver spoon in her mouth.' Billie needed to get away, she was losing it.

'Billie, listen–' Billie blocked out his words.

'Surely you know that? You've been briefed about every other damn thing in my life!' Billie was shouting now. 'I'm the one who has to work twice as hard to prove that I haven't got where I am today because of my golden family, my influential friends. Maybe, just maybe, *that's* why I make such forceful arrests!'

Billie stopped suddenly. Silent. Realising that a skeleton had just forced itself out of a very dark cupboard, a wrecking ball clenched tightly in its bony fist. She breathed out, utterly exhausted.

'I can help,' Max's voice was gentle, 'it gives us something to work on.'

'No! I've got to go.' Billie felt a hot surge of blood burning her cheeks. Embarrassed, she fumbled for her phone, panicking as she realised that it wasn't in her pocket.

'My phone.' Billie spun around, grabbing cushions from the egg-shaped chair. Max put his hand down the side of the seat and lifted out the mobile. Billie snatched it from his hand, checking it quickly. 'Damn!' She started pacing the room. She'd had it on silent. 'Ten missed calls. Jeez...' The phone rang immediately as she set the ringtone. She answered, in a state of agitation. Listening, she shook her head in disbelief. 'Yep. Okay. On my way.'

'Billie–' Max started.

'Out of my way. Major incident.' She snapped the phone off and raced for the door, wrenching it almost off its hinges. She already had one foot on Dr Max Strong's fallen nameplate, when another hideously unwelcome memory kicked in.

'So, okay...' She stepped off the nameplate, sheepishly. '...It's just up the road. Any chance of a lift?'

6

A BODY IN THE ATTIC

'Another murder?' Max Strong momentarily took his eyes from the road to glance at Billie, as she ended her mobile conversation with Boo. Billie looked around, slightly startled, amazed at the speed at which he had brought her to the scene.

'You could put a police vehicle on full blues and twos to shame,' she replied. It was a small offer of an olive branch.

The uniformed PC blocking the entrance to St Lucia's Nunnery, a quirky, old castle-like building, recognised Billie immediately and swept the scene-of-crime tape to one side.

'*Lucky Lane*,' Max stated as he turned in to the narrow drive with thick shrubbery on either side. 'TV series when I was a kid. Set at a youth club. This was the location.' Billie's face lit up momentarily. Her own happy memories overcoming her super-stressed demeanour.

'Don't I know it?' She couldn't help grinning. 'I was in a drama group at school and we were invited to be acting extras. Human wallpaper really. I loved it.' Memories of more innocent times came flooding back as the huge nunnery building loomed into view.

'I had an actual part!' Max grinned. 'Tiny one. I played a

child in the local foster home. Bad boy. If I remember, I found a secret door, behind a bookshelf in the first-floor office, with hidden stairs leading up to that bell tower on top. My character had a tantrum, threatened to jump off...' he shook his head, equally charmed by his own memories, '...bit of luck really, my mum was an actress in it.' The car came to a halt. Billie unbuckled her belt.

'So, another kid born with a silver spoon in your mouth,' she chided, 'shipped in to play your part and then chauffeured back to your smart home in a more salubrious location.' Billie was only partly joking. 'Just like me then. Suffer any scary flashbacks from your own terrible childhood, Doctor?' She swung the car door open, spotting Josta King heading her way, peeling off her forensic investigation overalls.

'Ah, long time no see!' Josta teased, as Billie emerged from the car. 'Think we'll start on the examination of this poor lady first thing in the morning. I still have the fuller version of Gracie-May's notes to write up. I'm afraid we'll need to reschedule our dinner date.'

'Any obvious similarities?' Billie was being offered her own overalls by a CSI trainee and started to pull them on as she spoke.

'I have my suspicions.' Josta spoke quietly, looking around, then stopped, suddenly distracted by the sight of Max Strong heading towards them. A uniformed PC intervened.

'I'm afraid you have to leave the location, sir. This is a crime scene,' he started.

'Darling!' Josta looked like a woman in love, as she propelled the PC to one side and held her arms out wide towards Max.

'You've met?' Billie was bewildered, watching as Max gave Josta a tight bear hug.

'In the womb, dear.' Josta grinned. 'My son, Max. I hadn't realised that you two were acquainted. Of course, he got his handsome features via his thespian mother's genes.' Billie suddenly recognised the striking features of Josta's actress wife, Lola Strong, in Max. 'Just as well,' Josta continued, 'the male contributor would have lost a beauty contest with a bulldog.'

'I'll leave you to it.' Max managed to peel himself away from Josta and turn back towards his car. Billie hid the hint of a smile playing on her lips as Max caught her eye and flushed pink. His turn to be embarrassed now.

'Don't worry about him, dears!' Josta announced to anyone in hearing distance. 'He was a captain in the British Army, Ireland, Afghanistan, Iraq. He's seen more fresh meat than the local butchers. Certainly totted up more corpses than me!' She finally wrestled herself out of her CSI overall, then spoke more quietly as Billie watched him turn the car around.

'Special Forces, dear. But he had to give it up. Terrible post-traumatic stress disorder. Retrained as a psychologist in an attempt to work out what exactly makes the mad men tick. He's in great demand the world over. If you get stuck up the creek without a paddle on this case, he might be able to shed some light on your friendly neighbourhood assassin.'

Ash approached, raising a quizzical eyebrow as he watched Max head back down the drive.

'Been worried sick, boss. We couldn't get hold of you. Nearly sent out a search party. You all right?' He exchanged glances with Josta who quickly busied herself. Billie tensed again. Could she have absolutely no secrets around here anymore?

'The Grass was the first officer at the scene,' Ash continued. 'Said she'd just dropped you off, hence the concern.' A burst of silent obscenities screamed through Billie's head. The Grass of all people! Billie followed Ash around to the back garden of the grounds. 'The victim's little dog managed to break free. The Grass had to do an emergency stop to miss it. Came up here to find the owner and–'

The vision of a stout elderly woman loomed into view. She was fastened in a crucifixion-type pose to a large, peeling wooden cross. They approached the body.

'Different type of victim, but similar modus operandi.' Ash grimly viewed the body.

The corpse had suffered several vicious knife wounds. Congealed blood merged into the pattern of a floral, knee-length dress, chunky legs dangling just a few inches above the ground. Clearly a harder victim to manoeuvre than a four-year-old child. Puppet strings similar to those that had been fastened to Gracie-May McGill, were binding her in place.

'Been ID'd already. The Grass went next door first.' *Hurrah for The Grass again*, Billie cheered, her bitter inner voice full of irony. She forced herself to get a grip.

'Great work,' she mumbled.

'Joy Summers. Retired civil servant. Came here to walk the dog regularly after helping out at the food bank up the street.'

Billie bent closer. The smell of death mingled with Joy Summer's Estée Lauder Youth Dew. She was searching for one particular telltale sign, as Ash continued. 'One thing's for sure, Daddy Dearest in the cells isn't the culprit. Body's still warm. Josta was out here like a shot and she said the body was pretty fresh. That was just an hour ago. Killer may even have still been in the vicinity.'

Billie gave herself a vicious mental beating. What the hell had she been doing, chewing the damn fat in *The Secret Garden* down the street, when a killer was hanging and butchering an elderly woman only five minutes away?

'Could be a copycat killing, of course,' Ash added, 'social media is going wild and there are lots of crazies out there.'

Billie circled the body closely then stopped dead. There it was, cut into Joy Summer's mottled and swollen ankle, a few inches below a bright strawberry birthmark. A small, ragged M. It was the confirmation that she had been hunting for.

~

It was nearly midnight when Billie arrived home. She had long ago sent Ash off to join his wife and lovely kids. Who could blame him for wanting to keep family close on a day like this one? Kate emerged into the hallway, eyes red and puffed. She looked relieved to see Billie.

'Hey, brought some fish and chips back with me.' Billie grinned. 'And some of that disgusting chav curry sauce you love so much.' Kate's whole body appeared to relax.

'Oh my God, you know me so well!' Kate wiped her hand over her red nose and headed after Billie into the lounge.

''Course. You're my sister from a different mister!' Billie joked, reflecting that taking in a lodger to share her parents' large sprawling home in a smart suburb, whilst she cleared it out, was the best decision she had made for a long time.

As light relief from the endless pressure of wedding and funeral arrangements as well as work worries, she had indulged in girl bonding time over takeaways and terrible TV soaps. It had felt like a breath of fresh air, saving her sanity at a time when she had feared she was drowning in a sea of anger and grief.

'David and his mum came around.' A waft of fried fish, grease and peppery faux curry filled the room as Kate unloaded the takeaway, whilst Billie kicked off her boots.

'Bugger. I forgot about tonight.' Billie didn't know whether to feel yet more guilt or utter relief. She chose the latter. She'd had her fill of guilt for one day. She rammed a chip into her mouth, suddenly starving. 'He was bringing his mum around to finalise the flower arrangement on the church door.' Billie rolled her eyes in disbelief as she peeled off a crispy layer of batter from the fish, dangling it into her mouth.

'And to see the wedding dress.' Kate giggled. 'I blocked the door. Insisted that you wanted to keep it top secret. His mum was spitting flames.' Kate poured the yellow-green chip-shop curry over her chips. Billie pulled a face and then dunked one of her chips in.

'Ha, I'll bet!' Billie munched away, dripping curry sauce down her top.

'Two weeks to go,' Kate reminded Billie. 'You *do* want to get married, don't you?' She suddenly looked serious. Billie shrugged.

'Why not? It's been decided since birth. Both sets of parents planned the forging of their two perfect families, during sittings of the Rotary and golf club committees.' Billie grabbed a tea towel and tried to remove the cow splat from her top. 'The son of one of Northumbria's top judges, with the daughter of a former chief of police. Ash says it's not much different from his arranged marriage. That seems to have turned out all hunky-dory.'

'But do you love him?' Kate continued. 'To be fair, he is very handsome.' Billie seemed to focus on the wiping of her top, preferring not to spend too many seconds thinking over the question.

'I guess so. He's okay. A bit manipulative but not as bad as his bloody mum.' Billie started tucking in again. 'We rub along. We've been together since pre-school. I guess I love him like a brother.' Billie shrugged. 'That'll do. I meet enough bad boys at work.' Kate pulled a face, her mouth half full of chips.

'Jeez Billie, are you sure about this? I mean, my God! I've got a brother, but I wouldn't want to walk up the aisle with him!'

'They're the only family I've got left.' Billie was serious, before stealing one of Kate's chips and dipping it in her sauce.

'Except for you, of course. I want you sitting next to me at the top table.' Kate wiped her mouth miserably.

'They told me they want me out. By the weekend. David and his mum.' She swallowed hard.

'Wha–?' Billie stopped mid-bite, furious. 'How bloody dare they? Take no notice. This is my house!'

'They do have a point. David says that you need to get on with the building work–'

'What building work?' Billie interjected. This is exactly what annoyed her about David's family.

'As his mum says, you'll be newlyweds. You don't want me hanging around like a body in the attic.' Billie caught Kate's hand with her own.

'No worries, I get along great with bodies in attics.' She giggled as their hands glued together for a second with grease. 'You're *my* body in the attic and you're staying.' She decided that she'd start the way she meant to go on with this marriage.

'Thanks, that means a lot. This morning, it really shook me up.' Kate's eyes filled with tears. 'People swarming all around in white suits wanting samples of my hair, saliva...' Kate shivered. Billie wrapped up the remains of her takeaway, suddenly feeling a little queasy.

'Don't worry about it.' Billie felt sorry that she had messed up her friend's day, big time. 'Same for me. But it's just for forensic exclusion purposes. We were all over the body. This way our DNA doesn't get mixed up with the killer's.' Kate looked as though she might be about to throw up her food.

'Think I'll turn in.' She rubbed her face and headed for her bedroom.

'Better day tomorrow,' Billie called after her, reassuringly. She headed for her own room. Despite the fact that she should have been bone-tired, she actually felt alert and excited, not by prospects of promotion, or her impending wedding, but about the two new cases that had come her way today. *This* was what she was born to do and no wedding or promotion was *ever* going to stand in her way.

From Kate's room Billie heard the first strains of the children's choir, singing their haunting a cappella version of the magpie counting rhyme. As she kicked off her clothes and pulled on an oversized T-shirt nightdress, she reflected that it was a beautiful, soothing melody. She hoped that it would help her new friend sleep without nightmares tonight.

Billie suddenly had the urge to open the big black box sitting in the corner of her bedroom. It had been her father's, previously kept locked in the wall safe in his study.

Despite Billie's refusal to show her grief in public, she still found it hard to shake off the shock of her parents' so sudden deaths. She could have done with her dad's steady guidance right now. He'd always been happy to talk about her cases long into the night.

As Billie unlocked the box and lifted the lid, she gently took out medals and certificates, charting her dad's super-successful career in the police force. She fondly remembered her mum pinning the medals onto her dungarees as a child, whilst Billie had marched around pretending to arrest people. She smiled, tipping the box upside down onto her bed until it was empty. Suddenly the balsa wood bottom gave way, revealing further treasures tucked below. Billie frowned, pulling the false bottom out. There seemed to be more paperwork inside, photographs and a certificate.

Billie laid the hidden items out in front of her crossed legs on the bed. She immediately recognised herself, as a pre-school child in the centre of the largest photo, in best party dress. Next to her, with beaming smiles, were versions of her parents, thirty years younger, dressed in best bib and tucker. They appeared to be in a court room, the insignia of the Crown and a bench in shot behind them. Billie turned the photo over. Her mum had a habit of identifying photos in her precise copperplate handwriting. Here it was.

Billie Aged 4. Adoption Ceremony.

Billie blinked hard, unable at first to believe her eyes. Then she dropped the photograph and backed away, off the bed, before hurtling to the bathroom. There she forcefully threw up her supper. When the shocked convulsions finally died down, Billie straightened up, catching her exhausted reflection in the bathroom mirror. A total stranger stared back.

7

THREE WISE MONKEYS

'You look like you've seen a ghost.' Kate, wrapped in fleecy pink dressing gown and slipper boots, placed a steaming mug of coffee on the huge, old English oak outdoor dining table which sat overlooking the manicured lawn. 'Are you okay?' Kate dumped a crumpet directly on the table next to the mug. Thick strawberry jam oozed over the sides and onto the wood.

'Yeah.' Billie looked up and smiled, grateful yet again for the company of her new lodger. 'Just what the doctor ordered.' She took a bite of the crumpet. 'This table was made for crumpets and jam. God knows how many I've knocked back sitting here...'

Billie took another bite, suddenly lost in the memory of long hot summers, paddling pools and play dates, her parents' cocktail parties and the smell of her mother's pink perfumed roses all around. The recollections suddenly turned sour. In truth she had been an intruder, here under false pretences. Where had her real childhood gone? Kate pulled out a chair and sat down, tucking into her crumpet.

'Better get the next size up when you eventually buy that wedding dress,' Kate joked. Billie raised her eyebrows.

'Maybe...' Her mind had started racing. She had wanted to

talk to David last night, explain that considering her stupefying discovery, maybe they should wait to get married, maybe... but David hadn't picked up his calls, probably long asleep at their penthouse flat in town, or perhaps sulking that Billie had upset his mother, yet again.

'My music didn't keep you awake did it?' Kate looked worried. Billie blinked away her crazy thoughts. She patted her friend's hand.

'No, it helped me nod off.' *Finally*, when her body had simply been too exhausted to deal with the shockwaves that had continued for hours. Kate seemed to have the magpie rhyme recording on a loop, and it had eventually soothed Billie into a fitful sleep, broken by strange dreams.

Images of a terrifying man cackling and flapping his arms like wings in her face had caused her at one point to cry out and wake up in the darkness. Nodding off once again, her sleep was filled with visions of a gentle magpie, hopping across cool green grass and Max Strong's dark-lashed eyes staring into her very soul. She had woken up hot and dishevelled, knowing that her life would never be quite the same again.

Now as a new day began, Billie realised that she had only one certainty left in life, her overwhelming love for her job. Her determination to bring this latest killer to justice wiped out every other feeling that had threatened to overwhelm her in the witching hours.

'I've got an early start with my crazy kids. Outward bound today.' Kate pulled a pained face. 'Going to need all the sugar I can get. Last lot had only ever seen ducks in the fairground, made of plastic. So as soon as we came across an idyllic scene of real mother and babies floating along a lake, they started picking up stones and belting them. End of a lovely afternoon ramble in the countryside.' Kate laughed. Billie mused that she seemed to be as passionate about her work as Billie was about her own vocation.

'Can I tell you something?' Billie ventured.

''Course. I'm your sister from a different mister, remember?' Kate joked.

'I've just found out I was adopted.' Billie swallowed hard. Hearing the word applied to her own life in the cold early morning light, made her fill with emotion. She had to fight to stop tears welling up.

'What?' Kate stopped munching her crumpet.

'Are any of your wild kids adopted rejects?' Billie asked. 'Is that what makes them fight against the rules and do crazy things?' Kate paused before putting her hand over Billie's.

'Nope. But most of them probably wish they had been. It's realising that no one at all cares about them that makes kids go wild, Billie. Knowing the truth, that their real mum and dad would choose drink or drugs or violent lovers in a heartbeat over them, no question. Why wouldn't they go totally loco?'

Billie had to admit that first-time offenders from average homes were startlingly few and far between in the criminal justice system.

'Adopted kids, they've been given a chance. Take it from me, my life has been full of the kids who were left behind. You were one of the chosen ones, Billie babe. Think about it. You got all the luck.'

Hours later and with a second autopsy under her belt, an avalanche of work on her slender shoulders and nothing at all in her stomach since her dawn breakfast of jam and crumpet, Billie had a moment to reflect that Kate might have had a point.

'It wasn't my fault nobody else wanted the kid.'

Billie fought an internal battle with herself not to spring over the table of the interview room and smash little Gracie-May's former foster daddy in his pudgy tear-stained face. Luckily, Ash was by her side and Billie was well aware that Nigel Barnes, the defence lawyer appointed for Conner Grey, was waiting eagerly for her to make one wrong move.

The sudden bang of a fist on the table between them even made Billie jump.

'But it was *your* fault that she suffered a terrifying death!' Ash was arguably even more worked up than Billie over this homicide. He'd begged her to play good cop in the interview routine today. It had been a hard sell, even though she knew that he was trying to protect her from herself. Now it looked like he was on the brink of giving her a run for her money.

'My client has now been through several interviews and continues to maintain that he was categorically *not* responsible for the death of Gracie-May McGill!' Nigel Barnes gave his best 'indignant brief' performance. Truth to tell, as long as he did his job by the book and got his fee, he would be just as happy as the rest of them to see his client rot in hell.

'She was fast asleep when I left. I was only a few hundred yards up the road. My back garden's longer. If I'd been a doctor in an airy-fairy restaurant, instead of a pub, this wouldn't be happening. I wasn't keen on the kid, but I wouldn't have wished any harm on her!' Conner Grey shook his head in bewilderment.

Billie took a deep breath, calling on all of her childhood acting experience to play this particular good cop.

'Kids can get you down, that's for sure.' She gave her best sympathetic look towards the heaving lump of flesh who was trying maggot-like to wriggle off their hook. 'Just needed a bit of peace and quiet, did you, Conner? Can't tell you how many times kids have driven me to the brink...'

Nigel Barnes rolled his eyes. He knew the various police interrogation presentations like the back of his hand. He also knew that Billie didn't have any kids.

'My nieces, nephews...' Billie shook her head in exasperation, flicking a triumphant glance towards Nigel Barnes when Conner Grey fumbled in his pocket for a hanky and blew his nose.

'Right enough,' he agreed. 'She was a handful that one. Been placed everywhere. We told the social worker we couldn't take another kid, but they still dropped her off, like a hot potato. We needed a break, time for ourselves...'

'Your wife needed a break sure enough. Was it from your behaviour?' Ash threw down a crime-scene photo of Gracie-May. Face of a sleeping angel, body destroyed by the Devil himself. Conner Grey squeezed his eyes shut in horror. Wiped his mouth.

'Having endless kids palmed off on us, never knowing their history. This one hadn't even been nappy-trained,' he continued tearfully.

'But you took the money!' Ash interjected. 'And you didn't spend it on food. Autopsy showed that all she had in her stomach was a few jelly babies!'

Billie grabbed Ash's wrist under the desk, squeezing it in warning, to calm down just a little.

'I didn't give her any jelly babies! Said on her notes she was sensitive to sugar. I've always been very careful about that sort of thing. Anyway, she was hyper enough without jelly babies...' He shook his head, looking to Billie for sympathy. 'These days they're allergic to everything. You need a degree in science – one's allergic to gluten, one to dairy, then there's nuts, chocolate, fresh bloody air. Costs a fortune keeping them in special diets...' Billie's ears had pricked up.

'So, who did she get the jelly babies off?' This was the latest of several interviews with the man who should have been caring for Gracie-May, trying to find a link to the killer of both the child and Joy Summers. This might finally be one tasty morsel that would come in useful.

'What about these two? Didn't call on any of your old favourites to come around while the wife was playing away?' Ash slapped down the photos of the two girls who had accused Conner Grey via Facebook. He looked startled. 'Word has it you took a real fancy to them.'

'No I never!' Conner Grey looked to Billie for help. She might be repulsed by the man, but she believed him. Nigel Barnes sighed and looked at his watch theatrically.

'My client has done his utmost to assist you with your inquiries, but really, I'm afraid your time is nearly up.'

Ash glanced at Billie as he gathered the photos back up. Nigel Barnes started to tidy his briefcase.

'Can I go? The wife needs picking up from the airport.' Conner ignored Ash, looking instead to Billie to throw out a crust of kindness.

'Sorry. The afternoon court van isn't travelling that way,' Billie checked the clock on the wall, 'bit of luck, we'll get you squeezed in before close of play. Conner Grey, we are charging you with the offence of cruelty to a child – abandonment, neglect and failure to protect.'

'What's that mean?' Conner, in panic, asked Nigel Barnes.

'Means that you are heading to the nearest magistrates' court, where three wise monkeys will decide whether to keep you on remand in the holiday home known as Durham Scrubs, or release you on bail until your no doubt very public trial. Either way we will be back in touch.' Ash was full of helpful information today.

'But how long will I be in if they find me guilty?' Conner was hyperventilating now.

'If?' Ash rolled his eyes in disbelief. Billie could see he was having trouble shaking off the bad cop character. He almost had her believing that he really was a cruel son of a bitch.

'Maximum ten years on that charge and it's not looking good.' Billie smiled sweetly as she delivered the blow, reflecting that she, on the other hand, wasn't acting at all.

The incident room looked like it had been at the centre of an explosion. Paperwork was piled high, jackets were slung onto chairs without care by the MIT team, having rushed back from various enquiries. Billie was pleased to see that no one appeared to have been wasting a moment. In truth, it was hard to forget how urgent their work was.

One side of the main room was decorated with blown-up photos of the desecrated bodies of Gracie-May McGill and Joy Summers, silently screaming out for a helping hand in death, to make up for the lack of one at the moment they had so desperately needed it.

On another wall, two equally enlarged photos stared down. Billie found them almost as painful. Joy Summers had smiled warmly at the camera, as though to a special friend. Billie wondered if that friend was still around, heart shattered into a million painful shards that would destroy their world forever. She kicked herself yet again for having been so close and yet so far from preventing the cheerful woman in the picture from being displayed on this wretched wall of fame.

Gracie-May's photo was so powerful that Billie had already moved it once, determined that it wouldn't catch her unawares again. It was the teddy bear that had caught her off guard, the fluffy toy that should have been the child's comforter, but which had instead been used to suffocate Gracie-May to death.

In the photo it was dangling by one arm and staring with its one eye, straight at Billie as she had stepped out of her room. The flashback, if she were grudgingly to indulge just for a moment, Max Strong's theory, involved once again a teddy bear so similar to the little girl's that it could have been the same toy. Gracie-May was clinging to it like a lifeline, her huge blue eyes staring out warily from behind a tangle of unbrushed curls, a grimly beautiful picture of a little girl for whom all hope of a saviour, even in life, already appeared to have gone.

Billie avoided the moving eyes as she weaved through the mass of clutter. A takeaway delivery of nearly stale bakery items, ordered late in the day, arrived as she clapped her hands to get attention.

'Okay. Tuck in, folks. Let's have a round-up of where we are so far.' The team swooped on command, headed towards the vast box of food, resembling starving wolverines. Billie could tell that they, just like her, had forgotten to take any meal breaks so far today.

Ash barrelled into the group like a rugby centre half, nabbing the last two croissants left. He handed one to Billie. The desiccated pastries looked like they had started the day before dawn and were seriously suffering the effects now.

'Thanks, boss.' He grinned as they both tucked in, scattering crumbs all over the floor. 'That's the theory of how the feeding of the five thousand was so successful.' He munched away, spilling more crumbs.

'What?' Billie was still trying to avoid the soulful stare of Gracie-May. The tiny creature's eyes seemed to follow her around the room no matter where she stood. She brushed away a barrage of bread flakes from her top.

'It wasn't loaves that were responsible, it was croissants. The total of crumbs from five croissants is at least a thousand times the quantity of the originals. Sorted.' Billie shook her head in mock dismay.

'Your wife owes me a medal for giving her a break from your banter all day.'

As the MIT team tucked in, Billie quickly ran through the results from door-to-door enquiries and statements from the motley crew of Magpie fans from the pub. She bit her lip. All in all, it didn't amount to much.

'No DNA matches, other than elimination samples... any luck bigging up the CCTV?' she asked Jim Lloyd, the exhibits officer. He clicked on his laptop, bringing the short footage sequence up onto a big screen behind Billie. She turned, hoping to God that she wasn't going to have another incident. The teddy in Gracie-May's hand was swinging happily, its one unblinking eye on a level with Billie's own. It started to fragment. Billie blinked hard, breathing out a sigh of relief as her vision returned to normal.

'Good work,' Billie commented.

'She looks drowsy.' Ash's voice was full of compassion. 'Should have been tucked up fast asleep with her teddy.'

'Could have been drugged,' Billie replied. 'Boo, have the toxicology reports come in yet?'

'Just checking, boss.' Boo turned to her PC and started speedily clicking her keyboard.

'Looks like he's got a black-and-white scarf and hat on as well as the hoodie.' Billie squinted her eyes. The CCTV enhancement was good but still a zillion miles off from HD and the clip was literally four seconds long.

'Could there be some warped religious motive? Gracie-May was on the Angel and Joy was in the grounds of St Lucia's, a former nunnery. Both were hanging roughly in the shape of a cross.'

'Good thought. Let's keep that in mind when we are interviewing.'

'Toxicology just coming in.' Boo looked up from her screen. 'Small amounts of flunitrazepam in the blood of both victims.'

'Rohypnol,' Billie answered, 'that would account for the drowsiness. Could have been given via a drink easily enough. Ash, can you check out everyone who came into the food bank? Find out if Joy Summers was looking drowsy and if anyone new was talking to her just before she left?'

That wouldn't be as straightforward as it seemed, Billie mused to herself. The food bank operated a drop-in free lunch invitation on the day that Joy had been helping, so strangers could have visited, no questions asked. Quite rightly, the staff were very protective of their vulnerable clients.

'The other possibility is that the drug was administered via both victims' last known meal. In Gracie-May's case, jelly babies were her only known food intake that day.' The team seemed to collectively shake their heads in despair.

'Joy Summers had a quantity of undigested shepherd's pie in her stomach.' Billie wondered if that would have been the woman's dream last supper. 'Her cause of death was the initial knife wound to the heart, rather than suffocation, but like Gracie-May, seven knife wounds were present in addition to the strange cuts in the area of the ankle.'

'There were some jelly sweets in bowls for the kids visiting that day. I remember seeing them when I went into the food bank looking for the dog's owner. It would have been easy to administer the Rohypnol via those,' The Grass piped up from the back of the room, where she stood in isolation.

'And how exactly would you get a jelly baby to take its medicine?' Derek Blythe asked scornfully. A hardened CID veteran and big admirer of Billie, he wasn't going to forget her grassing up her boss in a hurry.

'Just soak them in a tray with the drug. The same as we all used to do with vodka back in the day when we were partying.' The Grass took off her specs and wiped them, revealing two white marks on either side of her nose; skin that had never fully seen the light of day. Everyone else was struck silent for a beat, watching her.

'Whoa. You're a bit of a dark horse, aren't you?' Boo couldn't help herself. 'Thought you would be tucked up by ten with a barrowload of books and a mug of weak cocoa, not raving on drugged-up sweets.'

Even Billie couldn't avoid laughing. She caught Ash's eye. He grinned back.

'It wasn't actually jelly babies.' The Grass looked suitably studious as she explained, 'We used those fuzzy jelly sweets in all sorts of shapes. The point is that they soak up fluid like sponges and pack a kick when combined with the sugar in the sweets, so you could smuggle them with you anywhere – boring lectures, raves, through airports...' The MIT team continued to stare in wonder.

'I imagine Rohypnol could be absorbed in the same way. It's clear, taste-free, portable and quick to administer.'

Billie had to admit that The Grass wasn't necessarily as green as she was cabbage-looking.

'Good point.' Billie hated admitting it, but credit where credit was due and The Grass's revelation of her past misdemeanours had lightened a day that had started so darkly.

'Just had some fresh intel delivered, ma'am.' Jim Lloyd's fingers whipped over his keyboard. A piece of video footage appeared on the big screen. Everyone stopped eating. The location was in darkness, but the star of this grizzly show was in close-up and brightly lit by the phone camera shooting the scene. It showed Gracie-May swinging from the Angel of the North. The footage went blank, then came on again, this time from the foot of the sculpture, with the tiny body swaying in the cold night air above. Billie's heart started beating fast.

'Placed on the dark web, ma'am, early hours. Funny thing is, where it was accessed and reported.' Jim Lloyd shook his head in disbelief.

'Spill,' Billie demanded.

'HMP Durham, ma'am,' he answered, 'inmate was tipped the wink to view it. Even put a hardened con off his breakfast bad enough to report it.'

'Boo, get on to the prison, we need to find out who uploaded this. It has to be the murderer or an accomplice.'

'On to it.' Boo picked up the phone to make the call.

'Could I have a word, ma'am?' The Grass approached Billie as she stared at the screen, willing herself to see something that she might have missed earlier.

'It's just about the motorist yesterday.' Billie gritted her teeth. Patience was a virtue, her mother had always reminded her. 'He was wearing NUFC clothing, some of the witnesses said. That was why yesterday I asked you–'

'Yes. Hat, scarf, same as half of the city.'

'And possibly the murderer.' Ash was right, The Grass was like a dog obsessed with a bone.

'Are you going to tell me something new, Green?' Billie started off in the direction of her office. It was going to be a late night.

'When I saw the car, there was a big bag of jelly sweets on the passenger seat.' The Grass blinked hard, no doubt recovering the scene from her mind's eye as Billie continued into her room, shoving a pile of paperwork away to sit at her desk.

'Have you ever been to a live football match, Green?' Billie glanced at her desk phone. Lights were flashing up a vast queue of unanswered calls.

'I'm more a Roller Derby girl, ma'am. I'm in the local team.' Billie tried to hide a sudden surge of amusement. She'd once been on an investigation that required interviewing members of a female Roller Derby team. They were crazy, strong and very sassy women with attitude, who wore camp costumes and used witty pseudonyms when playing the hard contact sport. God only knew what name The Grass used. Billie forced herself not to go there.

'Sweet stalls are everywhere around the stadium. Lots of jellies, acres of black-and-white kit. Gracie-May's murder was judged to have taken place between midnight and 3am. The accident took place around 6.30am–'

'Six twenty-eight, ma'am.' The Grass stood to attention, her hands behind her back, looking straight ahead. 'Just think it might be worth checking out, ma'am.'

Billie had only to ponder for a moment, before deciding that it wasn't such a bad idea. Send The Grass off on a wild goose chase after every single Magpie fan who had a bag of jellies in their possession. It would certainly keep her off her own back for the duration of the case.

'Be my guest, Green.' Billie succumbed to a tight smile. 'Shut the door when you leave, would you?'

'Ma'am.' The Grass scampered off like a woman on a mission. Billie picked up her mobile which had started to ring.

'I hope you'll be ready on time!' It was the unmistakable voice of her fiancé, David, sounding rather agitated.

'Wha... I tried to ring you–' Billie started, before David cut in.

'Check your voicemail. I've rung you about a dozen times today. The VIP reception has been brought forward to six thirty. I'll pick you up at six.' Billie's mind blanked. 'You haven't forgotten my dad's big party tonight?' Billie's mind still hadn't quite switched from murder to celebration. 'For his knighthood?' David said the words loud and clear, putting an incredulous twist into the tone.

'No, 'course not,' Billie lied, running her fingers through her hair as she looked at her calendar on the wall. The date was outlined in red felt-tip pen for emphasis.

'I'll be waiting outside in an hour. I hate coming in when that scruff of a lodger's around.'

David ended the call. Billie grabbed her bag in a frenzy, racing out of the door, almost knocking The Grass to one side as they left the exit to the car park together.

How on earth could she have forgotten the major celebratory event for David's family? The race was on to change chameleon-like into a sparkling socialite, mingling with people living a world away from the murder, death and destruction on the seedier side of town. The last time she'd set eyes on her party dress, it had been scrunched up in a ball at the bottom of the wardrobe. Crushed velvet was about to take on a whole new meaning.

8

DEAD ON TIME

'Wow, look at you, Wonder Woman!' Kate popped her head out of her room as Billie breathlessly clattered down the stairs in stilettos, a halo of red curls lifting in the wind tunnel caused by the speed of her descent. She looked radiant in a long, deep-green velvet dress which clung to her slender body.

'Thanks so much for steaming this. I owe you!' She smoothed the dress down on her hips.

'No problem.' Kate smiled. Her expression changed as she flicked her head back towards the open door. 'Lover boy's waiting.' Billie felt a surge of irritation that David had chosen to sit outside in his Jag rather than come into the house. He checked his Rolex as she swung her long legs into the car, waving goodbye to Kate.

'Dead on time for once.' He pecked Billie on the cheek. Her heart was still beating rapidly with the pace at which she had needed to move to hit the deadline.

'You're looking pretty handsome tonight if you don't mind me saying so.' Billie started to relax. David was indeed looking gorgeous. He'd apparently been at the gym every night – whilst she had been clearing out her parents' place – getting himself wedding ready. He pulled the car away smoothly.

'That dress again. It's been a good servant to you.' He glanced at Billie's outfit. Her heart sank a little.

'Thanks for the compliment.' She rolled her eyes.

'No, really, you look great in it. Hey, you'd look great in a bin bag. It's just that Mum was hoping you would get something special for tonight.' Billie could feel a black mood descending. David's bloody mum. She should be getting an award for control freakdom.

'Shame you didn't take her up on the offer of that modelling course she tried to get you for your twenty-first birthday,' David added. 'You could have been dressed from head to toe in Balenciaga for the past ten years.'

'As if.' Billie felt herself deflating inside, wishing she was off to the pub with Kate, who said she was having a reunion with old friends, instead of heading to this self-congratulatory fest of bright lights and dim people.

'I've been looking at pictures of our honeymoon hotel. Maldives here we come!' David smiled. He could have been a model himself, all white teeth, golden tan and expensive fragrance. Beach ready, Billie reflected, whilst her pale skin made her look like she had been sitting under a heavy weight since time began.

'Um, just thinking about that,' Billie took a deep breath, 'we couldn't put it back a few weeks?' She braced herself, certain of the answer. David jumped the amber light before it hit red, putting his foot down.

'You *are* joking, right?' He glanced at Billie. He wasn't laughing. Billie had prepared her argument.

'It's just that I've suddenly got a heavy workload on. Two murders rather than the one we expected to tie up quickly.'

'It's our honeymoon, for Christ's sake...' David overtook a cyclist, nearly knocking him into the gutter.

'Well if anyone had asked *me* before they booked it!' Billie snapped back.

'It was a surprise from Mum and Dad as you know!' David shook his head in irritation.

'So your mum just went ahead and booked the flights, and chose the hotel, before asking me if it was a good time,' Billie countered in equal annoyance.

'Well, maybe she thought, strange though this may sound, what better time for a honeymoon, than straight after the wedding?' David's voice was tight. If he put his foot down on the accelerator any further Billie wouldn't be surprised if a traffic patrol car suddenly loomed into view in the back mirror.

'And could you please stop having a go at Mum? Everyone's just trying to do the best they can after everything you've been through – near-death experience, disciplinary proceedings then your parents' accident. It's all too much for you. If you ask me, the quicker you hear about this promotion and get behind a desk, the better.' Billie felt suitably guilty and equally piqued, as well as tight-lipped about her intention to wriggle out of the promotion.

The rest of the journey continued in stony silence as David's car sped out of the smart leafy suburb of her parents' former home, picking up even more speed through the rough side of town. Billie stared out of the window, ticking off familiar places in her mind, scenes of high drama in her working world, amongst people considered lowlifes. It felt an oddly comforting view. She silently wondered if she had started out in streets like these.

Billie had forced thoughts of her adoption shock out of her mind as much as possible, determined to focus on getting justice for little Gracie-May and Joy before facing her own wrecked history. Now though, in these moments of strained silence, she couldn't help wondering how the hell her early life had led her here, to a fast car with a man who, after a month living apart, felt a million miles away in spirit. Billie pondered that a stranger would think they were at the fag end of a long and empty marriage, bickering away in a desperate attempt to inject an iota of energy into a badly flogged horse.

David finally pulled the car up outside of a smart hotel on the glittering quayside of Newcastle's city centre, under one of the seven spectacular bridges spanning the River Tyne. Spangled lights from restaurants, art galleries and concert halls were like coloured jewels reflected in the dark rippling water of the river. They sat still for a moment, before David caught hold of Billie's hand, kissing her curled fingers.

'Sorry, look, I don't want to fight, darling. It's been a stressful time for both of us. It's my ear that keeps getting a bashing over flowers, wedding breakfast menus and hymn sheets, remember.' David smiled that endearing smile of his.

Billie reminded herself that every relationship went through ups and downs. She and David had just been through quite a few downs in a row recently. She kissed him on the tip of his nose as a sign of reconciliation. God, she could be such a cow. It was true that she had left all the wedding arrangements to everyone else, rather than negotiate with David's mum. Maybe he was right about Kate too. She had been neglectful of their relationship. She made a note to herself. Must try harder – and get a bloody wedding dress, pronto.

'What were you ringing me about last night?' He was making a big effort to be all ears. Billie decided that this wasn't the time or place to drop her birth bombshell.

'It's okay. We can talk about it later,' she answered lightly.

'Then it's time to celebrate,' David ruffled Billie's hair, 'drink champagne. Give my old man a night to remember.' Billie glanced up at their penthouse across the river, with its garden roof terrace giving a bird's eye view of the waterfront and the magnificent court building where David spent most days of his dazzling career. She was looking forward to staying there again tonight. Maybe she should sell her childhood home? After all, it had been built on a big fat lie. Maybe it would be the first step towards a fresh new start?

Billie reached for her velvet evening bag as she turned the idea over in her head. Searching under her feet to no avail, she flipped open the glove compartment, rifling through. She pulled out a bag of opened jelly sweets.

'What is it about jellies today?' Billie shook the bag in David's face. He frowned.

'What do you mean?' David picked up her evening bag which had slipped down the side of the seat and handed it to her.

Billie laughed as they left the car. 'Drunken jellies. We clearly missed out on so much fun, concentrating on being fast-tracked to the top in our jobs.' Billie linked David's arm as they headed towards the hotel entrance. 'Time to catch up. Let's have some jolly jellies on the tables at the wedding reception!'

'Sounds good to me.' David pulled her closer. Lost in a renewed sense of togetherness, neither noticed the dark shape of a lone figure climbing onto the railings of the iconic Tyne Bridge.

Billie gave the new Sir James Silver a heartfelt hug as she congratulated him on his appointment as a high court judge and his resulting knighthood. He had been her dad's best friend, partners in crime on the golf course and Billie had no doubt, in the courts, too, as they had worked up to the top in their chosen vocations, one nabbing the bad guys, the other locking them up.

'You look exquisite, Billie, my love.' He kissed Billie on both cheeks.

'Darling, couldn't you have found a dress with sleeves?' David's mother whispered as she followed suit, glancing at Billie's scarred arm as she stepped back. 'Hair definitely up for the wedding. I've already run through ideas with the hairdresser.'

Billie bit her tongue, instead keeping a smile fixed on her face as she grabbed a glass of champagne from a passing waiter. She glanced across the room; to her utter delight, she spotted Josta King standing to the side of a spectacular buffet table. She was eyeing up a huge joint of beef placed near her.

'Hands off the knives,' Billie whispered in her ear, having crept up behind Josta, who chuckled heartily.

'I must admit I'm tempted. Whether to test a theory or slash my wrists I couldn't say. I've had tête-à-tête with corpses who were livelier than some of our fellow guests here tonight. But social connections are vital in the world of crime, as in all areas of life. C'est la vie, my dear.' Billie guessed that Josta's stunning and gregarious wife, Lola, was probably mingling, charming the entire room en route.

'You need a drink.' Billie turned to look for another waiter.

'Here it is – at last!' Josta boomed happily. 'The delay no doubt due to my escort being something of a babe magnet.'

A wide smile crossed her round features as Billie spun around to see Max Strong handing a large glass of Bordeaux to his mother. He looked impressive without appearing to have particularly tried, wearing an exquisitely tailored black suit, white shirt open at the neck. His dark eyes took in the view of Billie, mouth turned up at the corners as he gently spoke, holding out his hand to shake.

'DSI Wilde. How delightful to meet you again so soon.' Billie felt her face flush and damned herself. At least he didn't take the opportunity to remind her of the time of her next appointment.

'His other mother's off on the highways and byways of the far reaches of the kingdom.' Josta gratefully took a swig of her drink. 'A fringe theatre that I forget, in pursuance of spreading Shakespeare's word. How she suffers for her art.'

Billie and Max exchanged amused glances. The moment was suddenly broken as a hand roughly shook Billie's shoulder, causing her to splash her drink down her dress.

'Billie! I do hope you aren't discussing murder.' Billie brushed the spill away, as David's mother barged past Josta, giving the older woman a disapproving and dismissive stare. She caught Billie's wrist, yanking her away towards a group of judges and their wives. Billie felt her temper flare. With some difficulty she forced herself to keep control. Such behaviour would have resulted in the perpetrator being hurled onto the floor, cuffed and very much the worse for wear, had it taken place whilst she was working. David's mother clapped her hands, putting on her best show of joyfulness.

'Tonight, we have more good news to share! As you know, Billie is about to be married to our son, David, and we are very much looking forward to seeing you all at the wedding.'

Billie wondered if David's mum had been knocking back the champers too quickly. She hardly knew anyone in the group now grinning inanely at her, save for a couple of judges she vaguely recognised from court appearances, gowned and bewigged on those occasions in all their judicial finery. So much for the intimate wedding she had craved.

'Sorry, I don't recognise any of you with your clothes on.' It was an attempt at a gag to stop her flooring David's mother, but it simply caused the judges to drop their smiles and the wives to look rather nervously at their husbands. Billie felt her face flush.

'Billie has just been promoted to Assistant Chief Constable. The youngest person of that grade in the whole of the UK!' Billie wanted the ground to open beneath her. She had clocked the Chief across the room when she had first arrived. Had he spilled news of the appointment to David's mum on purpose, knowing she would spread it like wildfire, cutting off Billie's planned escape? Who exactly were these people who claimed to care about her?

'Um, I haven't taken the job,' Billie answered, sipping her drink. 'Got a bit too addicted to murder, I'm afraid,' she added as way of explanation. A few people chuckled at her weak joke. Others looked bewildered.

'But you will,' David's mum said loudly. It sounded like an order.

'My job. My damn decision.' Billie flicked her head up. Her stare was steely. 'Now if you'll excuse me.' Billie turned and walked away, straight into David's waiting arms.

'Darling! Was this the news that you rang to tell me last night? Congratulations!'

'No,' Billie answered as she headed for the door. She wanted out. Her life wasn't her own. But then it appeared that it never had been. Suddenly David's mother was in between them, her face in Billie's, the smell of more than a couple of glasses of champagne on her breath.

'How dare you show me up in front of our guests?' Billie was closer than she had ever wished to be to David's mum. Behind the carefully made-up face were sad bloodshot eyes sitting in skin wrinkled like an apple way past its sell-by date. A woman forced, by lack of personal achievement, to live a life of reflected glory. The strain was clearly beginning to tell.

'Simply stating the facts.' Billie tried to sidestep the woman, an act of steely will, considering that she had never been one to walk away from someone picking a fight.

'Facts? You want some hard facts, dear?' David's mum's voice was getting louder. 'You came from the gutter. Dumped. A scruffy little Jane Doe. You would be nothing if your parents hadn't taken pity and given you sanctuary in their lovely home. Not without a lot of hard work on the part of David's father, too, I might add. But breeding comes out. I told David this wedding was a mistake!'

Billie was stunned. People around had turned to stare, as David's father approached, smiling apologetically to his golf chums in their social climbing suits. The thought flitted through Billie's mind that they were like the little dress-up dolls she had played with as a child, wearing a different outfit for every occasion. Ageing Barbie and Ken dolls. Nothing seemed real anymore.

'All these big family events are proving a little too much for her I'm afraid. She's getting a bit highly strung. Come along, dear.' David's father led her away. Being a bit deaf these days, Billie guessed that he hadn't heard his wife's bitter words clearly. But David had. He was looking sheepish. He certainly hadn't contradicted his mother.

'You knew.' Billie could feel fury rising in her chest.

'What?' David shrugged.

'About my adoption!' His face revealed the truth. 'How long have you known that I was adopted?' Billie demanded, pushing his arm away from hers.

'Um, well, I dunno... forever, I guess.' David tried to sound nonchalant. 'When I was a kid, mum always said not to mention it. She said it might upset you, so I just never did. I assumed that you had always known and simply didn't want to discuss it. Mum explained that it's just one of those dirty little family secrets.'

'What?' Billie nudged past David. 'No, I can't do this. It's all just one big lie!' Billie headed towards the big French windows leading to an outdoor area overlooking the river.

'Billie, don't be foolish,' David tried to reason. She ignored his pleas, desperately needing to get away.

Outside, Billie took gulps of fresh air mixed with smoke. She moved as far away as possible from the other guests, taking refuge behind a huge potted palm whilst damning herself for not heading for the main exit. The only way out from here without vaulting over the railings enclosing the space, was back through the main room. She leaned against the wall, closing her eyes.

It was the hint of lemon aroma that alerted her at first to the nearness of Max Strong.

'You okay?' he asked gently, as he joined her.

'I've felt better,' Billie admitted. She wasn't in the mood for smart talk and anyway, he'd no doubt witnessed the whole embarrassing incident.

'Larkin was right – they do tend to fuck you up, your mum and dad.' He smiled as he referred to the famous Philip Larkin poem, 'or mum and mum in my case,' he added with amusement.

'Did he write anything about mothers-in-law?' Billie rolled her eyes in horror. Max smiled.

'I could easily beat you in a humiliation at a party contest,' he shared, 'take my fifth birthday. I was hoping to impress my school mates, big time. We were all into *Star Wars*. I asked for a Millennium Falcon cake, magician dressed as Darth Vader, lightsabres in the party bags. The whole kit and caboodle. What did I get?'

Billie shook her head; she had no idea, but his engaging chat was lifting her spirits despite the situation.

'A cake that looked like an autopsy table complete with dead body on it...' Billie laughed despite herself, '...and a murder-mystery-themed party. The prize being to find my thespian mother rather indecently dressed and fully dead in the linen cupboard, complete with a trick axe in her head and copious amounts of fake blood pouring from every orifice. Some of the tea towels and pillowcases still have red stains ingrained into them.' He shook his head in dismay at the memory. Billie couldn't help laughing.

'If I was a kid, I would have loved that,' she argued.

'Let's just say, The Force wasn't with me on that birthday. Kids went home traumatised. Some were having screaming nightmares for weeks afterwards. Our house became a no-go zone. One parent claimed his kid needed counselling afterwards.'

'Don't we all?' Billie cheered up, before remembering her situation. 'I've just discovered that I was adopted,' she blurted out, feeling shocked at her need to tell and ridiculously small and alone for a moment. Max Brown's hand brushed her bare shoulder. She wanted him to keep it there. He did.

'That must be tough,' he answered quietly. They stayed in that position for a beat before Max broke the moment. 'You've got a lot to deal with right now, Billie. Your murderer sounds like a piquerist for starters. Someone who derives sexual gratification from torturing victims with multiple cuts or stabbings.'

'We haven't found any evidence of sexual interest in connection with either victim.'

'Not at the scene of crime perhaps, but it will be there.' Max sounded certain. 'Knifing is as much a turn on to piquerists as George Clooney is to most women.'

'Nor do I remember mentioning mode of death,' Billie added.

'Had afternoon tea when I picked my mother up earlier. You only have to open the fridge to sum up the situation. The chicken had succumbed to a frenzied attack and a pound of sausages had been slashed almost to smithereens.' Billie couldn't help giggling, imagining the scene. 'Once you get your suspect, do a body search, because if they can't get their hands on a victim, they will slash themselves. The scars will be there. Billie, you need to be careful.'

His hand slid away from her shoulder tracing the scar down her arm, just as David appeared before them. He took in the scene, looking less than impressed.

'The speeches are about to start,' he ignored Max, 'you need to come in.'

The other guests had already dutifully made their way back inside. Billie's mobile rang. She rifled in her bag and took it out, recognising the ancient 'Dixon of Dock Green' theme tune that she had set for work calls.

'DSI Wilde,' she answered. David reacted in irritation. He glanced at Max dismissively, whilst holding out his hand.

'Let's go. We don't want to upset the apple cart any further.' Though Max Strong was taking in the scene, Billie had immediately blocked out everything but the call.

'Okay. Tell him to stay *exactly* where he is and stay calm. I'm going to call him right now.'

'Billie!' David glanced behind. The speeches were starting, David's father was being introduced.

'I've got to make a call,' she quickly scrolled through her witness contact numbers and clicked on one, 'it's Conner Grey.' Max raised an eyebrow in question. David shook his head, even more annoyed. Even though Gracie-May's foster dad had been plastered all over the internet and evening newspapers he hadn't made the connection. 'He's been let out on bail. Headed straight to the Tyne Bridge and he's threatening to jump.'

All three turned their heads to the iconic bridge looming a few hundred yards away, suddenly aware of the commotion upon it. Police cars, lights flashing, had stopped traffic on either side. A group of shadowy figures were illuminated every few seconds in the revolving light as they crowded around the central area.

'So? Good riddance to bad rubbish.' David tried to grab Billie's hand. 'One less chav to clog up the courts.'

Max looked as though he was about to hit David, but it was Billie who pushed him away.

'He wants to speak to me.' The phone connected via video. Conner Grey could be seen in close-up, sitting on the iron railing of the bridge, wild-eyed and sweating.

'Billie! This is your last chance–' David was cut off in mid-threat as Max moved quickly to block his movement and propel him backwards, forcefully pinning him against the dark wall. He whispered in his ear.

'No, this is *your* last chance. Get yourself out of her face right now, or I promise, you will be the one down there feeding fishes in that very dark and deep water.' Max stood back, keeping steely eye contact. David, shocked, straightened his tie and with one final pause to stare at Billie's back, finally turned away and slunk back into the main hall.

'Conner,' Billie started, 'I'm here. Look at your mobile screen. You wanted to talk to me?' There was a sudden commotion behind Conner as someone tried to intervene.

'Get back, or I'll do it!' Conner, in panic turned away. Billie ran her hand through her hair, feeling her heart beating fast.

'Try to stay calm,' Max whispered as he rejoined Billie. She was struggling now to keep the phone in her hand whilst trying to take the opportunity of Conner's distraction to speedily climb over the waist high barrier enclosing the outdoor area, in her long dress. Max vaulted over and swung her into his arms and away from the gilded prison of the back-slapping hotel, onto the quayside and hard reality. 'Show empathy for his situation,' he whispered in her ear as he stood back, out of view.

'Empathy?' Billie felt panic rising. 'I was the one who gleefully told him he would probably face ten years in prison!' she whispered. Conner's distressed face suddenly loomed into view on her mobile phone screen once more.

'I've told them I'm only speaking to you!' he shouted, adjusting his heavy weight on the rail where he balanced precariously. Billie wondered how on earth he had managed to get up there considering his size. She guessed old climbing habits died hard. 'You knew where I was coming from this afternoon...' He looked as though he was about to cry.

'The wife's left me,' he started, 'met some guy in Benidorm, even before she heard about all of this!' His nose started running. He moved his arm to wipe it, almost slipping. Billie could see the reaction from those standing in view behind him on the safe side of the bridge.

'I'm listening, Conner.' Billie tried to keep eye contact and stay calm as Max nodded to her in encouragement, leading her carefully towards the bridge. 'Talk to me.'

'I'm gonna jump anyway,' he continued, tears rolling down his chubby, waxen face now, 'but I want you to know that I didn't do anything with those other girls. Trolls all over the internet saying disgusting things but it's not true – it's *not* true...' He trailed off, sobbing now.

'That must be hard for you, Conner.' Billie was terrified that one wrong word would send him hurtling down into the dark swirling water.

'It is!' he agreed, as Max carefully led her along the pavement. Never had she been so grateful for a strong but gentle grip on her wrist. 'They're right about Gracie-May.' He rubbed his eye with one hand, almost slipping again. He stopped speaking, balanced himself. 'I should never have left her. It's all my fault. I just meant to stay for the first half of the match, then after I had a pint...' His chest heaved in an attempt to catch his breath. 'She normally slept right through with that stuff they gave her to knock her out at night...'

Lisdexamfetamine, Billie remembered. It was an ADHD prescription treatment, which had also shown up in Gracie-May's toxicology report, but Josta was certain it hadn't contributed to her death. She tried hard not to let her mind wander on to thoughts of other treatments, such as regular cuddles and bedtime stories that may have better comforted the unsettled fallen angel.

'I know that's no excuse...' he added.

'We all make mistakes, Conner.' Billie glanced at Max. Was she saying the right thing? He gave her a thumbs up. She wasn't lying. She'd cocked up herself big time tonight. If she'd only managed to shut her mouth when David's mum had opened hers...

'But I've done my best with all the other kids. We've fostered nearly fifty of them and most have kept in touch, so the marriage wasn't all bad.' He gulped and took a big sigh. 'One of them, Micky, he was a shy little runt of a kid when he was placed with us. I taught him to play football, took him to games and last night,' he shook his head, 'last night I was so proud. He had his first match for the Toon first team.' He started to sob again.

'That's why I went an' left her. I wanted to see our Micky walk out onto that pitch. I always told him he'd be a winner, told him to believe in himself. God knows he's had his ups and downs on the way. I said, remember – shy kids get nowt...' Conner broke down again, heaving wails of tears as he rocked forward. Billie's heart leapt into her chest.

'So don't do this, Conner. It sounds like you did Micky proud. Don't take the edge off his success. You would break his heart.' She sighed, feeling she was way out of her depth here. Conner wiped his face on his sleeve.

'You really think so?' he sniffed. 'Naw, I'm just history now.'

'I know so.' Billie stood still now. Max brushed his hand gently over hers. 'Because I was a dumped kid as well and the people who took me in, well I owe them everything. They've just died so I know that if you do this, Micky's heart will be like mine, broken. Probably forever.' She blinked and glanced at Max, tears filling her eyes. She meant it.

'I'm sorry to hear that, love.' Conner looked with concern at Billie, distracted from his own tale of woe. 'I knew you would understand.' He seemed to calm a little.

'All that stuff you've just told me now, well the court will take it into mitigation,' Billie added, feeling absolutely mortified that she had been so judgemental of the man earlier. Could her smart-arse interview have been the reason that Conner Grey was at this moment hanging so precariously off the Tyne Bridge?

'The jelly baby thing, I wasn't lying about that, I wasn't!' he added. 'It was on her notes not to.'

'I believe you.' Billie nodded.

'But after I left the police station, I remembered about two weeks ago, on different days, someone did try to give her sweets, in the park. Might have even been jelly babies. I told them to back off.' Conner adjusted himself, seemingly to find a more comfortable position. He looked away, recalling his memories. Billie's ears pricked up.

'Approached her both times by the swings. Gave her a shove. Seemed a bit strange but lots of the kids have family trying to make contact when they're first taken into care, even if they've got a court order to keep away. So I told them to bog off.' Billie's heart started beating faster.

'Conner, can you remember anything about the person? It could be important.'

'Yeah. Remember them well cos they got a bit bolshie the second time.' He looked straight at Billie as he recounted his protectiveness. 'I picked her up and took her straight home. Didn't want her witnessing any argy-bargy stuff.'

'Look, I'm heading to the bridge right now, on the lower quayside path. There's a pub down here. Will you meet me, have a drink and a chat? It will go well for you in court–'

'I don't care about the bloody court, I'm a dead man walking,' Conner burst out. Billie closed her eyes. Had she said the wrong thing? Max Strong's reassuring hand stroked her own. 'But if it helps you catch the monster that did that to the kid, well, it'll be something.' Conner Grey turned his head to the police standing behind him.

'She wants me down there,' he flicked his head back, 'can you help me over?' Billie got a flash of relieved faces and strong arms reaching out as the mobile phone was passed into someone else's hand. She took a moment to breathe out, glancing at Max. He dropped her hand.

'You did great!' He smiled softly.

'I don't want any of you lot coming. Just me and her!' Conner's voice could be heard breathlessly demanding, as he was hauled over to the safe side of the bridge. A police constable's face loomed into view on the screen.

'Ma'am?' he questioned Billie. She nodded, running her hand through her hair.

'Send him down. I'll meet him,' she ordered. Conner's face suddenly popped into view again, having taken back control of the phone.

'I'll just shake this lot off,' he spoke in hushed tones, as though he and Billie were partners in crime. He gathered pace, the group of emergency workers receding from view behind his profile.

'I see you down there now.' He waved. Max Strong slunk away into the shadow of the bridge out of view.

'Good lad, Conner.' Billie gathered her wits about her. This could be the breakthrough she needed. 'I'm buying. Bet you're ready for a pint?' She had to keep a connection, give the impression that she was his new best friend forever.

'You can say that again.' Conner managed a sheepish smile. His head bobbing in and out of view as he gathered pace in her direction. She glanced up and spotted his shape dodging down the steep side street off the main bridge crossing. He stepped off a kerb, looming back into view on her mobile screen once again. 'The funny thing about that person trying to feed her sweets was—'

Billie heard the screech of tyres and a loud bang as the picture on the screen fragmented – split-second views of sky, metal and tarmac.

'Oh my God!' Billie cried. Max sprang out of the darkness. Together they sprinted towards a white van, which had probably been speeding down the rat run side road, to avoid the bridge closure.

'Conner!' Billie cried, as Max rushed ahead of her, dragging Conner's body from under the front of the vehicle. 'Conner!' she cried again, struggling to help haul out his weighty bulk, as the dazed driver stood frozen in horror. Billie dropped to her knees, ready to resuscitate if needed, but as Max laid down Conner's upper body, his head flopped over to face Billie – what was left of it anyway.

'I'm sorry.' Max shook his head, but he didn't need to say the words. Conner Grey's brains were spilling out onto the cold, hard tarmac. The precious information he held about Gracie-May McGill's possible killer now just another grizzly secret about to be buried with him.

9

DIRTY LITTLE SECRETS

Billie was sitting upright in the pre-dawn darkness of her bedroom, arms cupped around her knees, when she heard the front door open. She rubbed her eyes, feeling her face, dry and puffy to the touch, due to the tidal wave of emotion that had surged through her body on arrival home hours before.

Max Strong had dropped her off at the doorstep, ensuring that she had entered safely. Billie hadn't invited him in. She had already made a fool of herself on leaving the scene of Conner Grey's death, by allowing tears to stream down her face as she and Max had made their way back under the dark shadow of the Tyne Bridge. He had suddenly pulled her close and touched his lips momentarily on the top of her head. The movement had no doubt been a straightforward comforting beat of kindness, but like an idiot she had responded, brushing her lips against the base of his throat. He had sprung away, it felt to Billie, as if in horror.

Neither had said another word about the contact, instead covering their jointly disturbed emotions with intermittent expressions of shock over the death of Conner Grey. However, when she had tried to hail a cab, clearly in no mood to rejoin the party, he had insisted on dropping her home. Their parting had been excruciating, with Max reminding her quietly of her next appointment. She felt crushed with embarrassment at the memory.

As the bedroom door now opened, Billie felt her body tense. Instead of the expected figure of Kate back from the rendezvous with her friends, the dark shadow of a male figure filled the space.

'Billie?' It was David. Billie let out a sigh of relief, for a split second, before remembering his words from the night before.

'Billie, it's me,' he sounded slightly drunk. 'Look, I'm sorry... I didn't mean what I said about that guy on the bridge...'

'What about me being the family's dirty little secret?' Billie felt anger replace melancholy.

David crossed to her bed and sat down on the edge. He had a bottle of opened champagne in his hand.

'Look, it all came out wrong. I don't care how you came to be here, I just want to make you my wife, live happily ever after with you, end of.' He took a swig from the bottle, before offering it to Billie. 'I've just been so stressed. Work, the wedding – my bloody mother...' He shook his head.

'Yeah, well she made her feelings clear on my background; seems I was the only one not in on my own secret life...' David kicked off his shoes noisily.

'I thought that you didn't care. As for my mother, don't dwell on anything that *she* said, she was so pissed tonight that she ended up falling into the ornamental fountain.' He sniggered at the memory. Billie couldn't help a small smile as she imagined the scene. She relented a little, took a drink of champagne. The fizzy bubbles went straight to her head. 'And that guy. What a creep! He was hitting on you,' David wound his arm around Billie's shoulders, 'and you're mine, all mine.' He posted a wet kiss on her cheek.

'Rubbish! He's the police shrink that *you* lot all insisted that I see. He just happened to be at your dad's "do". Suddenly you've all landed me with a full-time therapist checking that I'm not going totally crazy, even off duty.' Billie crossed her eyes in jest, pushing away the memory of Max's fingers brushing her shoulder and the warm, smooth, lemon-scented skin at his throat when her lips had touched the naked spot at the opening of his shirt.

'Well that's all right then.' David shrugged off his jacket. 'Look, when we get the wedding out of the way, I'll do whatever you want to put things right about your adoption. Just don't go finding some chav family and moving them in. It's bad enough with that lodger you've dragged in from the gutter.'

'Stop picking on Kate!' Billie bristled. David kissed her on the nose playfully.

'All right, all right. I'm just having a bit of fun. You need to chill out, young lady.' He undid his shirt and peeled it off. Billie couldn't help clocking how super fit her future husband was looking.

'Please stop judging me and finding me lacking, when you become Mrs Silver, Billie Wilde,' David teased, pulling a hurt face. Billie had to admit that bearing in mind tonight's terrible events involving Conner Grey, his words had a ring of truth. 'Have you got your handcuffs with you, officer?' he quipped playfully, as he jumped into bed beside her.

Rays of warm sunlight heralded morning, along with a gentle kiss on Billie's forehead as David woke her with orange juice and a bowl of freshly peeled fruit.

'Wow. Is this what I can expect every day from married life?'

Billie joked. 'Though, you could, of course, be feeling guilty about something?' She raised a quizzical eyebrow.

'Don't be silly,' David sat on the end of the bed, 'I realise that I should have been more attentive recently, with everything you've been through.' He kissed Billie's fingers. 'I've got a gift for you.' He reached down and hauled up a huge box. 'You don't have to accept it. Take it back and change it if you don't like it...' Billie lifted off the lid. An exquisite wedding dress lay inside. She grinned sheepishly.

'How did you know?' She bit the bottom of her lip as she smoothed her fingers over the beautiful ivory silk of the gown.

'Your lodger can't lie to save her life, that's why.' David laughed. 'I just knew when she was trying to wrestle my mother from your wardrobe door the other night, claiming that you wanted to keep your dress secret, that it simply didn't exist. So, I saved you that trouble at least...' He trailed off, not knowing how Billie was going to react.

'It's beautiful.' Billie had to admit David had amazing taste. She hadn't known where to begin.

'It's unlucky to see you in it before the wedding,' David kissed Billie on the nose, 'but believe me, I'm so looking forward to taking it off after the event.'

Later, as Billie stood at the door wrapped in David's old shirt, watching her future husband heading to do battle in the Crown Court, she had to admit that she was starting to shake off the terrible feelings of anger, grief and guilt that had threatened to engulf her lately. David looked sleek and smart as he climbed behind the wheel of his Jag.

'Don't forget, wedding rehearsal tonight,' he called, blowing her a kiss as his car accelerated smoothly away.

Refreshed and reinvigorated, Billie finally felt positive once more about the future. Whatever had happened in the past, was exactly that – history. It was time to move forward.

As she turned to go back indoors, Billie felt something in the front pocket of David's shirt. Pulling out a key she frowned. The name on the tag was The Turret Room. She smiled. Maybe it was another playful present planted by David. It sounded very much like the sort of name that the honeymoon suite might have, in the castle venue where they were due to get hitched. Seemed like her last-minute doubts and jitters were unfounded. Married life looked like it was going to be a bag of fun surprises after all.

10

A KILLER SIGNATURE

Billie almost sent a wayward press photographer flying into the bushes as he leapt in front of her car. She flung him a disparaging look, all the while damning herself that she'd given him just the shot he wanted for tonight's newspaper coverage. Ever since her first case as DSI, she had attracted attention, not just for the murder cases that she had investigated but for the fact that she would never fit an identikit picture of the typical detective, despite her supposed family pedigree.

As she entered reception Billie immediately spotted the figure that had caused such excitement outside, the town's newest hero, footballer Micky Flannigan. This morning, he looked less like a winner and more like a little boy who'd just lost his dad. Billie felt her stomach lurch as she held out her hand to shake.

'DSI Billie Wilde. You look like you could do with a cuppa.' Micky nodded, all puffy eyes and blotchy skin in his famously branded team tracksuit. She might be looking at the new local poster boy for the game. But right now, her prediction to Conner Grey the night before appeared to have come true. Micky

Flannigan looked utterly heartbroken as Billie ushered him into the canteen.

Having positioned him behind a large fake palm, facing away from the admiring eyes of every male police officer in the room, Billie joined him. She handed over the quietly requested nearest thing to fresh orange juice that the canteen had, for the star who had kicked the spectacular winning goal and put the team on track for a trophy.

'Thanks.' Micky accepted the drink politely. 'Uncle Conner always made sure I drank a glass of orange juice every morning.' Tears started to well up in his eyes. Embarrassed, he quickly swiped them away with his sleeve.

'So here's to Uncle Conner.' Billie chinked her mug of steaming coffee against Micky's glass. 'He spoke about you, last night,' Billie started, 'he was proud as punch for you with everything you've achieved.' Micky took a sip of his drink.

'It's him that should be sitting here being proud,' Micky shook his head in disbelief, 'I know he shouldn't have left Gracie-May, but that was my fault.' He turned his face to the wall, tears welling up in his eyes again. 'If I hadn't been picked for the first team...' He trailed off for a second, deep in thought.

'You mustn't blame yourself for that,' Billie reassured him, 'look around here, see how many people are thrilled that you were chosen. The killer is the only one to blame for Gracie-May's death.'

'It looked like I'd missed my chance at the big time.' Micky picked up a paper napkin from the table and blew his nose. 'Always played as a jobbing freelancer for any club that would have me until now. Sometimes had to take other work. I'm getting on a bit for a crack player. I'd got him a ticket but with her there, he couldn't come... he just didn't want to let me down.'

'Look, we all feel terrible.' She wasn't lying. 'Had we realised how fragile he was... but we had to interview him.' Micky took another sip of his orange juice and nodded.

'I know the drill. Was a bit of a bad lad myself as a kid. Had a few police cautions. Always wheeling and dealing and nicking, anything to get attention.' He looked up and smiled sadly at Billie. 'My family spilt up, you see. It would have been all right if that hadn't happened. Might have been an England player by now...' He trailed off for a moment. '...Word has it you talked him down, from the bridge last night.' He looked Billie in the eye, she felt her face flush, well aware that her actions had unwittingly led him to his death a minute later.

'It was talk of you that stopped him jumping, Micky. I want you to be quite clear about that. He was keen to help us with information to nail Gracie-May's killer. What happened afterwards was an accident.'

'Those bloody girls online,' Micky answered angrily. 'He never laid a finger on them! The two of them came to stay at the foster home when I was there. He did his best. They were on the game from being kids, take your bloody eyes out and come back for your sockets given half a chance. They are the ones who want locking up!'

Billie ran her fingers through her hair, she couldn't actually begin to fathom who should be locked up in that scenario, but some of her sympathy had to go out to the two damaged individuals who had made the accusations, drugged up young women who appeared to have needed to steal, lie and sell their bodies to survive, for practically their entire lives.

'Conner mentioned someone approaching Gracie-May in the park a couple of times, possibly offering sweets. Did he mention that to you at all?'

Micky shook his head. 'Naw, he didn't, but come to think of it, someone did come up to Gracie when I offered to take her to the park, just last week. I was visiting and Uncle Conner had to rush off to hospital with one of the short-term kids. Disabled lad. He had a funny turn and Aunty Joan was shopping for her trip to Benidorm then she was off to bingo.' Billie was immediately alert, pushing to one side the overwhelming sorrow that she had been involved in the untimely death of a man who seemed to have been capable of giving most saints a run for their money.

'Can you tell me exactly what happened, Micky?' Billie got her notebook from her pocket.

'Em, well me and Gracie were just having a kick about. I was being goalie and letting her score all the time. She was made up.' He smiled at the memory. 'And this guy came up, wanted to shake my hand. Said he'd seen me play in a match with my last team. I scored a hat trick...'

'Did he show any particular interest in Gracie-May?' Billie was aware that judging from the admiring stares all around her here in the canteen this morning, the incident might well have simply been a starstruck fan spotting his favourite footballer.

'Nope, though the woman he was with lifted her onto a swing and gave her a push.'

'A woman? There were two of them?' Billie persisted. 'Can you describe her at all?' Micky stared into the distance, shaking his head.

'Not really. I think she was wearing a grey hoodie. Could have had dark hair, but it was all tucked inside of her hood, quite tall, well-built... I can't say for sure cos the guy was gushing all over me, asking about the team and whatnot,' he explained.

'And she didn't offer Gracie-May any sweets at all?' Billie persisted. Micky shook his head.

'Not that I remember, but I can't say for sure. I had my attention on the guy.'

'Remember what he was wearing?' Billie decided that the incident was probably nothing.

'Black-and-white hat and scarf pulled up high and he was wearing thick glasses. He looked a bit crazy to be honest.' Micky was thinking hard. 'In fact, he was a bit crazy, cos he asked me to do this funny thing.' Billie looked up from her notebook, all ears.

'Rolled up the sleeve of his jacket and handed me a pen and asked me to sign my name on his arm. Said he was going to get it tattooed over.' Micky shook his head, even allowing a small incredulous smile at the oddness of the request. 'So I signed, but I warned him it wouldn't be much of a tattoo, cos, well,' he looked embarrassed as he glanced up at Billie, 'I couldn't read and write until Uncle Conner taught me, so I just use one letter when I'm signing. It's the same shape I write in the air when I score – a sort of signature.' Micky looked bashful. Billie's heart had already started beating faster.

'Can you put your signature on my pad here?' Billie tried to keep her voice calm as Micky took her pen and drew the ragged capital letter.

'It's an M. Just the first letter of my name like.' He smiled, slightly self-conscious. 'I still can't even make that neat.' Billie stared at the letter on the page, speechless for a moment. It was an exact copy of the killer's signature, carved into the bodies of both Gracie-May McGill and Joy Summers.

The enlarged autograph of Micky Flannigan held the attention of everyone in the incident room. 'So, we may be getting somewhere at last.' Billie looked at the photos of the two victims on the wall, as though attempting to restore their confidence in her efforts. Joy smiled back, looking cheery as always, Gracie-May and One-Eyed Ted still appeared seriously wary. Billie thanked God that the flashbacks triggered by that huge photo seemed to have eased off.

'Check HOLMES again. See if we have anything on a male and female perpetrator acting together. Keep a lookout for a male with a tattoo on his right forearm just like this one and check for cuts elsewhere on his body. Apparently, some sad cases cut themselves up if they haven't got someone else handy and clearly, we've got someone who likes a blade.'

'He still shouldn't have left the kid alone!' Ash sounded defensive, no doubt remembering his forceful interrogation the day before. The death of Conner Grey loomed over them like a dark cloud. Justice was one thing but losing someone in the manner that Conner Grey had met his end, was a devastating tragedy.

'True, but let's remember he didn't kill her. The real bummer is that we didn't get more info out of Conner earlier. His last words were *"the funny thing about that person trying to feed her sweets was–"'* Billie swallowed hard, determined to forget the terrible vision of Conner Grey's brains scattered all over the road.

'He might have been referring to the M tattoo, if it was the same guy who approached Micky,' Derek Blythe offered.

'True. Anyone else got any ideas?' Everyone shrugged, shaking their heads in puzzlement and frustration. 'Any thoughts, Ash? You haven't come up with any of your own funnies this morning and it's almost midday.' Ash didn't react in his usual jovial manner.

'Who knows? Maybe he was wearing a clown outfit and juggling.' He shrugged, disgruntled at the question.

'You okay?' Billie asked.

'Yep, boss.' Billie made a mental note to check why Ash was clearly out of sorts today. Rina Hoy, the statement reader, who never let anything pass her eagle eyes, waved her hand from the back of the room.

'Might mean nothing, but both girls working upstairs at the pub said that Conner Grey didn't attempt to engage their services, he was simply clapped out on one of the beds they wanted to use. Seems he was attempting forty winks during half-time. He told them he was exhausted with childcare but wanted to watch Micky play. Sad thing is, they report that he nodded off again, back in the bar and didn't even see Micky score the goal.'

A silence fell on the room for a spilt second, as the team took in the terribly poignant morsel of information. Billie felt as though she had been winded. David's teasing words about being too judgemental rang in her ears. She took a deep breath, determined to keep focused.

'Any progress on Gracie-May's former foster families?' Billie asked around the room. The whole team were chasing up leads on the ten families Gracie-May had been placed with from birth.

'We've come across a few dicey characters with links to her care network, some in the nick. We're working through them all, ma'am, quick as we can,' Derek Blythe offered.

'Good work. Remember to look out for the tattoo and recreational cuts.' Billie reflected that something had changed last night in her trust of Max. Here she was spouting his theories, when only the day before she had ripped his alleged profiling expertise to shreds.

Rubbing the scar on her arm, she recalled his hand on her wrist, gently leading her along the quayside, his encouraging nods as she had tried to keep it together to stop Conner from launching himself from the bridge. She shivered, not sure which of the two recollections had triggered the reaction.

'Anything in Joy Summer's background to link her to Gracie-May?' Billie asked Ash. He had a history of being meticulous in his approach to inquiries. She trusted that if anything was there, he would find it. Ash shrugged.

'Nothing so far. Been mostly a carer for her old mum until she died a couple of years ago.'

The Grass put her hand up, like a child in the school classroom, eager to get the teacher's attention.

'I managed to find the stolen car from yesterday's accident and searched it, ma'am. I was correct. There had been a bag of jellies on the seat. The owner of the vehicle has been traced and confirmed that they didn't belong to her. I took fingerprints for elimination purposes.'

'Go Sherlock Holmes,' Derek Blythe clapped mockingly, 'the mystery of the missing jellies has been solved!'

'I've got the rest of them here.' The Grass held up an evidence bag containing an open packet of jellies, with a couple remaining in the bottom.

'Got a bottle of vodka at the ready to get soaking, have you?' Derek Blythe joked. He clearly wasn't the forgiving sort.

'Permission to send to the lab, ma'am,' The Grass persevered, blinking wide-eyed at Billie. A memory of the man who had been driving the crashed Mini started to take shape in Billie's mind... it sounded like the person Micky Flannigan had described, but surely that was a crazy idea? She would wait to find out results from the lab before jumping to such unlikely conclusions.

'Yes. Crack on with it, Green, then help DS Blythe with enquiries.' Derek Blythe pulled a face at Billie.

'How kind, ma'am,' he joked as The Grass shot off on her mission.

'Let's get to work.' As the team broke up and set off on their different tasks, Billie caught Ash's arm.

'Sure you're okay, Ash?' Billie was missing her usual daily banter with her wingman.

'Yep. I've got to get to the food bank to follow up on some interviews.' He checked his watch and started to move away. Billie had wanted to talk to him about her adoption shock, ask his advice on the situation. He might be about to be David's best man, but he was also her best friend. She guessed he was secretly gutted about Conner Grey. She decided to cheer him up.

'Hey, you'll be pleased to know that I got my wedding dress at last.' She grinned.

'Great,' he replied, 'at last I can use that scene-of-crime suit I've been keeping back for you.' It was a weak joke, but Billie hoped he was cheering up a little.

'I'm guessing you gave David the nod to buy it. Don't suppose you're going to spill the beans about this little secret either?'

Billie slipped her hand in her pocket and pulled out the key she had found in David's shirt, with the tag marked *The Turret Room*. She put it down on the tabletop. Billie could tell by Ash's reaction that the key hadn't been meant for her eyes. Boo sped to a halt alongside them holding a printout.

'Got the name and address of a woman who actually tried to take on the care of Gracie-May when she was a newborn. She had some sort of link to the birth mother.' Boo handed over the paper.

'Bingo!' Billie read the information. 'Bags me a ride to the seaside.' She looked up again; Boo was already on the other side of the room checking out information with one of the team and Ash had left. Billie realised that he had taken the key with him. Clearly, she was not meant to be in on the big surprise coming her way.

The sun was shining brightly as she headed for her car, her mood lifting for the first time in weeks. The double murder investigation seemed to be finally taking shape and her relationship with David had suddenly regained its sparkle. She would just hurl away the improper thoughts of Max which kept threatening to upset her equilibrium. Finally, there was a sense of light at the end of a long dark tunnel and as for her surprise rendezvous in The Turret Room? Billie smiled in anticipation. She hoped it was going to be another night to remember.

_____

11

PRECIOUS WOUNDS

A *small seaport town, famous for all kinds of wickedness.* The quote from Methodist founder John Wesley in 1742 made Billie smile, as the picture postcard seaside village of Alnmouth suddenly loomed into view. Billie stopped the car in a passing place on the winding hedgerow-hugged road and stepped out to take in the truly heart-stopping view. To her it was the least wicked place on earth and her work had certainly taken her to a few evil locations.

Below, the ancient settlement was perched on a spit of land stretching out to sea, with gaily-painted houses looking down over the river mouth. At high tide, the tumble of ancient grain stores, now turned into houses, pubs and cafes, were cut off from Church Hill, a high grassy mound topped with a wooden cross. It marked the spot where the original village church had collapsed and slithered into the sea during a terrible storm. Today, storybook-white fluffy clouds scudded across the blue sky. Fishing cobles bobbed close to the beach, hauling in the lobsters and crabs that this location was famous for.

The view caused a sudden wave of emotion to surge from nowhere. Grief-stricken brackish tears skittered down Billie's cheeks. Alnmouth inhabited so many of her ice-cream sweet, sea-salty happy family memories.

True, she had discovered that it wasn't the life that she had been born to live, but the immediate shock and anger towards her mum and dad for keeping such a big skeleton in the cupboard, was beginning to calm. The hideous truth of Gracie-May McGill's upbringing and Micky Flannigan's early life swept away any romanticised idea of the alternative childhood that she may have left behind.

As soon as the current investigation was over, Billie vowed to discover the story of her early life but approach it in a positive frame of mind. Whatever she might discover, she was in no doubt that she had genuinely loved her so-called mum and dad. She desperately ached to have them back, if only to hug them close rather than admonish them for their dirty little family secret, as David's mother had memorably described her. Billie blew her nose then got back inside the car. The hauntingly seductive village always pulled her like a magnet, despite John Wesley's warnings. If this was as wicked as life got, Billie mused, then bring it on.

~

'DSI Billie Wilde.' Billie held up her ID, as a tall, handsome woman in her mid-sixties opened the door. A look of shock crossed the face of Margaret Craig.

'Police?' She nervously ran her fingers through her faded strawberry-blonde hair.

'Mrs Craig? I have a few questions to ask you about the recent death of Gracie-May McGill. Can I come in?'

'Yes...' Margaret Craig appeared flustered. 'It's my birthday,' she mumbled apologetically, as she led Billie through the hallway and across the elegant lounge to the open French windows, where an impressive cake sat on a white ironwork table. Matching chairs were perched on the small patio. Below, a terraced garden swept down to the River Aln estuary, opening to the sea below. The view was exquisite.

'Oh, happy birthday! I won't keep you long if you're expecting visitors.' Billie nodded to the table. Margaret Craig smiled wistfully as she led Billie out onto the patio.

'Unfortunately not. This isn't exactly the time for celebration, DSI Wilde, not after the news of Gracie-May.' Margaret Craig pulled out a chair and beckoned Billie to take the other. 'The cake is a yearly ritual, sent from a friend who is rarely in a position to join me on birthdays. To be honest, I didn't expect this one to arrive today. A pleasant surprise.' Her eyes twinkled a little as she glanced at Billie, who guessed there was a tale to tell with that friendship.

'You must be a very special acquaintance then.' Billie eyed up the cake. 'Looks like lemon. My favourite.' Margaret Craig beamed at the news.

'Mine too. You must share. I've just made a pot of tea.'

Billie knew how vital it was to tread carefully with people who might have information. Of course, in some cases it could just be a case of battering the door open and pinning them against the wall, needs must and all that. But other people needed gentle coaxing, to get them over the initial tongue-tying issue of having a police officer firing questions at them. She had lost count of the number of times a prime morsel of intelligence had been plucked, from what would appear to an outsider to be a rambling conversation about nothing much.

Whilst the elegant birthday girl poured tea, Billie cast her eyes over the spectacular view from her home. Billie's route had taken her past the tiny village primary school, complete with woodland and beach classrooms. It was painful to think how close Gracie-May McGill may have come to enjoying a perfect childhood, with memories of the area as precious as Billie's own.

Margaret Craig glanced up at Billie as she handed her a porcelain cup of tea. Her eyes were blue and bright. Billie was guessing she must have been something of a beauty in her time.

'I was devastated when I heard the news.' Margaret Craig stared down, shaking her head slowly as she sipped her tea. 'I blame myself.' She sighed sadly. 'Maybe if I had argued more forcefully to be the one caring for her... I haven't been a great mother figure, DSI Wilde.'

'Please, call me Billie. Can you take me back to the time that Gracie-May was born? Did you know her parents or any other family members?' Margaret Craig looked away sadly, her memories clearly less than joyful.

'I knew her mother, a lifetime ago. I looked after Shannon for a while when she was young. Truth to tell, I wasn't much older. Moved in with a bad boy and his kids. That's me,' she said through a sigh, 'the queen of dreadful judgement.' Margaret Craig took a sip of her tea, lost in thought for a moment. Billie could sympathise. She'd made some questionable judgements herself recently. 'I was forced to keep him in drink *and* drugs. Then he ran off. Left me to care for his two, Shannon and MJ, in a house no better than a squat. I didn't have the tools. I was struggling to make ends meet and I already had a toddler of my own.'

'That must have been hard.' Billie made a note. She wondered where he was now, this 'bad boy'. Could he be an evil killer? 'Can you remember if he was into climbing, or did he work in a job that required scaling buildings?' Margaret Craig chuckled despite her harsh memories.

'He had trouble climbing out of bed. To my knowledge he never had a job, not *ever*.' A look of shame suddenly shaded her fine features.

'I was up at dawn cleaning a nunnery and out at night pulling tricks. Can you believe it? I brought the drugs home for the boyfriend and the bacon for the kids. Upshot was I wasn't focused enough on childcare.'

'You're being a bit harsh on yourself. You sound more like a victim of domestic abuse to me.' Billie touched the older woman's hand. In her police career she had met so many women who blamed themselves for a violent partner's cruelty.

'Well, you make your bed... to be honest, sometimes I gave as good as I got. I was a bit wild in those days.' The older woman was lost in thought for a moment. 'I recognised you as soon as I opened the door. I read about you in the paper, apprehending that man who was raping and murdering elderly women.' She gave a quick nod to the ragged scar on Billie's arm.

'Nearly killed him more like. I've been in the doghouse for that one.' Billie raised her eyebrows. She still couldn't bring herself to apologise for the force she had used. Margaret Craig smiled in admiration.

'I'm sure that your parents were very proud of you.'

'Tried to get me promoted off the streets more like. They're dead now, though, so...' Billie didn't know why she was telling this woman her life story.

'I lost my own child,' Margaret Craig whispered quietly, 'it broke my heart in two. I almost went crazy with grief, but I couldn't turn back time. When I got the chance to go abroad and start a new life, I took it. My bad boy's kids went back to their mother. She was out of rehab by then, demanding that they be returned to her. I just ran away from it all.'

Billie could feel the sorrow, sweeping through the woman's very bones. She could sympathise, having had her own issues with overwhelming grief lately. There had been moments when she had felt like running away from it all too.

'But you did well in the end.' Billie gestured to their

surroundings. Margaret shrugged, clearly less than impressed with herself.

'Mostly my husband's money. Nothing for me to be proud of, I'm afraid. He made big bucks in oil drilling. He's dead now too. We'd just moved back to England and this house, when he hit a hole-in-one on the village golf course then keeled over. I guess you can say that at least he died happy.' Billie sensed that Margaret Craig seemed infinitely less full of grief for her husband than her child.

'Did you get in touch with Shannon when you returned?' Billie tried to focus on the need for useful investigative information. Margaret Craig shook her head, a little too vehemently Billie thought.

'Oh no, not when my husband was alive. He didn't really like me going out much or getting in contact with people that I knew before I met him. He insisted that I give up work, said that he wanted to look after me.'

'Did you have children together?' Billie felt an overwhelming sadness for the woman, who at a casual glance would appear to have led a charmed life in beautiful locations.

'No. My husband said that all we needed was each other and the few friends that he had through work. He even chose my clothes for me.' A quick snapshot of her wedding dress, chosen by her own future husband, flashed through Billie's mind. It made her shiver as did the mention of specially chosen friends… wedding guests, even.

'Of course, now in these more enlightened days, DSI Wilde, I am aware of coercive abuse, but at the time I wasn't sure if I was just going mad. He certainly gave that impression if I tried to break free from his seemingly loving grip. He would constantly insist that I was fragile, that I needed looking after, he was just showing his total love for me…' She trailed off for a moment as Billie dwelt on similarities within her own relationship. Where did one draw the line between devotion and emotional abuse?

'When he died it was like a breath of fresh air, I'm ashamed to say,' Margaret Craig continued. 'I can't help feeling that I was complicit in the warped situation. Did I ask for it? Did I choose to stay in return for familiarity and fear of my own abilities? Did he truly not realise what he was doing?'

Billie felt sorry for this poor woman, who seemed to have had her life defined by controlling men in their many forms. She checked the brief notes that she had been handed on Margaret Craig.

'But your husband didn't start your successful chain of nurseries? Is that how Shannon knew where you could be found?' Margaret Craig shrugged.

'I guess so, we'd just launched and had some positive coverage in the press. I'd had the idea for some time, but my husband always said it would be too taxing for me. He wasn't even cold in his grave before I started the business. I'm sure a psychologist would make something out of *that*.' She looked up at Billie, who immediately tried to wipe away a vision of Max, the feeling of his fingers curled around her wrist. 'Was it the need to show defiance now he was dead, or atone for letting my own baby down?'

'Well, it looks like you've given lots of babies a fine start now.' Billie was pleased that at least Margaret Craig seemed to be enjoying a happy ending of sorts in this enchanting village. She bit into her lemon cake, showing delight in the taste. 'Shannon must have had some happy memories of your care, for her to hope you would look after Gracie-May,' Billie added.

'Social services got in touch. Gracie had been born in hospital the day before, but Shannon had left immediately, keen to get her next fix no doubt, as the baby was born addicted to heroin.' Margaret sighed heavily, tears springing to the back of her eyes. 'She left a letter next to the baby, asking me to take care of the child.' Billie pulled out a tissue from her pocket and handed it to Margaret. 'How sad is that? The most rubbish parent figure in the world was the best she could hope for.' She dabbed at her eyes. Billie waited whilst she regained her composure.

'I loved Gracie-May at first sight,' Margaret's voice shook as she spoke, 'and even though I was technically way too old to look after a baby, the wishes of Shannon carried some weight. There were apparently no other close relatives in a position to help. I even brought Gracie home for a day or two...' Margaret trailed off, taking a sip of her tea.

'Then what happened?' Billie urged.

'I was diagnosed with breast cancer. Treatment had to start immediately – operation, chemo, they whisked her away deciding that her best chance was adoption, rather than the risk of a few months with a clapped-out old horse fit for the knacker's yard.' Margaret Craig gave a wan smile.

'But you look great now.' Billie wasn't lying.

'I fought like a demon to get better, prove that I was up to looking after Gracie-May and when I got the all-clear, I begged to have her back, but it was too late. Shannon couldn't be found to back up my case. Word had it she had passed away in some drug den in Europe. I was told that the baby was now in a stable placement. Not being a family member, I had no rights.' Margaret blew her nose. 'Until the horrific news, I hoped that she had found a forever family.'

'Don't blame yourself.' Billie poured more tea into Margaret's cup and handed it to her, feeling guilty that she was forcing her to dredge up such memories on her birthday, of all days.

'I would have loved to have lived long enough to see her walk down the aisle. My husband didn't do weddings.'

'Come to mine then, next week.' The words were out of

Billie's mouth before she could think, but she had already asked Kate to fill one of the seats vacated by her mum and dad, much to David's mother's fury.

'What? But I couldn't...' Margaret Craig looked surprised.

'Why not? See it as a birthday present!' Billie desperately wanted to donate a sunny day to this woman. She scribbled the details on her notepad and ripped out the page, placing it on the tabletop. 'There's a seat next to me going free at the top table. It would be doing me a favour. Almost all of the other guests have been invited by my husband's family.' Billie bet Margaret Craig scrubbed up well. She could just imagine David's mum's face when another glamorous woman took her place at the top table.

'If you're sure, I would be absolutely delighted!' Margaret Craig said. 'Though, if you haven't been able to invite any of your own friends, I do hope you aren't falling into the same trap as me. Are you sure this is the man for you?'

A quick vision of Max flickered through Billie's mind's eye, catching her by surprise. She mentally batted it away, replacing it with a memory of David from that morning. Before she had time to answer, her mobile rang. She recognised the work-themed ringtone.

'DSI Billie Wilde,' she answered.

'Hi, it's Sandy,' the Chief's PA carried a smile in her voice. 'Just a reminder that you are due at your counselling session in thirty minutes. I've been told to keep a record and I don't want you sent to the naughty step again,' she teased.

Billie checked her watch and sighed. A flush of embarrassment coloured her cheeks as the memory of Max's reaction to her ill-judged kiss the night before flashed through her mind.

'Trouble?' Margaret Craig asked.

'My middle name.' Billie rolled her eyes, standing up. Margaret Craig smiled in recognition.

'A woman after my own heart,' she joked as she led Billie through her elegant lounge filled with photos. On a table nearby the door, a beautiful indigo-blue bowl embellished with a crazy paving of gold decoration took pride of place. Margaret Craig handed it to Billie. 'For you.' She nodded towards Billie's scarred arm. 'I really admire the Japanese art of Kintsugi – fixing broken vessels with gold metal to show how precious old wounds are. That's an impressive war wound that you are carrying. You have gold running through your veins, DSI Wilde. You should display your scars with pride.'

Billie left the village feeling calmer than she had done for weeks, realising that Margaret Craig was the first, indeed the *only* person who had not given negative feedback on the way in which she had apprehended the murderer who had targeted elderly ladies. From The Grass, who reported that she had used too much force, to the Chief, David and his parents, who wanted to ensure that she never got into that situation again, Billie had fought furiously against being made to feel that she had done the wrong thing. She guessed that the elegant Margaret in her lovely home was also hiding a lifetime of old wounds.

As Billie drove away leaving her heart, as usual, in Alnmouth village, she reflected that though she had not gained any great insights into Gracie-May's short life, she felt better about her own. She would enjoy Margaret Craig's company at her wedding and at least the time spent in Alnmouth meant less time in the shrink's seat. Was she about to be judged by Max for the events of last night, told that she had done the wrong thing, yet again?

12

THE BOWELS OF HELL

DO NOT ENTER UNTIL INVITED TO DO SO. *Welcoming*, Billie thought, as she viewed the new notice hanging on the closed door to Max Strong's consulting room. Billie paced the small waiting area outside, considering whether he had fitted the new sign especially for her. She couldn't remember stamping on that wording the last time that she had tried to leave in a hurry. Her face flushed at the recollection of that tantrum.

A bowl of jellies sat on the table. Billie nabbed one and popped it in her mouth, wondering how jellies had suddenly become all the rage. She realised how easy it must be to spike the things. She was suddenly hungry and it was hard to stop eating once she had started. She took another sweet whilst punching numbers into her mobile.

'Boo? Anything new turned up while I've been at the seaside?' she asked, glancing at her watch and the closed door. Five minutes into her shrink time and Max wasn't exactly welcoming her in the door with open arms.

'Bit of extra info about Joy Summers. She was a Sunday

school teacher at the church Gracie-May once went to. Might fit in with Ash's suggestion of a religious angle.'

The door swung open and a woman stared straight into Billie's eyes before pointing tight-lipped at the mobile then to another sign behind Billie. It read TURN MOBILE PHONES OFF. Billie ignored the woman, as she continued her call with Boo.

'Okay. Let's follow that up. If Ash's around ask him to go over to the Sunday school location and find out if anyone has been hanging around there, get any descriptions, etc.'

'On to it.' Boo ended the call. Billie popped the phone in her pocket. The woman folded her arms looking less than impressed.

'This really isn't a very good start,' she began.

'And you are?' Billie countered, wondering madly if she had entered the wrong building.

'Dr Jill Adams,' the older woman grimly replied, before waving her arm to indicate that Billie should enter the room.

'I'm here to see Dr Max Strong.' Billie almost pulled her ID out and waved it in front of the woman's face, before remembering that she wasn't conducting a criminal investigation, though she suddenly felt like a suspect.

'I will be taking over your sessions from today.' Jill Adams shook her hand in the direction of the chair. Billie stood stock-still.

'What?' She blinked. Had she misheard?

'It's been agreed by Dr Strong and sanctioned by the chief of police himself,' Jill Adams continued, 'so let's get on. I have another client at 3pm.'

'Where's Max?' Billie demanded. There wasn't a hope in hell she was going to succumb to interrogation by this woman.

'Dr Strong decided that it was inappropriate for him to

conduct further consultations with you. Your file has been handed to me.'

Inappropriate? Billie screamed silently. *Just because of one quick ill-judged kiss in a stressful situation? He'd kissed her on the head, first, hadn't he? Had she imagined that?*

Billie felt a hurtful stab in her heart, flushed away by a surge of embarrassment, which was quickly knocked aside by anger. Had he told this woman about last night... what was her name?

'You're joking.' It wasn't a question. Jill Adams didn't look like a comedian. She was now flicking through Billie's file.

'Anger issues have been flagged up. I can see they are going to be high on the agenda.' Billie cut across the speech Jill Adams was about to make.

'Here's something for your agenda – take that file and stick it deep where the sun doesn't shine!' Billie wasn't just piqued, she was livid, as she turned and stormed out. Cool fresh air hit like a hard slap to the face, as she slammed the door behind her, alighting onto the pavement outside. She reached in her pocket and answered her mobile which had been ringing relentlessly almost from the moment she had ended the conversation with Boo.

'DSI Wilde,' Billie snapped. Boo was back on the line.

'Finally managed to track down the inmate of HMP Durham, who was sent footage of Gracie-May, ma'am, but you'll have to be quick. He's being held on remand over a big drug-smuggling case. Just locked up a couple of days ago but he's obviously enjoying the experience so much that he's back at the magistrates' court today, on charges of GBH. Beat another inmate up in the exercise yard, yesterday.'

'Don't tell me, underneath it all, he has a heart of gold.' Billie second-guessed the argument that his defence lawyer would be putting up.

'Even hardened cons don't like to give a child killer an easy ride, hence his offer of intel,' Boo reasoned. 'His name's Glenn Baxter. He'll be heading straight back to jail after the hearing, so you'll have to see him before the prison van heads off. He's a bit nervy about talking, asking for all of your police ID to be removed. Plan is to pretend that you're his shrink, there to help with the sentencing report.'

'On my way,' Billie answered, shaking her head at the irony of the situation. Hurrying to her car, she silently ranted that no one deserved to see a shrink like Dr Jill Adams. She wasn't going to forgive Max Strong for this in a hurry.

A descent into the bowels of hell could be a fair description of the journey from modern court reception hall, on the upper floor, housing slick security, upholstered seating and even a snack bar selling different formations of coffee, to the gloomy dank cells way below. Billie sensed an unsettling change of ambience during the downward spiral of staircase. Reaching the bottom, it felt as though all hope had been abandoned, left triumphantly waving goodbye from the lofty landing far above.

In the oxygen-throttling world below stairs, the waft of expensive perfume from highly paid lawyers gave way to the overwhelming smell of cheap bleach, cloying sweat and the stench of fear, salty with tears and bitter with disappointment.

This was the squalid space where mad, bad and sad examples of humanity awaited their fate at the hands of the magistrates' bench. This collective of three allegedly fair-minded citizens were, in theory, volunteering their life-changing judgements from the perspective of people exactly like those being charged. In practice, the two tribes, above and below stairs, could have been created on different planets, such was the total disparity between their life experiences.

'Court's over. The rest of them are loaded in the meat wagon, so don't spend all day with lover boy,' the vastly overweight custody officer muttered. She rubbed her back as she scuffed along the bare floor of the empty corridor, her worn-out uniform stretched over hips howling out to knees for a double date at the replacement clinic.

The walls were the sickly pink shade of children's medicine, the type that required kids to be pinned down by parents before it could be administered. Grime and graffiti offered the only decoration, that and a smattering of unidentified sticky substances, the content of which Billie made a concentrated effort not to dwell upon or come into contact with. The custody officer finally heaved to a halt outside of a cell at the very end of the utterly depressing walkway.

'Ten minutes max,' she warned, before turning a key in the metal door. She didn't bother to open it, before wheezing her way back in the direction that she had started from. Billie wondered if she would be capable of making the return journey in that time.

'Take no notice of The Zombie. No one's in a hurry to get where I'm heading,' a male voice piped up from inside the cell. Billie yanked the heavy door open. In the corner, the man, with his back to her, was just finishing off at the urinal.

'En suite? You bagged the luxury quarters,' Billie commented, indicating that if he had opted to use the toilet facilities right then, in an attempt to unsettle her, it hadn't worked. Still turned away, he zipped up his jeans with the air of someone familiar with the technique necessary when one hand was cuffed to the other.

The moment gave Billie an opportunity to appraise the prisoner. Tall, broad, head shaved, muscular. Even from behind, she could sense that he wasn't a man to get on the wrong side of. She didn't fancy the chances of the person who had inflicted the fresh cut across the back of his head, or the purple, now-turning-yellow bruise around his eye, as his profile came into view.

It was the full-on figure of the man, however, that stopped Billie in her tracks. As he stepped out of the shadows into the unforgiving glow of the fluorescent light above, she registered, with horror, the other painful-looking wounds on his body. He smiled; a slow, controlled smile that could appear menacing if it was pointed at the wrong person.

'Shame I won't be free to escort you down another back street tonight.' He looked straight into Billie's eyes. She felt her face flush in mortification. It was the guy from The Dive Bar, the one who had been beaten up! She decided to ignore the comment. She glanced away, focusing instead on a side wall where a scrawl of graffiti warned **You've got what's coming bitch**! next to a drawing of a huge penis.

'I'm investigating the murder of Gracie-May McGill. I have viewed video footage sent to you in connection with her death. Can you tell me who sent that footage and how you came to receive it whilst you were locked up in prison?'

'Should have known you were a copper.' Glenn Baxter slowly rubbed the scar on his head. 'So, you don't need a lesson on how easy it is to get stuff inside. I could get a full circus with elephants and a lion tamer in the clink if the mood took me. There are these clowns called...' he bent close and whispered in Billie's ear, '...naughty screws, but judging by the way you were dancing the other night I'm guessing you know *all* about them already...'

Billie reached out and grabbed Glenn Baxter's shirt, pushing him towards the long concrete shelf topped with mauled wood which passed for lavish seating in the court holding cells. His reaction unnerved her. He started laughing.

'Oh no, officer, no, don't get your friends to beat me again!' he mock-cried in sotto voce.

'Need any help down there?' Billie peered through the small rectangular window in the cell door. The custody officer had turned her body to face the door and was calling whilst wincing at the effort of the action, still not having made it back to her station yet.

'Everything's fine,' Billie called back, kicking herself for getting into this damn situation. If she had sent Ash out to the court it would never have happened.

'Do you want to help with this investigation or not?' Billie was struggling to keep her temper in check. 'We're talking about a pre-school child, who was murdered in the worst possible scenario. Do you have kids?' she demanded.

'Yep. I've got a little princess myself.' Glenn Baxter's face reflected regret for only a split second, but Billie noticed it.

'So think of her. Think how you would feel if you never got to see your daughter again.' She sat down next to Glenn Baxter, determined to get a name from him.

'I don't get to see my daughter,' the now subdued prisoner flatly stated. Billie wondered what he must have done to have access denied to his own child. 'Not since I chose to stay in UCO.' He said the words so quietly that Billie almost missed them. She was stunned. Was he making it up? Was Glenn Baxter an undercover police officer?

'You do understand that I'm risking my neck here?' His voice was deadly serious, his accent dropping from street slang to that which Billie guessed was his normal voice. 'But then we both like to live dangerously, right? Hanging around with lowlifes on our secret investigations. Forget a happy family life in our game...' He sighed and leaned against the back wall. Billie decided not to correct his assumption that she had also been at work the night before.

'I turned up at home in the full druggie kit one night. My little one just started screaming. She had nightmares for weeks about the bogeyman in her room.' He shook his head. 'She didn't even recognise me. Then the wife decided she didn't recognise me anymore either.' He shrugged. 'Can't say I blame her. At least I don't have to look for a new gaff right now. Got myself booked into a nice little shared cell,' he joked.

Billie readjusted her preconceptions of the man. She shivered as she thought of the squalid quarters awaiting him. She'd seen inside enough remand prisons to know that tabloid headlines describing extravagant prison living bore no resemblance to reality. A Victorian-era squat was more likely, in which so many innocent-until-proven-guilty men and women rotted, awaiting their fate.

'Check me out with the Chief. He's looking into who kicked the stuffing out of one of his leading UCOs.' Billie suddenly had a picture in her mind's eye of the photos spilling out of The Grass's folder and the interest that the Chief had taken in them. It started to make sense now.

'Well I can assure you that it wasn't me,' Billie replied.

'You want to be more careful, stay off the drink on the job. You need eyes in the back of your head in those places. I was trying to protect you, not jump you. Turns out you should have been protecting me.' He rubbed his head again. Billie grimaced.

'Sorry about that,' was all Billie could reply. She could take the lecture, much as she didn't need it. But then she couldn't tell him the truth, that she had been totally off duty and had still only consumed a single drink. Glenn stretched up and looked through the window.

'Anyway, Chewbacca's on the homecoming run, so let's be quick – the footage was sent by an old jobbing con called Geordie Stix. Real name George Strachan. Got sent down years ago for fiddling with kids. Latterly his USP has been small-time drug smuggling, hides the goodies in sweets...' Billie caught her breath.

'Do you know where he lives? Is he a climber?' So many questions and she could hear the shuffling gait of the custody officer getting ominously closer.

'Bit of a character. Fancies himself as a Charlie Big Spuds, but he'd have trouble fighting his way out of a paper bag. Runs a scam when he's inside, swapping drugged-up jellies for fags. As a consequence, he suffers from COPD. No way could he have scaled the Angel. Had a thing about birds – the feathered kind. Ran a club inside called the Jail Birds, would you believe? Special interest in magpies.' Glenn rolled his eyes. 'Jeez, I gave up my family for this...' He shook his head.

'What about *his* family?' Billie persisted. Glenn shrugged.

'Think he had some history in Lincolnshire, as well as the North East. Said he was planning a big get-together when he got out.' Glen was talking quietly but fast now. 'Fishing trip,' he said. 'Went on about wanting to catch a big fish then go bird watching. To be honest, I've got bigger fish to fry inside myself, so half the time I paid no attention–'

'Time's up. They're kicking off in the sweatbox.' The custody officer was only yards away now, jangling her keys. Glenn Baxter took out his mobile and scrolled through.

'Quick, give me your number,' he demanded. Billie complied. 'I'm giving you a picture he sent at the same time. Doesn't look up to much, but I'll let you be the judge.' He hit the send button then stepped behind the half-height urinal wall. 'Turn away if you're squeamish. I've got to hide this in a dark place.'

'Anything else?' Billie grabbed Glenn's arm as he re-emerged. He stopped for a moment, glanced to see that the coast was clear and bent forward.

'Yes. You owe me dinner in a more upmarket location than

the last one, when I next get out. I'll be better-looking by then,' he quipped. Billie nodded. She could hardly refuse the last wish of this condemned man.

He moved out of the cell first, following the long-suffering custody officer who clipped one of his handcuffs onto her own wrist and unlocked a back door. Billie could see the prison vehicle parked only metres away. It was rocking on its wheels as disgruntled prisoners banged on the inside. Glenn Baxter winked as he was led out, leaving Billie stunned at the encounter.

The information that he had just given could be gold dust to the enquiry. It pointed to Geordie Stix possibly being right at the centre of the murders of Joy and Gracie-May. How many other cons drugged jelly sweets, used fishing equipment and had a record of hurting children? Billie felt her pulse quickening – could the M shape, carved into the victims, be a nod to the magpie, his favourite bird?

Billie clicked open her mobile and glanced at the photo sent by Glenn Baxter, nearly dropping the device in shock as she did so. The picture revealed was a 'selfie' featuring two grinning people, propped against a bar, pints in hand. Other football fans milled around in the background. Billie immediately recognised the location as The Bird in the Hand pub. Conner Grey's tall, skinny drinking mate wore thick jam-jar spectacles, a Newcastle United knitted hat and scarf over a hooded top.

Without a doubt Geordie Stix was the man who had crashed his Mini right in front of Billie. The culprit who had pointed out Gracie-May's body, swinging like a tiny fragile bird from The Angel of the North, and then done a runner. He also fitted Micky's description of the man who had asked for his autograph, when playing football in the park with the little girl.

Billie mentally reviewed the CCTV footage of the person leading the miniature angel to her death. Could he have drugged Conner Grey's drink that night, to allow Gracie to be taken? Was 'the funny thing about him', that Conner had been just about to reveal when he was killed, that the man he had berated at the playpark had later bought him a drink in the pub? A spiked drink? Billie quickly made a call. Boo answered.

'Boo, put out a search and pick-up shout for a George Strachan, known as Geordie Stix. We need to interview him urgently. Prime suspect. He's recently been freed from jail so get hold of probation, he might be in a hostel.'

'If he's our man, it's a shame he wasn't kept in custody. Are you on your way to the murder location now?'

'What?' Billie was immediately alert. 'I've had my phone switched off during the court interview.'

'I've left a message. There's been another one.' Boo was normally as cool as a cucumber, but Billie could sense the shock in her voice. 'Team have just rung in to confirm that they've arrived at the site. It sounds like a real shocker. You don't suffer from vertigo, do you, ma'am?'

13

THREE'S A CROWD

The well-known children's rhyme, 'Sing a Song of Sixpence', kept hopscotching through Billie's head as she stared up at the astonishing view over 400 feet above. Swinging in the whipping wind, against a dramatic grey-smudged sky, a man was hanging from a huge, bright-yellow crane positioned on the riverside docks. His dark, shadowy bulk and outstretched arms reminding her of a blackbird.

Billie couldn't help thinking that had he still been alive when hoisted, the last view of this victim's life could have been magnificent – all the way down the River Tyne to the foam crested waves of the North Sea and perhaps even as far upriver as the seven famous bridges straddling the water between the architecturally awe-inspiring settlements of Newcastle and Gateshead.

But clearly this guy was way out of luck even before he'd had his head put in the clouds. Instead of the part of the nursery rhyme still skipping through Billie's head, in which a blackbird pecks off a maid's nose, Billie could see a more gruesome vision as he was slowly lowered down. The huge circling seagulls had feasted on the victim's eyes, leaving his bulbous drinker's nose still intact. Billie couldn't help thinking that truth was often stranger than fiction.

The corpse was bathed in blood, the sightless orbs having cried rivers of red down his cheeks and onto his chest, where his open shirt revealed a gaping knife wound. The rest of his body had absorbed more scarlet bodily fluids. Billie guessed by the quantity of gore, that the killer blow was not the first and that he may even have still been breathing when hoisted high, but she would leave that deduction to Josta with her legendary knife expertise. Charlie Holden joined her, raising his eyebrows as the body came to an upright standstill in front of them.

'Good grief. I wouldn't say the first two victims were company, but this third one makes one hell of a crowd.'

Billie nodded in agreement. It was clear that their killer was intent on a spree and getting ever more dramatic in the execution of their crimes. She hoped to God that Geordie Stix would be lifted fast. She felt sure that he could spill some very bloody beans on the slayings.

'Ash, any intel at all?' she asked. Ash looked up from his mobile which he had been scrolling through, slightly startled. Billie sensed a curious detachment from the scene. She reminded herself to get to the bottom of his recent change in demeanour.

'Nothing yet, boss.' He returned to his mobile duties.

'Nothing remotely religious about his location,' Billie mused to no one but herself. The Grass, who maddeningly, had yet again been the first officer at the scene of the crime, had quickly scuttled off behind a piece of heavy machinery to throw up, much to the amusement of a couple of uniformed coppers.

'Cut the cackling,' Billie snapped. 'If anybody doesn't feel sickened by this situation, they shouldn't be anywhere near a murder case. Move back and make sure that all the access gates are secure.'

The officers quickly set off as directed, suitably chastised. Billie had no idea why she was defending The Grass, who emerged white-faced back into view, save for the memory of her own embarrassing moment at Gracie-May's autopsy. Josta joined Billie, pulling on her gloves ready to get to work.

'Looks like our little fishing friend has been at play again,' she said.

'The bindings?' Billie thought again of Geordie Stix and his interest in fishing, thanking God for the information given by Glenn Baxter. She did owe him dinner. Big time. Josta nodded at the visible wounds.

'Postulating, of course, at this stage, but at first sight the knife wounds look like those suffered by the earlier victims. I've narrowed it down to a particular fish-gutting knife, normally used by trawler men in Grimsby.' Billie felt her heart beating faster.

'Grimsby, Lincolnshire?' She took out her notepad and started scribbling.

'Made in Sheffield, but mostly used in the Yorkshire and Lincolnshire coastal areas. This particular knife might possibly date back to the 1940s, an old type – wooden handle, with a smaller brass area at the end. Quite thick blade... do bear in mind these things often found their way into homes long after they had done any fishing-related business; dumped in toolboxes or used in the kitchen as vegetable peelers. Passed down through families – quite the collector's item for those interested in fishing. I have one in my own collection, it used to belong to my grandfather.'

'Josta, I could kiss you!' Billie breathed a sigh of relief that she had something else that linked Geordie Stix to the crimes. The older woman twinkled.

'Don't want you smudging my lipstick, darling. These days appearance is everything,' Josta joked. She was fully kitted up in a white scene-of-crime overall complete with hood, gloves and foot coverings. On her short stout body, she wasn't exactly rocking the latest fashion.

As the crane steadied the body on the ground, a phone suddenly rang loud and clear, toppling from the jacket pocket of the murder victim. It landed at their feet. Billie and Josta exchanged glances. Josta was already ripping open a swab packet. Billie loudly called for silence. Josta took the swab and pressed on the answer button. A woman spoke.

'Hello?' Billie leant forward to listen. 'Hello?' The same voice again.

Billie answered, 'Hello, who's speaking?' The phone went dead. But not before Billie had committed the brightly lit caller's number to memory. 'Get all the intel off there and get it to me ASAP!' she directed Charlie Holden. He nodded, already reaching for an evidence bag.

'Ash. Go to the autopsy.' The examination needed a senior officer present, but it wouldn't be her. She was moving, pushing her way through the crowds, breaking into a sprint as she headed for her car. She recognised that number and she recognised the voice of the person who had made the call, though she desperately wished that she hadn't.

Billie made the journey in record-breaking time, jumped out of the car and started to hammer on the front door of the tall, brightly coloured building overlooking the river estuary.

'Hello?' she shouted through the letter box, hoping to hear footsteps along the hallway leading to the door. The house appeared silent. Billie peered through the narrow slit. No keys on the table, though perhaps they had been found a new home, rather than their earlier resting place, in the beautiful Kintsugi bowl that Margaret Craig had given Billie less than two hours earlier.

'Margaret?' Billie hammered on the door again. A small bent-over man, pushing a Zimmer frame, emerged shuffling from the next-door property.

'Keep the racket down. Have you come for the party?' he asked, squinting at Billie.

'Party?' Billie approached the man. 'What party?' Margaret hadn't mentioned any party.

'It's her birthday.' The elderly man grinned, showing exactly one tooth in a mouthful of gums. 'She's just gone off to the theatre. To the ballet.' He nodded sagely, before hobbling back inside and slamming the door with a loud bang.

Billie was reminded of a little painted wooden weatherman, on an ancient cuckoo clock that her mum and dad had been given for a wedding present. Two figures, one an old man, the other an old woman, who had appeared from little doors either side of the pointer on the hour, every hour. When the wooden woman had toppled over one day on her hourly journey, beheading herself on the hard black-and-white tiled floor of their hall, the wooden man had just kept on going in and out, all alone. He'd been following the same route all by himself now for about twenty years and had even outlived her parents. Just for a second, the old, bent, whittled figure appeared to have come to life right here, before her eyes.

Billie tried to still her mind for a moment, though a million thoughts were bouncing around her brain. How did Margaret Craig know two murder victims? Why had she been ringing the crane victim just after Billie's visit? Could she be in danger or even somehow involved in the killings?

Billie reminded herself that she had just invited the older woman to her wedding, for God's sake! The idea that she could be a murderer didn't bear thinking about. If that did turn out to be the case, Billie decided that David was right, she did need to be taken off the streets and stuffed behind a desk – for the safety of everyone.

She ran her fingers through her hair as she finished her tour of the outside of Margaret Craig's house, finding absolutely no signs of life, wondering if she should put out an alert to find the woman. But on what grounds? She needed to think. Straight.

If Margaret Craig had gone out to celebrate her birthday, could the latest victim be the mystery man, the one not expected to send the birthday cake this year? Maybe that was the reason for her call to him. Had she been stood up?

Billie wondered how long he'd been hanging around on the crane. She flashed her mind back to the gruesome scene. He hadn't looked as though he was dressed for a night out and he smelled pretty gruesome too, in addition to the oppressive perfume of death that had cloaked his body. He couldn't possibly be the elegantly groomed Margaret Craig's type, could he? Billie punched some numbers into her mobile.

'Boo. Anything yet from Charlie on the mobile phone belonging to today's victim?' Boo seemed to have an uncanny talent for appearing to have the information at her fingertips whatever the request.

'Charlie's still at the scene, but the phone's been brought back for intelligence... not a great deal on it. New phone. Just a couple of calls to a betting shop yesterday, but two voice messages today from the woman that you visited earlier, same home number both times. Calls seem to have been made both before and after your visit to her. He doesn't seem to have picked up either of them and each message asked for him to get in touch urgently.'

'Can you send a message to Green for me?' Billie replied. 'Get her to swing around the local theatres and put out calls for

Margaret Craig. She's at the ballet, wherever that's on. I need her brought in to base for another chat.'

It broke Billie's heart to have to spoil her new friend's birthday treat with news of yet more death, but she seemed to hold information which was vital to the investigation. If that was come by innocently, then she could also be in deadly danger.

Billie headed back to the neighbour's house and banged on the door. She heard the slow shuffle of the Zimmer frame and slippered feet making their way towards her. The old man opened the door and peered out.

'I've told you, the party's next door.' He pointed his thumb sideways.

'It must be later tonight. Did Margaret say what time she would be back?' Billie persisted. The old man shrugged.

'She's gone to the ballet.' He picked up a piece of paper from the telephone table by the door. 'That's my number on there.' Billie took the scrap with the printed details on. The man slammed the door shut, just as the grandfather clock behind him struck the hour.

Billie hoped that Ash was getting more useful information from the corpse on Josta's mortuary slab.

14

AN EFFECTIVE WEAPON OF MURDER

'What do you mean he didn't attend the autopsy?' Billie paced Josta's kitchen. It was unheard of for a senior officer not to be present at such a procedure and she had specifically asked Ash to be there. What on earth was going on with him these days?

'Don't worry, dear girl. I managed and the young officer, Green, volunteered to come along in his place. I think he had family issues. One of the children is ill.'

Billie silently swore. She had better get hold of The Grass before Ash found himself reported in a similar way to her for a breach of procedure. The Grass answered on the first ring of her call.

'Ma'am.'

'Have you picked up Margaret Craig?' Billie hoped that she had been too busy with her extra task to make any written complaints.

'I'm afraid not, ma'am.' The Grass sounded genuinely sorry to have failed in her task. 'There aren't any ballet performances today at any of the main theatres or concert halls, nor any bookings in the name of Margaret Craig for any performance at all in a local theatre.'

'Damn!' Billie cursed. Of course, the old man may have been mistaken and theatre tickets could have been booked in any name. On the upside, as it was her birthday, Margaret Craig was likely to be safe in the company of friends. Billie still didn't want to consider that her wedding guest was anything other than an innocent person who had wandered into the middle of the investigation.

'Okay. Leave it. Take an early night.' Billie glanced at her watch. It was 7pm. Early for a MIT copper anyway. Surely even The Grass would rather be putting her feet up in front of the telly with a glass of wine, than writing up a report on Ash's autopsy no-show and therefore Billie's lack of ability to handle her team. The Chief would pounce on just such an opportunity to take her off the case.

'I'm with Dr King now, updating.' She ended the call. At least The Grass wouldn't be able to claim that Billie had missed something important. She was prepared to drive to Alnmouth for a third time later tonight to interview Margaret Craig, but she had to admit that right now she was feeling the effects of having eaten nothing but a handful of Max Strong's jellies all day. She glanced at Josta lifting a vast pizza from the oven as she punched in Ash's number. His messaging service kicked in. Billie clicked off her phone.

'We're going veggie tonight,' Josta exclaimed as she ripped fresh basil leaves onto the colourful pizza. The smell was amazing. It made Billie's stomach rumble.

'Don't tell me, even you've seen enough dead meat for one day?' Billie managed to summon a smile as she teased, though her head was spinning with the number of issues she had to follow up; not least why Ash had disappeared without calling her first. Her tummy fluttered again, this time with concern over her friend's ill child. She adored all three of his girls and desperately hoped that they were okay.

'It was quite a grizzly examination, but young Green held up well. I understand your wariness of the girl, but you may want to cut her some slack. She took an avid interest in the inspection and is full of surprises. Did you know that she once ran away and joined a circus?'

Josta chuckled to herself as she opened drawers and rifled for napkins and utensils. 'It's amazing the conversations that open up during tea and biscuits before an autopsy. Anything to take minds off the impending introduction to the dead.'

'The Grass?' Billie made a mental note that this day was getting stranger by the minute. Josta handed her a huge bowl of salad to lay on the table.

'Apparently quite the high-wire queen. She claims that she had family troubles. Ran away from home.' Josta started cutting the pizza with an unusual knife.

'Cuts like butter as you can see. I'm certain that *this*,' she waved the wooden-handled fishing knife, 'is the favoured blade used by our marauding killer.'

The door opened and Max entered. He stared at the knife in Josta's hand for a split second, before nodding politely to Billie.

'DSI Wilde.' A hint of a smile played on the corners of his lips. Billie quickly turned away, her heart starting to beat fast. She could hardly take him to task for the way in which he had dumped her as his patient, here in his mother's kitchen.

'Max, darling,' Josta's face lit up at the sight of her beloved son, 'I was just telling Billie what a great warhorse our family fishing knife has been. Didn't you take it with you on your battles around the world? Does it make a hugely effective murder weapon in your opinion? Don't worry, dear, it's been washed,' she added in a mischievous aside to Billie.

'Mother, Isabelle is just in the bathroom and you know how

she gets upset at your deathly anecdotes.' Billie felt a stab in her heart at the name of Isabelle. Did Max Strong have a partner? Why on earth did she care anyway? Josta was unfazed.

'Rubbish. She's addicted to whodunnits. You know nothing about women.' She winked at Billie who, infuriated at herself, blushed bright pink as Max brushed by her on his way to kiss his mother on the cheek.

An intoxicating hint of lemon perfume mingled with the tantalising kitchen smells of an intimate romantic evening in a trattoria. Billie shook the thought away, focusing instead on the hefty file on the kitchen countertop. She needed to put any further thoughts of Max out of her mind and crack on with the investigation.

Billie opened the file and glanced at a few of the grizzly photos within, including a close-up of the latest victim's ankle, with the signature M carved on it. A speed-read of the first page showed that he had also been an alcoholic with serious liver problems and something of a drug habit. The Rohypnol identification was there as with the others.

'Jellies again?' Billie asked Josta, suddenly remembering those that she had wolfed down in Max Strong's waiting room earlier that afternoon.

'No sign of any, but easy to drop something into his drink and the indications are that he'd had quite a few by the time he was hung out to dry out as it were.'

Billie glanced at Max. He was staring at her intently. Without Ash's insights from the examination, she desperately wanted to have a fuller conversation with Josta about her findings, but she wasn't about to share further confidential information with Max Strong.

The door opened and an elderly lady hobbled in, unwrapping a smart silk scarf from around her neck.

'Ah, Billie my dear, meet Isabelle Church. Max gallantly

offered to be her chauffeur on hearing that her date had failed to turn up this evening. She is swapping the joys of Tinder for the trials of pizza with me.' Isabelle Church shook her head in mock disapproval.

'Tinder indeed. Josta, your jesting will get you into trouble one of these days.' She smiled at Billie and held out her hand. 'So pleased to meet you, Billie my dear. Max has been telling me all about you.' Billie glanced at Max. His turn to flush pink.

'I believe that you're the one tasked with solving these terrible murders. Dreadful business. All over social media...'

Billie's stomach tensed again. She was acutely aware that it was, indeed, her job to bring the murderer to justice, yet here she was eyeing up pizza. Josta poured out generous glasses of red wine. Max handed one to Billie. She shook her head.

'No thanks. I'm working.' Her voice was politely clipped. She refused to look at him, as she tucked the file under her arm.

'I knew the latest victim, of course.' Isabelle took a seat. 'Geordie Stix was a tricky character, without a doubt.' Billie froze with shock. Isabelle paused for a moment to take a large swig of her wine.

'Geordie Stix?' Billie's voice came out as a whisper. *Her prime suspect was the latest victim?* She wanted to scream. Isabelle nodded.

'Many thought that he should have swung years ago for the child cruelty crimes. So perhaps being strung 400 foot up on the hook of a crane was a fitting end for him.' She took another sip of her wine.

'You are certain of that identity?' Billie's mind was racing.

'I have my contacts, dear, and my eyes. Footage of him hanging from that crane has been all over the internet. I'm a chaplain at the local prison. I saw him only a few days ago, just prior to his release. It's Geordie all right.'

'Did he have any enemies that you know of?' Billie asked. Isabelle nodded.

'Plenty, I'm sure. Geordie was no angel. But he did have his quiet moments of reflection, God rest his soul. He told me he had been badly abused by his own parents. As Aristotle said, "Give me the child until he is seven and I will show you the man". His parents were alcoholics and child beaters by all accounts, so what were we all to expect of him?'

'Isabelle is used to hanging out with abusers, Billie.' Josta took a swig from her glass. 'She used to be a nun and we all know how shameless they can be.'

'It's a shame that only one type of abuser swings, I will say that. There are plenty of people who present as leading lights of the community whilst in truth they are wolves in sheep's clothing. That's why I left before my novitiate period was complete. I lost my faith for many years due to the terrible exploitation of children, right there in the nunnery. Where was God then, I asked myself?'

'Was Geordie involved in that?' Billie persisted.

'Not directly. The nunnery housed single mothers, many of them prostitutes, who, having given birth, handed the children over to the nuns.'

'For adoption?' Billie frowned.

'Often sold off to the highest bidder.' Isabelle took another large swig of her drink. 'The nuns took a cut and the police, who ran the whole shabby show, took the rest. The young mothers were often distraught, as you would imagine, but who were they going to go to for help?'

Billie couldn't believe what she was hearing. Her dad had been chief of the local police force thirty years ago, if he had got wind of such behaviour... Isabelle broke through her thoughts.

'Fact was, that many of the police were fathering the babies in the first place, despite having wives and children at home.'

Billie shook her head. Her father had often regaled her with tales from the past, he'd never mentioned such a thing.

'But how could they get away with that?' Billie questioned with scepticism.

'Young, gullible social worker, in a relationship with the judge. She filled out the adoption recommendations. He signed them off. Who was going to argue with it?' Isabelle shook her head in dismay. 'After all, the chief of police himself was at the helm. Handsome chap, but brutish with it, I can't remember his name, Wills, White, something starting with a W... anyway, it's in the past now.'

Billie, feeling sick and dizzy, attempted to head for the door. The room started to spin around her. Of all the chiefs going back, only one had a surname beginning with W. But she didn't want to believe it. As her legs gave way, darkness encompassed her, but it is said that the sense of smell is the last thing to leave you, when your other senses have all checked out, so it was that the smell of lemony cologne enveloped her, when strong arms caught her body as it spiralled towards the kitchen floor.

Unconscious for only a matter of moments, Billie was aware, as she blinked her eyes open, of feeling her cheek against a hard, muscular chest, a heart beating firmly within it. Then, as her senses further awakened, of being carried. Max gently brushed her hair away from her face as he placed her body carefully down on Josta's vibrant red velvet sofa, at the far end of her huge kitchen.

'Here, take a sip of water, dear.' Josta was rushing over with a glass.

'She's looking very pale,' Isabelle chimed in, her face looming close. Billie forced herself upright.

'Sorry, it's okay. I just forgot to eat.' She sounded panicked, even to her own ears. A smooth hand brushed her cheek softly. She shrugged Max away, suddenly aware of her phone ringing loudly. Fumbling, she pulled the device out of her pocket, knocking the answer button onto loudspeaker as she did so. The caller was David's mother, incandescent with rage.

'Billie! I demand you get here at once!' Billie blinked, not comprehending the angry words for a moment, before their meaning sank in.

'I'm on my way!' she cried, clicking off the phone and grabbing the arm of the sofa. The faces of Max, Josta and Isabelle registered disbelief.

'Where on earth are you going, Billie?' Max's gentle voice was full of concern.

'My damn wedding rehearsal!' Billie answered, fumbling madly for her car keys.

15

THE WORK OF THE DEVIL

'I told you I could drive myself!' Billie shook her head in exasperation at Max Strong, furious at herself for being talked into letting him drive her to the church.

'I was worried, Billie,' he glanced across at her, 'though you seem to have some colour back in your cheeks now, thank goodness.'

Billie's mind was racing again. Could her father *really* have been at the centre of a child-selling scam? The very thought chilled her to the bone. She shivered.

Max zipped through a light, just as it was about to change to red and accelerated, overtaking a lane of slow-moving vehicles.

'And you're worried about *me* driving?' Billie forced the other thoughts from her mind.

'Worried about the innocent members of the public you would have taken out behind the wheel in that state. One serial killer around here is enough.' Billie sulkily bit into the pizza slice that Josta had wrapped and shoved in her hand. It did taste good.

'First Isabelle then me. Is this your new job then, if you're no longer a shrink, chauffeur to frail single women?' Max laughed.

'Frail, you?' He shook his head in amusement. 'Have you tried refusing an order from my mother?' He glanced at her through long dark lashes. 'I'm simply determined to get you to the church on time.'

As Max spoke, a Jag accelerated out of the scenic driveway of the church they were approaching, causing him to break forcefully. David, stony-faced behind the wheel, sped off. Billie exchanged glances with Max.

'Stood up. Not for the first time today,' she observed wryly. 'At least I was early for my appointment with you.' Billie opened the car door and jumped out, heading through the church gates.

'You're doing this on purpose!' David's mother was tearful with rage as Billie crunched up the gravel drive, relieved to be able to put one foot in front of the other thanks to the blood-stabilising effects of the pizza. She thought about depositing the last mouthful in the bin that she was passing, but unable to fight the urge, instead stuffed the remaining morsel into her mouth.

'David's just left!' his mother practically screamed at Billie. She was flanked by David's genial long-suffering dad on the right, vicar on her left. Billie smiled at him sheepishly, wiping her hand on her jeans before shaking his.

'Hi, I'm Billie. Sorry I'm late,' she added with sincerity.

'Now David's late for an important appointment!' his mother wailed. David's father put his arm around her as though she were a sickly child.

'Now dear, calm down. Billie is here. She has undoubtedly been busy with work, as you can imagine,' he added, smiling kindly at Billie. He was always the peacemaker.

'And what exactly do you do, Billie?' the vicar asked politely.

'Chase murderers mostly,' Billie answered.

'David's job is important too!' David's mother gibbered, still furious at Billie.

'Everything okay?' Billie hadn't noticed Max park his car on the driveway behind. He joined the group.

'And you are?' David's mother demanded, looking accusingly between the two.

'My shrink,' Billie announced, smiling at the vicar, 'seems I'm so crazy these days, he has to follow me everywhere.' A look of shock swept across the vicar's pallid face. 'Though it seems that I'm so unhinged that he's actually just resigned. So, he is free,' Billie looked directly at David's mother, 'if anyone else wants to take him.' There was a stunned silence for a moment before David's father chuckled.

'You are such a tease, Billie. Come along, let's run through the show, then get you home, dear.' He squeezed David's mother's shoulder. 'You need a drink, a large G and T is just what the doctor ordered, to calm your pre-wedding nerves.'

The relieved vicar, along with David's parents, started to walk inside. Billie shot a glance at Max. He raised his eyebrows.

'Nothing like making an entrance, Billie.' He smiled that slow smile of his. It made Billie shiver. She decided the feeling must be annoyance.

'Thanks for the lift. You can go now.' She flung the words out, realising that she didn't actually want him to go, now. Maybe not ever. She mentally damned that outrageous thought, burying it deep under one of the ancient gravestones flanking the church door.

'Just checking that you're okay, Billie,' Max answered quietly. The vicar suddenly poked his head back out of the door, directing his words at Max.

'We're a groom down, so I wonder if you would mind doing the honours?'

A look of shock flashed over Max's face. It didn't go unnoticed by Billie. Or the vicar.

'It's quite all right. Just a rehearsal, so we know where

everyone must stand, etcetera. You're quite safe. I won't make anyone sign the marriage register.' He grinned genially.

'I think Dr Strong is rather busy–' Billie started, before Max interrupted.

'No, it's fine, um, as long as we won't be too long. I do have a meeting...'

Billie felt sick. Never had anyone made it so clear that he didn't want to take that role. Even if it was only play-acting. She wanted the ground to swallow her up.

'Can't David's dad stand in for him?' Billie asked, giving Max a dismissive look. She didn't want him actually thinking that she did want him to take the place of her fiancé.

'I'm afraid not.' The vicar had a rod of steel at the core of his gently persuasive demeanour. 'He will be leading you up the aisle, playing the role of father of the bride, bearing in mind your sad circumstances.'

The words made Billie rock on her feet. Who exactly *was* the father of this bride? A loving, newly deceased dad, or a dangerously corrupt copper? She felt a dizzy moment of panic before Max's firm hand gently took her wrist, leading her into the church.

'Come on, Billie. Let's just do this.' He smiled, brushing the side of her lip with his thumb. 'Pizza sauce,' he whispered, before he led her to David's father and walked onwards to the front of the church, taking his place at the top right of the nave.

Billie took a deep breath, wobbly once again, not knowing whether it was due to the revelations about her father, the fact that she had witnessed an eyeless man being lowered from a crane, or that she was about to walk up the aisle to play husband and wife with Dr Max Strong. As she took in a deep breath on hearing the first notes of Handel's 'Wedding March' and moved forward, she decided that she seriously had to get a grip of her life. Max stepped out into the pulpit and stretched out his hand. She took it in hers.

'We are gathered here today to witness and celebrate the wedding of...' The vicar trailed off, bending forward to Max who mumbled something in his ear. The vicar nodded and stood straight.

'Maximus Augustus Strong.' Billie whipped her head around to Max, a giggle rising in her throat.

'You're joking. Maximus Augustus?' she whispered, her head close to Max's, catching that lovely lemony smell as it cut a dash through the dusty, musty aroma of the church. The vicar continued loudly.

'To Philomena Wilde.' Max raised an eyebrow, bent his head close again. His eyelashes caught the skin of her temple in a butterfly kiss.

'Blame it on the parents – Phil,' he teased back. The vicar coughed to garner attention.

'Then we go on through the introduction and the reading from the Apostle Paul, the first letter to the Corinthians, chapter thirteen verses four through to seven...' The vicar continued flicking through his script. Billie glanced back at Max. He smiled and squeezed her hand. The vicar's voice faded into the background as Billie and Max held their gaze. The vicar nudged Max, breaking the moment.

'I, Maximus Augustus Strong, take you, Philomena Wilde, to be my lawful wedded wife.' He nodded at Max, who dutifully repeated the words, smiling softly at Billie as he did so.

'To have and to hold from this day forward, for better for worse, for richer, for poorer.'

Max's dark-brown eyes stared into Billie's own as he echoed the words. She was momentarily transfixed.

'In sickness and in health,' the vicar continued.

A shadow crossed over Max Strong's handsome features.

'Which you repeat.' The vicar was obviously growing impatient. 'And then, after me.' He nodded to Max. 'To love and to cherish until death do us part.' Max dropped Billie's hand; panic etched across his face. He shook his head.

'Sorry, I can't do this...' His voice was stressed, he stepped back.

'Not long now,' the vicar persisted.

'No, no...' Max took a few steps backwards. 'I've got to go.' He turned and bolted back down the aisle, tearing out through the huge ancient oak door. A spiral of church leaflets scattered across the floor in the mini whirlwind caused by his hasty retreat. The door slammed shut with a deep bang behind him. There was a silence. Then the vicar attempted a joke.

'Let's hope that you won't be jilted on the day.' The smile didn't reach his eyes. Billie caught sight of David's mother, out of the corner of her eye, slapping her hand to her head in utter disbelief. She desperately wished for the floor to open and swallow her into the crypt below. The persistent vicar caught her arm and pulled her forward.

'Now, you and your devoted husband will follow behind me to the altar to sign the register.'

It was at the moment when Billie stepped away from the vicar and into position for the binding signatures, that she heard the noise immediately above her head. She snapped her eyes towards a short gallery way up high, above the choir. A vast statue of Christ was teetering forward from its base. Was that a shadowy figure that caught her eye or simply a trick of the light?

Billie had no time to decide. Suddenly the vast stone statue hurtled downwards. She leaped out of the way, taking the vicar with her, in a move worthy of a rugby international. With an almighty crash, the statue smashed into smithereens on the very spot where she had been standing only a moment earlier.

Billie was on her feet in seconds, hurtling towards a side

door that she hoped would lead to the gallery. Narrow curved stone stairs stretched upwards. She took them two at a time, aware that her breathing was fast. She had to be alert. The perpetrator could still be hiding in the corner of the gallery and no way was she planning to follow the route of Jesus.

In moments, Billie emerged into the gallery. It appeared empty. Below, she could see the shaken vicar wiping the body of Christ from his robes, see David's father running to help, and his mother dissolving into histrionics, just for a change.

Here, up on high, prayer books were scattered like breadcrumbs leading to an open door at the back of the gallery. Billie kicked it wider and ran through a small empty vestibule. Another door leading from that airless room was also wide open. Billie stepped over more words of God; this time song sheets, strewn in an unholy mess all over the floor. She emerged out onto a landing. Hearing a noise above, Billie registered that the ancient, enclosed, winding stairs would put her at a serious disadvantage should she come face to face with someone set on murder. The thought lasted only a moment before she took the first uneven step and stealthily crept towards the church steeple.

Suddenly a loud sound clattered from above, making Billie pin herself to the wall. The church bell started to peal out the hour. Eight o'clock. Billie exhaled. *The day flies by when you're having fun*, she ironically thought, stilling her fast beating heart for a moment, before plunging up into the bell tower.

The tower was empty, save for the huge bell hanging above her and open to the darkening cloudless sky all around. Billie rushed to the waist-height wall and looked down. The front drive to the church was far below. She could see no one. She ran to the opposite side of the space. Was that a shadow she spotted behind a huge ancient gravestone? Beyond it was a closed gate, leading out of the church grounds. Billie blinked, straining her eyes, waiting to see if a further movement was about to be made, something that might enable her to nail the person responsible.

Abruptly, Billie heard footsteps on stone, heading upwards. Her heart leapt once more, as she pinned herself against the wall, hoping to be concealed in the shadow of the huge bell. The only other way out of this tight spot was over the side and she was damned if she was going to be taking that exit. A tall dark figure emerged from the staircase. Billie braced herself.

'Oh, my goodness!' The vicar moved towards her clutching his chest. 'Is everything all right?' Billie exhaled with relief. Even in the dim light, she could see white dust still clinging to the vicar's hair and cassock.

'Such a shock!' He brushed down his robe in a fluster. 'Vandals. I keep ringing the police, but I'm afraid the house of God isn't high up on their crime hit list.'

Billie ran her fingers through her own hair. Bits of the sculpture could be heard scattering like crumbs onto the floor of the bell tower.

'This is a regular occurrence?' She relaxed a little, wondering if chasing murderers was starting to warp her view of every little incident.

'The lead of the church roof has practically been stripped bare,' the vicar moaned, 'and the collection boxes have to be checked twice a day. They've been prised open regularly...'

The vicar continued with his long list of crimes against God. Billie listened with one ear, making a quick judgement that the sort of misdemeanours he was cataloguing were thefts for the purposes of making money, not to cause injury.

'But nothing of this sort. No attempts to injure?' she interrupted. He shook his head in annoyance.

'No one has attempted to murder Christ before. That is true,' he huffed.

'Or you?' Billie persisted.

'Goodness me, no!' The vicar sounded astonished at the suggestion.

That only leaves the one of us. Billie already knew she was right, but a lifetime of police training couldn't help but kick in.

'I'm simply carrying out God's work!' the vicar exclaimed. Billie looked back over the edge of the bell tower wall. The closed gate was now wide open.

But someone is sure as hell carrying out the work of the Devil, Billie answered silently. She was even more determined than ever to find out exactly who that was.

16

A TERRIBLE MISJUDGEMENT

Billie looked up and down the dark road, mobile pinned to her ear, damning the fact that there were no taxis to be seen. She hastily felt her pockets, then sighed with relief. Thankfully, her car keys were with her. At least she wouldn't have to suffer the embarrassment of a health interrogation by Josta if she just quietly picked up the car then drove off. Even worse was the thought of Max Strong, opening his mother's door and then having to beg *him* to hand over her keys.

She had rung David's number several times, leaving heartfelt apologies on his answering service. He hadn't replied. Clearly, she was back in the bad books again. She couldn't blame him, having just been left standing alone at the altar herself. It didn't do much for one's confidence.

'Hello?' Billie had also tried Margaret Craig's home number, but she hadn't picked up. Her best bet was to ask a favour of the old man next door, if she could persuade him to help.

'I've told you before. No cold callers!' a woman's voice scolded, before the phone call was abruptly curtailed. Billie punched in the numbers again.

'Hello? This is the police, DSI Wilde,' she got in quickly,

catching the woman's attention. If she was his wife, then she might just have some vital info herself.

'He said she'd gone to the ballet?' The woman chuckled, having listened to Billie's explanation of her earlier conversations with the old man. 'He tells *everyone* that,' she explained. 'Everyone's gone to the ballet. He's got dementia, love. I'm his carer. I've just called in to put him to bed.' Billie's heart sank at the news.

'True enough, his wife *did* go to the ballet, but that was forty years ago. Had a heart attack when she was there, God rest her soul. She never came home. You can bet your bottom dollar that if you walked in five minutes after I walk out tonight, he'd tell you that I'd gone to the ballet as well. We've all gone to the ballet, dear. That's all he can talk about these days.'

'I'm sorry.' Billie kicked herself for missing the old man's condition. 'So, do you have any idea where Margaret Craig might be?' She sounded like she was pleading. In truth, she was.

'Dunno, love. The house is in darkness. Maybe gone to bed already? We don't stay up late partying out here in the sticks.' She laughed. 'But I do know that Margaret likes to be up early in the morning. I see her when I walk my little Jimmy. That's the dog, not the husband.' She chuckled again.

Wow, this one's a real side splitter, Billie couldn't help thinking, before reprimanding herself. She ended the call, then tried to ring Ash. He still wasn't picking up. She needed him to meet her at dawn, head up to Alnmouth. It was vital that she questioned Margaret Craig without any further delay.

For a few seconds, she allowed Isabelle's story to play through her mind once again. If her dad had headed up a baby-selling scam, could she be the child of a streetwalker? She could hardly bear to dwell on the thought. Luckily, the welcome sight of a black cab came into view. Billie strode into the middle of the road, flagging it down. As it pulled into the kerb, she heard a voice behind her.

'Billie?' She turned around to see Kate sitting on a wall in the shadow of a tree. A sickly yellow street light caught her blotched wet face as she leaned forward. She had obviously been crying and worse, a swollen black eye was revealed as she moved out of the shadows. Further scratches and bruises covered her face. Tears started to flow once more.

'Kate?' Billie was shocked to see her friend so dishevelled and distressed. 'What on earth has happened?' Kate dissolved into racking sobs as Billie pulled her close in a hug, so that it took moments before she could speak.

'He beat me up,' she sobbed.

'Who?' Billie demanded. Kate rubbed her face, turning around to look up the street where the dark residential road started to merge into the sleazy side of the big city.

'I dunno...' Kate started to cry again. 'Someone up there... I was taking a shortcut down one of those alleyways, by The Dive Bar.'

Billie looked along the road. She could see an opening into the narrow, dark and winding lanes, the dangerous maze tucked between the glaring yellow lights of burger bars and kebab shops. Strange that this deadbeat location was less than a mile away from the sparkling high-rise, glass-clinking, social-climbing entertainment venues of the city centre.

'Did you see where he went?' Billie held Kate close, waving away the taxi. This was her chance to pay back for leaving a fellow officer to get beaten up there, an opportunity to nab, with a bit of luck, one of the culprits responsible for the recent assaults. Billie could feel her friend shaking in her arms. When she got her hands on the person who had caused Kate so much pain, she would make sure that they got a taste of their own medicine.

'Somewhere up that one, I think...' Kate pointed to the first dark alleyway. Billie took Kate's hand and led her across the road. She was limping a little. Clearly, Billie noted, the damage cut deeper than simply the injuries on view.

As they entered the first alleyway, devoid of street lights, Billie and Kate were plunged into darkness. Halfway up the narrow, rubbish-strewn lane, light spilled out from the slightly open door to The Dive Bar. Billie had no wish to draw attention to herself in that location once again. Quickly pulling her hoodie over her hair and coaxing Kate to stay close behind, she briefly entered the vestibule, looking around.

'See him here?' She turned to Kate. Her friend shook her head. As she closed the door behind her, she had failed to notice a couple, carefully hidden in a shadowy alcove, or the fact that they had immediately recognised her.

'I don't know... it might have been the next alleyway along...' Kate started to get upset again. Billie wrapped her arm around her housemate's shoulders.

'It's okay. I remember a shortcut through here to the next lane.' Kate started sobbing loudly. Billie held her close as they felt their way through the pitch-black space, stumbling slightly over empty beer bottles. Billie suddenly heard a sound. A shuffling step that abruptly stopped. Was someone else close by? The thought scuttled through her mind that there were many types of rat around this location, not all of them animal. Whatever that noise was, it certainly wasn't the flutter of butterfly wings.

When the blow came out of nowhere, the force was so severe that it almost knocked Billie off her feet. Her head ricocheted against the wall behind her. She touched her nose, feeling blood between her fingers, the taste of metal on her lips. Another punch followed, catching her on the chin this time. She immediately went into fight mode, but in the pitch black, all she was immediately aware of was that her attacker was taller and built like steel, a dark, forceful shadow.

A hand caught her throat like a vice. She fumbled on the rubbish-scattered ground, felt the neck of a bottle, smashed it, then brought the jagged glass down hard on the person's wrist. The attacker released their grip, muttering a muffled curse. Billie slashed out again, making contact with a limb.

Suddenly she heard Kate scream. Billie's legs were being kicked from under her, from behind. Could there be two attackers? As Billie hit the ground a booted foot slammed into her head. It felt as though her brain had exploded. Then she heard footsteps, running nearer, or running away? Kate was wailing loudly. More grappling noises, more footsteps then a flashlight shining in her face. She shielded her eyes, from the light or from the next blow, she wasn't sure which.

'Billie?' Max dropped to his knees beside her, his face etched with worry. 'Billie, speak to me, are you okay?' More light flashing from another source, footsteps in high-heeled shoes running towards her, then the lane awash with light from a window above.

'Everything all right down there?' a voice shouted. Billie looked away from Max and squinted into the face of The Grass, her face painted with make-up, her hair fashioned into a slick gamine style. When she opened her mouth to speak, however, blood started to pour out from it.

'No! Help! Ring 999, we need ambulance and police!' Billie screamed at the fag-smoking man who had poked his head out of the window. She pulled herself up, grabbed her phone and punched in her fast-track number, before tearing off her scarf, as she attempted to stem the blood pouring from The Grass's mouth and neck. Max worked with her, his army training clearly on show.

'They're asking if she's breathing?' The man popped his

head out of the window again, phone held against his ear. The Grass was slumped now, against the wall, making gurgling noises.

'Tell them to get a move on!' Billie commanded, as Max checked the young detective's pulse. She prayed that help would arrive before it was too late.

~

The A and E department of the hospital was like zombie central. Clearly most of the people were walking wounded suffering from the effects of too much drink and too many drugs. Billie pitied the night staff, trying to do their jobs in such difficult circumstances. The nurse who approached them looked jolly enough, however.

'Don't worry, both of your friends are going to be okay. The neck wound is not nearly as serious as it may have looked, but we'll be admitting her for tonight. Poor girl had also bitten her tongue when she was punched, hence the amount of blood. There are heaps of vessels in the mouth, so it can appear scary at first sight, but such injuries usually heal quickly. I'm afraid the other girl will have to wait a bit to get patched up. Feel free to take a seat out here. She should be sorted in a couple of hours or so.'

'Shouldn't you get checked over too?' Max was looking at Billie with desperate concern, or was it revulsion? She licked her bottom lip. It felt fat. She didn't fancy looking at her nose either. But in truth she felt more shocked than physically injured. Had she just gatecrashed a date? In her wildest dreams she could never have guessed that The Grass would be in a relationship with Dr Max Strong.

'Nope I'm fine.' Billie's lie was clipped. Being left in the lurch at her wedding rehearsal still stung, even though she now realised that he had probably been behind time for his romantic rendezvous. She looked around for a seat. They were totally full. Many people appeared to have bedded down for the night, spreading themselves along the rows, others were wandering around in various states of inebriation, harassing the staff. Billie could feel the need for a few arrests coming over her already.

'Well I need a drink. Come on...' Max took Billie's arm and led her out of the hospital. Despite her disgruntlement, she didn't resist.

Along the street, a little wine bar beckoned, its freshly painted door flanked by huge terracotta pots overflowing with red geraniums.

Billie was relieved to see that the ladies' bathroom was immediately to the left, as they entered. She slipped inside to survey the damage. Luckily, cold water and the wine bar's whole supply of paper towels managed to clear away most of the blood from her face. Her nose was pretty sore but didn't feel broken. *That would have looked cute in the wedding album*, she joked to herself. She couldn't do much about the fat lip but reasoned that many women paid a fortune to have injections to give a very similar effect.

Next, she took off the hoodie, revealing a black top underneath. She tossed her head, creating a halo of red curls, reasoning that a sightless man on a galloping horse might, just might, think that she was simply popping into the wine bar for a drink with a friend like any normal person. Sometimes she sorely wished that she could just be one of those people.

'I guessed you might like something chilled.' Max clinked his glass of deep red Bordeaux against a large glass of white wine. His dark eyes caught the light of the candle flame flickering on the intimate table in the corner of the room. Billie shivered as the first sip of ice cool wine touched her tongue.

'Thanks.' She licked her swollen lip. Max Strong appeared transfixed for a moment before glancing away.

'Nice place.' Billie took another sip. The wine tasted expensive. 'Maybe you should bring your dates here next time, rather than a burger bar up a sleazy alleyway,' she pretended to joke. Max Strong took a sip of his drink, whilst looking at her, that hint of a smile playing on his lips again. He slowly shook his head.

'You look so alive, Billie. I almost sense that you love having danger all around you.'

Billie realised that he may have a point. She had always felt that she didn't fit into the role of picture-perfect, middle-class daughter from impeccable parents. Maybe her early life – was that her *real* life? – *had* been full of danger. Maybe trouble was bred into her. Not that she was going to follow *that* line of thought with a shrink who had dumped her not once, but twice in the same day.

'Sorry I spoiled your romantic evening,' Billie persisted.

'I'm still a bit worried about *that*.' Max leaned across the table and stroked his forefinger in a line at the base of Billie's throat. His eyes darkened as Billie gasped, touching the spot herself as his skin broke contact.

'Just a flesh wound,' she attempted to quip, 'luckily my scarf stopped it being worse.' She took a large swig of her wine, feeling her face flush in reaction to his touch and damning herself for it. She made a mental note to go easy on the alcohol. The last thing she needed now was to find herself jumping up and dancing like a lunatic around *this* venue.

'Please don't go and get yourself killed, Billie.' Max said the words softly but firmly, his hand catching hers. The candlelight made his eyes look aflame.

'I think the murderer is getting desperate. Three killings in as many days and maybe another attempt tonight–' Max's voice was urgent.

'Tonight was totally different. An everyday lowlife beat up my friend. You saw the state of her yourself. He got to me before I got to him and it felt like he brought a mate for extra muscle. Simple. Unconnected incidents.'

'Are you sure about that?' Max's stare was intense. Billie pulled her hand away from his and took another sip of her drink. That was the trouble with shrinks, she reminded herself. They made a career of messing with your head.

'They're losing control, the attacks are becoming less planned, attention-seeking, crazy...' Billie had a sudden memory of the statue of Christ careering down at speed towards her. What a way to go. She wondered what Max would make of that? Probably weave it into his crazy theories. She refused to be spooked by his words.

'Save your wild imaginings for the crazy heads you get paid to work on.' She decided that she had to keep those sorts of conjectures out of her mind in order to focus on the job. 'You'll recall that I am no longer one of those people.' He smiled, slowly, shaking his head. Billie vowed that she wouldn't let Max Strong into her world when he had booted her out of his, like a kid who hadn't performed well in class.

'History is littered with serial killers who failed to fit the personality type created by criminal psychologists – Ted Bundy for one,' Billie continued. 'That's why detectives like me keep you lot at arm's length. We don't want to waste valuable time and innocent lives on a wild goose chase. Nine times out of ten, we nab a killer who turns out not to match the useless profile at all.' Max raised his eyebrows.

'A damning verdict indeed, Chief Superintendent Wilde.' He nodded to a very pretty waitress who had been eyeing him up with admiration. She came over to the table like a shot. 'Another drink?' he asked Billie.

'No thanks. Working. I'm heading off in a minute.' She later realised that she should have stopped there, got up immediately and left him to flirt with the waitress who had raced off to get him another glass of red. But no, being her, she had to get in another jibe.

'Of course, rookie coppers like The Grass, might fall for your charms. Gullible, I would say. More your type.' Max Strong's eyes flashed for a moment, before he stared straight at Billie, lowering his voice.

'I think you're better than that comment, Billie.' She felt his words like a slap. How dare he pass judgement on her after one and a bit stupid shrink sessions?

'What would you know? You're not my friend, not my colleague and judging by the way you ran out of the church tonight, I'm not the sort of female that fits your ideal profile!' She felt her cheeks flare, angry that everyone from David's mother to Max bloody Strong felt they had the right to voice their opinion on her life.

He drained his glass, staring down hard at the table before speaking.

'I'm not in a relationship with Jo Green, Billie. I'm married...' He looked up.

Billie finished her glass of wine and swallowed hard. Why did that comment feel like a blow more forceful than any she had experienced that evening? After all, she was only days away from her own wedding.

The waitress placed down Max's second glass of red, all eyes and teeth. He ignored her, looked into Billie's eyes instead. His own were brimming with tears. 'Well, still married up here in my head anyway...' He rubbed his hand over his forehead.

'I met my wife in Afghanistan and we married within weeks.

Natalie was beautiful. Clever, adventurous and full of surprises...' He smiled, memories obviously skipping through his mind's eye. 'A bit wild and very brave, just like you...' Billie swallowed hard as Max looked away, pain etched across his beautiful features.

'...I was commanding my unit when Nat came out with us on patrol. She was the best paramedic in the army, saved so many lives and not just on our side either – locals who needed treatment for all sorts of things. But this one day, I made a terrible misjudgement, sent my patrol a few centimetres in the wrong direction, right into a mine field...' Billie could tell he had played the scene over and over in his head a million times, his mind was there now. She touched his hand. He moved it away.

'...then watched my beautiful Nat blow up into a million tiny pieces. Direct hit.' Max reached for the new glass of red wine and downed the whole drink in one. 'Nothing left. She'd just gone, like that. I went out of my mind.' He laughed without humour. 'Even thought about joining a monastery at one ludicrous point, God knows why, nothing can atone for the sin of commanding your precious wife to walk into such a horrific death.'

'Max, you can't blame yourself.' Billie knew her words were falling on deaf ears.

'My fault, Billie, and now I feel even more guilt, because from the moment that you walked into my room...'

Billie caught her breath, knowing what he was alluding to, recognising that she had been wrestling with similar feelings herself. He held back from saying more, but caught Billie's hand, a note of pleading in his voice.

'I couldn't bear it if something similar happened to you. For what it's worth, I think you are wrestling with situations from your childhood, issues that are causing you to act out of character, playing the hard cop. Don't end up like I did, becoming a person you don't like. You desperately need to reflect on your past and decide who and where you really want to be in life.'

Billie knew in that moment where she wanted to be in life and it wasn't walking up the aisle with another man.

'But you're right. You've seen through me. I *am* crazy. You need to keep away, for your own well-being.'

Max abruptly stood up. '*That's* why, Billie, I forced myself to pass you on to a different clinician today.' Then he was gone. Out through the door. Nothing left, but the hint of his intoxicating scent. Billie was frozen to her seat for a moment with shock, trying to process what had just happened. The waitress approached the table.

'Men huh?' She rolled her eyes. 'Tricky buggers. Fancy a top-up now?' Billie shook her head, trying to absorb the truths that had just been shared. She knew that Max was right to warn her about her own life, however much she had feigned disdain for his theories. The revelations about her real start in the world had brought into focus the contradictory feelings that had plagued her for as long as she could remember.

Did the flashbacks, that Max had so perceptively diagnosed, point to a harsh early life that had resulted in a part of her that was cruel and uncaring? Maybe there was something in her genes that looked for trouble at work or down dark alleyways in a reckless search for danger?

It was time to reassess her life, even her impending marriage. It hadn't escaped Billie that being stood up at the altar by Max Strong had affected her much more than the sight of David driving away at speed from the church. There were some big decisions to make. Where on earth should she go from here?

17

THE GRASS BEGINNING TO GROW?

I t was nearly 11pm when Billie arrived back at the hospital having picked up her car, thankful that the waiting area was a little quieter now. She took the opportunity to ring Ash's mobile number, yet again. The messaging service kicked in.

Billie felt a tension between her shoulders as she remembered Josta's earlier words about his having left the scene of today's murder. She desperately hoped that he wasn't over in the children's wing at this same hospital, keeping a bedside vigil with one of his girls. Whatever the issue was, Billie was becoming more concerned by the minute. It was simply unheard of for Ash to rush off from the scene of a major crime. Why on earth would he not have contacted her directly?

As she waited, Billie leant against the wall. She was dog tired as well as sore from her beating, but Max's words kept spinning around in her head. She accepted the truth that he had flagged up. She was, indeed, in danger of becoming someone she disliked.

The memories of her having been so judgemental towards him, a man recognised worldwide, it seemed, for his work and clearly brave, struck her like a sharp punch to the head. She had been playing the smart unemotional cop as usual, in order to hide her true feelings. Yet in recent days he had repeatedly stepped in to help her, all the while coping with his own terrible pain.

Billie felt sickened by her behaviour. It was time to be her authentic self. Going forward, she intended to spend more time with the people that she loved, rather than constantly chasing the tails of dangerous psychopaths. Billie seriously feared that some of their heartless traits could have been rubbing off on her.

She punched Ash's home phone number into her device. There had been no answer earlier.

'Oh, hi Billie,' Jas, Ash's beautiful wife, answered on the first ring, sounding cheery enough.

'Are the children all right?' Billie asked, concerned.

'Sleeping like angels, even the baby,' Jas answered.

'I got a message that one of the girls was unwell?' Billie breathed a sigh of relief for the children, quickly replaced by concern for Ash's whereabouts.

'Nope. All fine and dandy. We've been out to a family party. Shame Daddy couldn't make it yet again. You don't half flog your team. Remember, I could do with him here, helping to put the girls to bed sometimes. He said he would probably be working all night, on this murder thing.'

Billie wound up the call without telling Jas the truth – that her husband had left work mid-afternoon. She had an uneasy feeling as she quickly texted Ash directing him to pick her up at 5am the next morning and to confirm that he had got the message. What on earth could he be up to?

She was so tired and sore that nothing seemed to make sense, not least the reason why The Grass and Max Strong had been in The Dive Bar together in the first place. Billie checked her mobile yet again, slapping the wall in relief to see a text reply from Ash flashing on her phone screen. Short but sweet in the circumstances.

Got it. See you at five boss. Billie guessed that Jas would have more to say about that when he finally made it home. His problem. Hers was to get to Margaret Craig at the earliest possible opportunity, wiped out with tiredness or not. She clicked off the phone and waylaid a nurse who was chirpy and kind despite the late hour. Billie wondered how on earth they did it.

'Any update on Jo Green?' Billie asked the nurse. Whatever her feelings towards the younger detective, she had to admit that she owed her big time tonight.

'Refused to stay in for observation. Hopped off home as soon as we patched her up. Tough as old boots that one.' The nurse grinned. Billie had to admit a grudging admiration. Perhaps The Grass was beginning to grow on her? She forgave herself the silent pun. Kate gave a wan grin as, looking the worse for wear, she came into view, limping up the corridor.

'Thanks for waiting.' Kate linked arms with Billie. 'Sorry I've caused you so much aggro tonight,' she added.

'No problem. Still a few takeaways open. Fancy fish and chips on the way home?' Billie wanted to offer some comfort to her friend.

'You're on, sister!' Kate nudged Billie. 'Hey, there was a really hunky doctor swathing me in bandages. I was ready to make a night of it,' she joked.

As she got behind the wheel, Billie decided that this is what her life would be about in future, fun and friendship, not death and destruction. Kate climbed into the car, almost sitting on the beautiful bowl that Margaret Craig had gifted to Billie.

'What's with the cracked bowl, couldn't afford a new one?' she joked.

'Seaside souvenir. Gift from a special lady I interviewed in Alnmouth.'

'You get around. Is it to do with the murders? No, don't tell me, you'll have to kill me if you do,' Kate teased.

'She was a kind of step-granny to poor little Gracie-May McGill, but sadly missed the chance to look after her. She's really cut up about it. So, I've invited her to my wedding,' Billie announced, as she drove off. Kate looked shocked.

'You're kidding? Is this a good idea? David's mother will go crazy!' Kate warned.

'Exactly!' Billie giggled. 'You'll be sitting next to my new guest of honour, so you'll have a front row seat to the show.'

'No way.' Kate shivered. 'That woman scares me.'

'I think you've had enough terror for one night.' Billie turned the radio on to an upbeat music station. 'Well, not counting that horrific curry sludge you love,' she teased, pulling a face as they headed along the dark, starless road. 'I'm buying. I'll get you a double portion. You should be scared... very scared.'

Stuffed full of stodgy food, freshly showered and smothered in bruise ointment, Billie finally fell into bed in the early hours, soothed by the melodic tones of children singing the magpie rhyme, as they did every night, from Kate's recording in the room next door. She fell into a fitful sleep, dreams of Max Strong feeding her jellies, cut to a scenario in which he and The Grass were attacking her in the dark alleyway. At 3am she woke up with a start, sitting bolt upright in the dark. It felt as if someone had entered her bedroom.

'Kate?' she called. There was no answer. Billie stole out of bed and peeped into the corridor. There was no light on under Kate's door and the house seemed silent. Billie headed back to bed, her head still muggy from the mad dreams and earlier beating.

Had she been more alert, she might have noticed that a car engine had burst into life outside in the lane. Instead, plumping up her pillow and pulling her duvet over her head, Billie finally fell into a deep dreamless sleep.

18

SECRETS AND LIES

The pre-dawn sky, bruised purple, red, black and blue, reminded Billie of her own sore and discoloured body. The patterns mottled across her skin had appeared uncomfortably similar, in the unforgiving light above her bathroom mirror, that morning.

'Okay boss?' Ash had picked her up dead on time, appearing as cheerful as usual. She had settled stiffly into the passenger seat; glad she wasn't behind the wheel at this crazily early hour.

'Yep. What about you? I got some garbled message about why you had to leave the crime scene yesterday afternoon,' she fibbed.

'Sorry, I came over all dizzy. The lights were on, but no one was in,' he counter-lied. 'Jas sent me to bed the minute I got home. I slept pretty much straight through until this morning.' Billie wanted to ask if he could feel his nose growing. 'All those new baby nappy changes getting to me, I guess. I'll make up the hours, boss. Did I miss anything?'

Billie felt hurt. She had always considered Ash to be one of her best friends in the world, but here he was telling her a blatant lie. What was he hiding? He didn't seem aware of her late-night phone call. Either he hadn't been home at all, or Jas was giving him the cold shoulder.

'Yesterday's victim was known as Geordie Stix. The last person to phone him was Margaret Craig.'

'What was her message?' Ash switched on the radio. The weather forecast predicted storms ahead. 'You're still not home, the dinner's in the dog?' He chuckled. Billie bit her tongue. It sounded as though Ash was basing his quip on his own experiences. Could he be having an affair?

'Everything all right at home, with Jas and the girls?' Billie fished. Ash put his foot down, overtook a lorry sleepily pottering along the road.

'Fabulous!' Ash sounded way too cheery, even by his own high standards. 'Apart from me *always* being in the doghouse,' he added. 'She'll be feeding me bones next. Welcome to married life.'

'I'm on the naughty step and I'm not even married yet.' Billie touched her lip. It felt sore as she spoke. 'I upset David's mother by arriving late to the wedding rehearsal.' Ash glanced at Billie, raising his eyebrows.

'That how you got the fat lip?' He laughed. 'Thought you'd been ripping Sellotape with your teeth again.'

Billie chuckled. She was pleased to have the cheered-up version of Ash back again. David still hadn't returned any of the apologetic messages that she had left. Glancing at her watch, she decided to ring him in a while, around the time that normal people would be expected to be awake. She silently promised to make it up to her fiancé tonight. She also quietly vowed not to let Max Strong invade her dreams tonight as she spooned her fiancé close.

'Penny for them.' Ash had noted Billie's momentary silence. 'Not having second thoughts?'

'Just pre-wedding nerves,' Billie answered, reflecting that like all ace detectives, he never missed a thing.

The radio DJ finished his inane chatter, before mentioning the local schools' choir contest, which was scheduled to be broadcast on the station. A preview of Kate's excluded kids, singing their atmospheric magpie themed melody, filled the car. Billie mused that the rhyme seemed to follow her everywhere these days. The last line of the piece, '*a secret never told,*' had hit home, in light of recent revelations. She hadn't mentioned the discovery of her adoption to Ash yet, nor the horrific possibility that her dad was a corrupt cop, heading up a baby-selling racket.

Was she one of those babies? Mother a street walker, father... who knows where? Could she have brothers or sisters, sold off to the highest bidders? It was a sobering thought. Should she keep schtum about her suspicions? If they turned out to be true, would Billie ever want the sordid details to come out? What about her dad's impeccable reputation?

'Hey, have you got any secrets never told, Ash?' Billie asked, repeating the song lyrics. She was relieved that the sky was finally starting to lighten up.

'That would be telling,' Ash quipped, 'but yep, I do actually. I always secretly wanted to be a chef. Jas won't even let me near the kitchen.'

'A chef?' She laughed. 'How come you never mentioned that before?' Ash shrugged. He changed stations to a chat show. 'Can't always have your cake and eat it, can you? No point crying over spilled milk.' Billie mimed a drum roll and symbols.

'Everyone a winner,' she joked. 'How poor Jas puts up with your quips, I'll never know.'

'She had no choice. Marriage was all arranged without much input from either of us.' Ash suddenly sounded serious. 'Kids expected. Life plan mapped out. That's parents for you. It was hard enough insisting that I wanted to be a copper. No way could I chuck everything in and go after what I really wanted most...' he trailed off.

'To be a chef...' Billie finished, totally bewildered by the unexpected revelation. 'David always says that he could have been a footballer, if his parents hadn't pushed him into law.' She didn't believe it to be true for a moment. Was Ash being serious? He suddenly turned up the sound on the radio.

'*He* followed his dreams,' was his only reply.

An interview with Micky Flannigan, midway through, filled the car. With his recent success he was the golden boy of the moment. Billie applauded him.

'Go Micky,' she cheered, remembering the charismatic heartbroken man she had spoken to about Conner Grey's death. He had kept his dream intact; despite the torturous route he'd had to take to finally score that willing goal.

'What advice would you give to anybody out there chasing the spotlight?' the unctuous radio interviewer probed.

'Just go for it.' Micky's quiet voice lacked any sense of bravado. 'Even when you get knock-backs. I mean, I was always getting signed by all sorts of lowly clubs then being dropped. In between, I had to work on building sites, offshore rigs, cook in burger bars, you name it, I did it.'

'And now you're our local hero!' The radio interviewer was laying it on thick as he wound the interview up, but he wasn't far off the truth.

'So there you are,' Billie continued the conversation, 'Micky was a chef. It's never too late to make your fantasies a reality.' A vision of Max Strong flashed before her mind's eye. She mentally threw that insistent fantasy underneath a passing bus. Ash stretched over, switching the radio off.

'But it is, Billie.' His voice was full of sadness. 'My dream was so far away from this – wife, kids, mortgage, job that sucks all of your feelings dry. I'm too far up the wrong road to change lanes.'

Billie was shocked by the tone of Ash's voice, his words bursting with sadness and regret.

'Wow, you never said...' Billie rubbed Ash's hand in sympathy. He jumped. She looked down, noticing an angry bruise and gash around his wrist. Coloured livid purple and pink, it was clear to see beneath his crisp white shirt cuff, even in the early morning light.

'What happened to your hand? Have you been in a fight or something?' Billie asked, shocked.

'Oh, just one of the kids playing with my handcuffs. Tying me to the chair. Didn't want Daddy to go to work,' Ash clearly lied. 'I told them that Aunty Billie was going to buy them sticks of seaside rock to make up for taking me away for the day,' Ash teased. Billie so wanted to believe that.

She suddenly recalled the sensation of bringing down the broken bottle on the wrist of her attacker as he had gripped her throat the night before in the dark alley. She glanced at Ash's injury again, shook away the ridiculous thought forming in her suspicious mind, as the car phone sprang into life.

'Ma'am?' Billie heard the voice of The Grass fill the car. She checked the clock. It was still not quite 6am.

'Green. You should stay at home today.' Billie had a sudden memory of the horror-film scenario of blood projecting out of The Grass, the night before. The memory still made her shiver.

'I'm fine, ma'am. All patched up and at work now. I just wanted to say thank you for the gift.'

'Already? The wonders of online ordering,' Billie answered, 'that breaks some record.' Billie had revisited her conversation with Max as she had tried to sleep. There was no doubt that The Grass had helped save her skin. Whatever special relationship the young detective had going with Billie's short-time shrink, she at least owed her a small token of thanks.

Billie ended the call, glancing again at Ash. Did he have a

small bruise on his face too? Was she letting her imagination run wild?

'Present? *The Grass?*' Ash asked in exaggerated astonishment. 'What on earth did I miss while I was on my sickbed?' Billie noted that Ash was set on drumming that fib home. It made her guarded.

'I'm getting soft in my old age. She went above and beyond the call of duty yesterday, so I decided that she deserved a reward. New me,' she quipped, trying to regain her composure. Had Ash *always* told her a pack of lies?

'Can't imagine what anyone would get The Grass as a gift, spiked jellies perhaps? She knows how to handle them and she's pretty crazy.'

'Roller skates,' Billie answered truthfully.

'*Roller skates?*' Ash exclaimed, bursting into laughter, swerving dangerously to miss a huge tractor labouring slowly beyond a tight bend they had rounded, now they had moved on to the winding country road heading down towards Alnmouth Village.

'Don't ask,' Billie retorted. She shook away her momentary suspicion of Ash. Maybe he was engaged in an extramarital dalliance, lots of the pretty PCs were charmed by his easy camaraderie... She certainly didn't doubt his love for Jas and anyway, Billie recalled the gist of Max's words the night before, Billie you are better than that. He was right. She dropped her zany misgivings. Maybe the kids *had* been playing with his handcuffs.

'Okay, I'll tell.' She chuckled. 'It turns out that The Grass is quite the roller-skating queen.'

It was at that moment that Ash slammed on the emergency brakes. A young man, wild-eyed with horror, raced out in front of the car. As the vehicle skidded to a halt, the man bounced off the bonnet, rolling onto the lane. Ash and Billie leapt out.

'Are you all right?' Billie looked him over. For a moment, he lay like a rabbit trapped in headlights, frozen with terror and shock at the collision. Then he jumped up.

'We need help, there's a woman, down there, hoisted on the Church Hill cross. I think she's dead!' He pointed down a track across the field.

Cut off at high tide, the hill had once housed an ancient church, which had tumbled down into the sea during a major storm. All that was left was a simple, large wooden cross on the top of the high grassy mound, surrounded by swirling water.

Billie's heart was hammering against her chest as Ash bumped the car at speed down the potholed track, which gave the only landward access to the hill. As they got closer, she could see panicked movement around the base of the wooden structure. Three men were frantically trying to drag a shadowy body, looking for all the world like Jesus pinned to the cross, down to safety.

As the car came to a halt, the faded strawberry-blonde hair now visible, immediately alerted Billie to the identity of the unfortunate victim. In truth, she had known the instant that the young fisherman had called for help, who she was going to find at the centre of that mind-blowing scenario.

'Margaret Craig,' she whispered in horror.

Billie's mind was whirling as she jumped out of the car and started to scramble up the grassy slope to join the fisherman. Margaret Craig's beautiful, terraced back garden, where Billie had eaten birthday cake, stood directly opposite, across the watery inlet. The older lady appeared to be wearing the same clothing as the day before. Only now it was awash with blood.

Billie felt as though she was going to be sick. Had she missed something on her second visit?

The sound of emergency sirens could be heard coming ever closer, thanks to the quick work of one of the men. Billie prayed that help wasn't coming too late.

'Doubt that ambulance is going to be of much use.' Ash was breathless as he caught up with Billie. The men were already carefully lowering Margaret Craig's body down. 'Should I tell them to leave the body in situ, boss?' Billie noticed that Ash wasn't looking at the victim, he instead appeared more interested in the magnificent seascape on view from their lofty position.

'No!' Billie rushed to help, as Margaret Craig almost touched the grass with her feet. She caught her in her arms and gently lowered the blood-sodden woman to the ground. Dropping to her knees, Billie felt for a pulse, leaned forward, sensed the faintest of butterfly-like breaths on her skin.

'She wasn't here a couple of hours ago when I went out to set the lobster pots,' one of the men announced.

'She's alive,' Billie called, ripping off her jacket to try to stem seeping blood from the older lady's chest. 'Tell them to hurry! We'll need the air ambulance,' Billie shouted, nodding to the ambulance and police patrol car making their way down the potholed lane.

'It's all right, Margaret. It's Billie here. You're going to be all right.' She stroked her hair, whilst keeping her hand tightly on the main wound site. Margaret Craig opened her eyes just a little and connected with Billie's urgent stare.

'Hello love.' She managed just a hint of a smile. Billie bent closer in order to hear the breathless, faintly whispered utterances. 'I always knew that you would come home to me in the end...' Margaret's head lolled back, just as two paramedics arrived either side of Billie with their equipment.

'Cardiac arrest,' Billie cried, sitting back on the grass, stunned, as the medics went into action. Was Margaret Craig hallucinating? Had she just witnessed the last words of a dying woman talking to her long-lost baby, or... '*I was up at dawn cleaning a nunnery and out at night pulling tricks.*' Billie recalled the older lady's revelations during her interview the day before. Isabelle's story of a nunnery and her father's association with it had also barely left her mind. Had Margaret's 'lost' baby actually survived?

'Got to get her down the hill. We've called in the air ambulance,' the female paramedic advised Billie. 'Are you her daughter?' she asked. Billie realised that it was an easy mistake to make. She and Margaret were of similar stature, the older lady's hair a faded version of her own red mane. Billie's scattered thoughts finally connected in a bombshell, one that totally blew her mind. Could Margaret Craig actually *be* her birth mother?

'You okay, boss?' Ash pulled Billie upright. She felt unsteady on her legs. Her mind was racing. The female paramedic looked up from her work and registered Billie's ID.

'Gets to us all sometimes,' she commiserated, waving to the air ambulance which was coming in to land on a flat area between the huge camel-backed sand dunes.

'You're a copper? Never mentioned that last night!' One of the fishermen was grinning now at Ash.

'Eh?' Ash started walking away from him.

'Ash, I'm going with her in the air ambulance,' Billie interrupted.

'Really?' Ash seemed baffled. 'Looks like she's a gonner to me.' The fisherman nudged him.

'Last night. I was talking to you in the bar of the hotel. Next town along from here.' He flicked his head in the direction of the nearest settlement along the coast. 'You and your friend–'

'Got the wrong guy, mate. Come on, move along. We've got to secure this area,' Ash blustered. The man looked quizzical, shrugged and started to head down the hill. 'I'll stay up here, boss,' Ash continued, as a uniformed policeman joined them. Even in her wound-up state Billie clocked the conversation and Ash's obvious eagerness to get away from the fisherman.

'DSI Wilde,' Billie showed her ID to the uniform, 'this is a crime scene, almost certainly linked to the recent murders you will have heard about on the news.' The uniformed copper nodded, a glint of excitement in his eyes. Billie was aware that the most action they usually got around these parts, were holidaymakers scrapping over car parking places nearest the beach.

'I'd like you to stay here, take witness statements and make sure that nothing, not even a single blade of grass, is touched until the Crime Scene Investigation Team arrive. Is that clear?' The policeman nodded enthusiastically.

'DS Sanghera here will keep you company. As you will note, not even *he* will touch a single thing.' Billie ran her hand through her curls. She could feel Ash's eyes boring a hole into her back. Suddenly she was questioning her whole relationship with her closest friend. As she scrambled down the hill behind the paramedics, who were handling the stretcher with awe-inspiring skill as they headed for the waiting helicopter, Billie collared the fisherman who had been shooed away.

'What hotel exactly do you work in?' she asked.

'The Paradise. Next-door village,' he announced, 'been working in the kitchen there for years. Place was a dosshouse, but it's just been relaunched. New owner. Themed rooms, all the rage these days with the visitors. Seen him up there a few times already with his friend. I never forget a face. Don't know why he's denying it.' He grinned and winked. 'You're not the wife, are you?'

Billie took out her ID and waved it in his face. 'DSI Billie Wilde,' she announced, 'head of the murder investigation team, I'll be in touch for a statement. I know where to find you.'

She ran on under the moving blades of the helicopter and climbed inside, thinking it was one of the oddest journeys she had ever embarked upon. A woman whom she had a suspicion was her birth mother, was fighting for her life right here, next to her. Meanwhile, far below, as the helicopter took off, she could see the best man at her coming wedding, having his every move scrutinised by an eagle-eyed traffic cop. It was only 6.15am. Could the day get any worse?

19

A WOLF IN SHEEP'S CLOTHING

'Margaret?' Billie softly called the woman's name, in hope, rather than in any expectation, that she would get a response. If the fisherman's account was correct, she couldn't have been hanging in her horrible parody of Christ for the entire night. That knowledge offered Billie little relief from her pain.

Josta, who had been liaising with the hospital, had explained that the vile cuts and bruises imposed upon Margaret Craig's body, must have been inflicted over several hours of torture. The seven knife wounds had come later. Probably at Church Hill. The M shape, cut just behind Margaret's ankle bone, was bigger than the others. Did that mean something?

'Same person at work,' Josta had nodded, during her examination, 'same knife, by the looks of it. Identical to the one that I showed you in my kitchen. Amazing good fortune that the woman is lying here this morning, rather than in my mortuary.'

Billie couldn't agree that Margaret Craig had been fortunate. She rubbed her face, still unable to forgive herself for not having acted when Margaret's neighbour had handed her a clue on a plate. Maybe there had been people inside, right then, having a party, the likes of which Billie couldn't bear to envisage. She would never know the truth. Further enquiries by the MIT team had confirmed that the old man remained so heartbroken by the loss of his wife all those years ago, that he had totally lost his mind. Billie feared that she was losing hers too.

A memory of Max and the revelation of the terrible death of his wife made Billie shiver.

'Wouldn't hurt to get yourself checked out whilst you're here, dear.' Josta had looked concerned, glancing hopefully towards a pretty nurse who had popped in to check a monitor by the bed. 'Yesterday evening was the second episode of fainting this week and whatever has happened to your lip? Thank goodness you have an exotic honeymoon on the horizon. Just the ticket.'

Billie was saved by the bell, as her mobile bleeped a message. Her attention flew to it. Josta had often teased Billie that the dead gave away more than she did, so she wasn't surprised when the forensic pathologist finally threw in the towel and waved a beaten goodbye, following the busy nurse out. To Billie's relief, she had also closed the door on the subject of her abandoning the investigation and this precious patient, in order to sit on a faraway beach and catch a tan.

The idea that she could still go on honeymoon was preposterous. Billie knew that there was no way she could let all of these victims down. But what about David? He'd already made his feelings clear on the subject. Without doubt he needed a break too. His bloody mother kept going on about his work. Billie had tried to call him, whilst the emergency team had worked on Margaret Craig at the hospital, but he still hadn't returned her messages. Didn't *he* also put his work first, or was Billie just trying to justify her neglect of the relationship?

Boo had confirmed the MIT meeting for later that afternoon. They needed to have an urgent update on information, focus on anything they had missed, recheck anything that could be useful. Billie felt panic rise in her chest with the responsibility of the task. One thing was for sure. She couldn't trust Ash right now to take over the investigation whilst she gaily sashayed off on holiday.

As the machines bleeped around Margaret Craig's body, fighting to keep her alive, Billie allowed herself to think the unthinkable. Could Ash somehow have been involved in the attack on her the night before? She had argued with Max that it was a random event, but in truth, she wasn't so sure. Ash did have injuries to his wrist and face which fitted with the body locations she had smacked with the broken bottle, whilst attempting to defend herself. But why on earth would her best friend assault her?

What about the murders? He was definitely lying about his whereabouts after leaving the scene of Geordie Stix's murder and if the fisherman was to be believed, he could have been in the vicinity of Margaret Craig's attack, all the way through to Billie's 5am pick up. It was a mad thought. Billie shook it away once and for all. Was she going totally crazy? It seemed that even Max Strong couldn't cope with her and he was trained to manage the insane.

The only person who Billie felt she had an uncomplicated relationship with these days was Kate. She reflected that maybe the disciplinary hearing instigated by The Grass, had caused her to mistrust *everybody*. She was becoming a person that she really didn't like. Max's words from the night before resonated once again in her mind.

Her dear friend Ash was clearly going through a difficult time at home, what he didn't need was one of his best friends thinking he was a damn serial killer! What was wrong with her? When this was over, she *really* did need to seek out some help, someone of her own choosing. It was lucky that Max had dumped her as a patient. After hearing about the horrific death of his much-loved wife, she couldn't open up to him about her darkest or deepest feelings. Not truthfully, anyway.

Billie leaned forward, tucked Margaret Craig's sheets around her body. When she heard the door open and upbeat voices, she spoke without turning.

'No entry. This is a controlled area.' She had a PC positioned at the door and had insisted on a news blackout, but village gossip of a woman hanging from Church Hill had spread like wildfire, leading the local news. So far, everyone assumed that Margaret Craig had died, like the others. Billie didn't want the perpetrator to discover that she was hanging on to life by a thread, then fast-track to the hospital to finish off the job.

There was a kerfuffle, as the PC huffed and puffed back into position from his regular bathroom breaks. Billie turned to see Max Strong standing in the doorway. A cage full of butterflies were set free in her stomach.

'Billie.' His voice was like liquid chocolate. His deep-brown eyes looked directly into hers. The PC intervened.

'He can't come in here, it's a controlled area,' the PC loudly admonished the pretty nurse, now standing alongside Max. It was clear that he was attempting to redeem himself for having taken the opportunity to go AWOL whilst Billie was in the room.

'He's a doctor.' The nurse's blinding smile, seconds earlier directed at Max, dropped as she flashed a warning look at the copper. *Wow, if looks could kill,* Billie thought.

'Max, maybe we can talk later,' Billie started, *maybe in that little bistro again, tonight.* The words ran through her head hopefully, her earlier resolution immediately melting away. She wanted to apologise for her harsh words the night before, craved to tell him how deeply sorry she was about the tragedy in his life, hug it away... the urge was almost overwhelming.

'Unfortunately not, DSI Wilde. I believe we agreed that wouldn't be a good idea,' Max Strong replied. The pretty nurse butted in, as Billie reacted to what felt like a verbal slap in the face.

'Dr Strong is here to see his patient. You need to step out for a few moments please, detective.' Her voice was firm.

'It's all right, I'll come back later.' Max flashed a soft smile at the nurse, turning to leave without another glance in Billie's direction. She was stunned, not only with Max's clear and final rejection of her, but at the news that he had a connection to Margaret Craig. What vital information might he be in possession of?

Billie swallowed her pride and raced out of the door. Max was heading down the corridor towards the exit, engaged in light-hearted banter with the pretty nurse. Her precious patients could have been taking their last breaths for all she appeared to care, so focused was she on the dashing Dr Strong. Billie felt a stab of jealousy.

'Stop!' Billie heard her voice bellow out. It sounded like she was making an arrest. The doctor and nurse turned, one looking seriously miffed, the other absolutely still. 'I need to talk to you about any information Margaret Craig may have shared with you.' The nurse rolled her eyes at Max, slightly shaking her head in disbelief at Billie's demeanour. Max appeared totally calm, only the glint in his dark eyes gave away any sense of emotion.

'I'm afraid that information is confidential, DSI Wilde.' The formal use of her name for a second time, hadn't escaped Billie. 'You, of all people, should appreciate that.'

'I don't recall you having a problem handing over *certain* confidential files at the drop of a hat.' Billie pulled out her ID, flicking her head to the nurse to make herself scarce. 'As you point out, I'm a detective superintendent heading up a multiple murder hunt, one victim of which was a pre-school child. Your patient may also turn out to be a murder victim, yet.'

She wanted to drum home to Max Strong that she wasn't just

some sad and hopeless former patient, she was highly competent, with a vital job to do. 'I would have thought you would be jumping at the chance to help me with my enquiries.'

A hint of a smile played at the corners of Max's lips as he watched Billie's performance. It made her feel incensed and stupid in equal measure.

'The question is, would any information that I might divulge result in harm to certain other innocent people?' He raised an eyebrow as he stared straight at Billie. It was as though he was looking into her soul.

'I am informing you that disclosing such information would be justified in the public interest.' Billie made it clear that she was well versed on the guiding principles involved. She hadn't reached her lofty position in the force so quickly without knowing her stuff, preferential treatment due to family ties, aside. *That* little voice was never going to stop niggling away in the back of her head.

'I'll certainly give it serious thought, officer.' Max Strong turned and pushed through the exit door leaving Billie frozen to the spot. Her heart was beating fast. She knew that she probably sounded like a pompous idiot, but she couldn't let Max go. Was she deluding herself that the only reason was that she desperately needed information that could lead her to the killer?

The sound of a commotion coming from the corridor behind made Billie turn and head back quickly. The PC, no doubt aware of Billie's rapid approach, was loudly admonishing an elderly woman who was trying to enter Margaret Craig's room.

'What's going on?' Billie asked. She made a mental note to replace the PC with a female officer she favoured. Not only did she have way better people skills, but also a stronger bladder. As the elderly woman turned, Billie was surprised to find herself facing Isabelle Church.

'Oh Billie, my dear. I'm trying to get in here to see my friend, Margaret, but this officer is being a bit of a bore.'

'You know Margaret Craig?' Billie asked.

'Yes, it's such a shock. It was Margaret I was meant to be meeting last night. We were going to the ballet, at her nursery, the children were putting on a little show.' Billie mentally kicked herself. 'Then we were planning to go to a nice place we know, for afternoon tea. It was her birthday you see.'

Billie tried not to scream. She reminded herself that hindsight was a wonderful thing. 'But I was already at the nursery when she rang to say that some friends from the past had made a surprise visit, so she couldn't make it.' Billie's heart started beating fast. 'She sounded quite upset about missing the show. She loves those kiddies.' Billie glanced through the glass window into Margaret's room. She was still totally unconscious.

'Isabelle, can I take you for a cuppa in the café?' Billie already had her arm around Isabelle Church's shoulder and was propelling her towards the lift.

'That would be wonderful, dear. Are they licensed at all? This has been such a shock. I could do with something a damn sight stronger than a cup of tea, I can tell you.'

Billie was willing to ply Isabelle Church with absolutely *anything* – sex, drugs, rock 'n' roll and definitely the stiffest drink on the hospital canteen menu if she wanted it, because *this* might finally be the breakthrough she had been praying for.

'So, you've known Margaret Craig for thirty years or so?' Billie was racing through the pages of her notebook at speed as she jotted down information. Isabelle paused to take another bite of the biggest cream cake in the hospital canteen, along with a swig of red wine from her hospital-issue plastic cup. Billie noticed that shock hadn't dulled Isabelle's appetite at all.

'Now let me think, at least thirty-five years, dear. She was Maggie Byrd then, of course. I left the convent in '89. That was the year Margaret was forced to hand over the toddler, you see. I'm afraid God fell out of my favour then.'

'*Toddler?* Who to?' Billie felt her stomach churn. The paramedic's mistake in thinking that Billie was Margaret Craig's daughter had been turning over in her mind ever since. She also knew, from her father's hidden photo, that she had been adopted when she was an infant, rather than a newborn. Could her own personal truth be just an arm's length away?

'Ostensibly social services. It was the young social worker who finally managed to tear the child from Margaret's arms, but we all knew where the poor little thing really ended up. It sent Margaret mad with grief. She was given money and shipped abroad. Rich men in those parts paid major wonga for beautiful women to service their needs and Margaret has always scrubbed up well,' she shook her head sadly, 'not that she had any choice. Do these girls ever? She was damned by the men in her life whichever way she turned.'

'Can you explain why the child was placed in care?' Billie blinked, feeling hot, pictures she didn't want to see had started flashing through her head. She shook them away, vivid projections in her mind's eye of how the parting scene between mother and child must have been.

'She had been abused, physically and mentally, by Margaret's latest live-in beau. His own children, whom Margaret, bless her soul, also cared for, were sent back to various dysfunctional relatives. I don't doubt that they all ended up in the care system. He was sent to prison...'

Billie had a sudden image of being hung on a tree branch, screaming, flapping her arms in terror as someone laughed at her suffering. She caught her breath, knowing that it was a memory, not imagination.

'...Margaret only had one child of her own and *he* wasn't the father. That's why he really went to town on that child.' Isabelle shivered, knocking back the whole cup of wine. Billie drained the rest of the bottle into Isabelle's cup before she had even managed to lay it back down on the table. 'Yes indeed. On reflection, Geordie Stix deserved to die in such a horrific manner. He inflicted immeasurable damage on a lot of young lives.'

'Geordie Stix?' Billie dropped her pen for a moment in shock. Her mind was racing now. *He* had been Margaret Craig's abusive live-in lover?

'Terrible business. All the sordid details didn't come out in the paper, but it was very nearly a murder enquiry with the child. Real father whipped her away. All hush-hush, of course. His wife couldn't have children and was hankering after a little one, so he set the whole thing up to look like a normal adoption. No one, including his wife, I'm sure, was ever the wiser that he'd actually fathered the little poppet. Hopefully, the memories of her abuse faded away, wiped out by her new privileged life as the daughter of the chief of police.'

Billie stayed stock-still, even though her soul was screaming out a cry of recognition, of grief, of love and horror. Her mind was in turmoil, but to anyone around she appeared completely focused.

'You are absolutely sure about that?' She heard her voice wobble just a little.

'Indeed I am. So desperate was Margaret to keep some thread of connection, that she went to great lengths to re-engage with the girl's father when she returned back to the UK.' Isabelle harrumphed. 'I told her she was a fool, but what do I know about love, wizened old maid that I am?' She smiled at Billie.

'There must have been some sort of distorted affection there on his part, too, because he would occasionally take the child to Alnmouth, so that Margaret could see her. Strictly from a distance, of course. She would be allowed to sit close by on the beach and watch, whilst he and his happy family enjoyed a picnic. Just a different sort of abuser from Geordie Stix if you ask me. As I said yesterday, the top dog was a very cruel man.'

Billie shivered, blocking the picture of her loving dad building sandcastles by the sea, that had sprung into her mind. Isabelle shook her head in disbelief, as she continued. 'When Margaret's husband keeled over on the golf course, the affair gathered momentum once again. Lover boy visited every week. I told her it was sheer madness, but she said that it allowed her to keep up to date on the child. True, the relationship did seem to grow into something more than just casual sex. He had a cake and flowers delivered every year on her birthday.'

Billie remembered the cake. Lemon. Margaret had said it was her favourite. It was also her dad's. Billie wanted to laugh crazily, tell Isabelle that family genes are funny things, lemon cake being her guilty pleasure too.

'Odd thing was Margaret said the cake arrived yesterday, even though her paramour expired a few weeks ago – car crash. Must have had a standing order, so confident was he that he could keep poor Margaret on the go forever. Anyhow, like all of us in the end, he went to meet his maker and hopefully repent his many sins. That's why I was pleased, rather than dismayed, when Margaret said that she had acquaintances to visit.'

Billie was struggling now, to stay calm. She wanted to run out of the brightly lit canteen, scream into a dark corner, gather her thoughts, but she felt that the key to unlocking the name of the person responsible for this mayhem and murder was in her grasp. She wouldn't, in fact she *couldn't* give up the hunt now. It was the last remaining truth she could count on in her own life.

'Did she name the visitors by any chance?' Isabelle was getting restless now, gathering her bag, finished with her gossip-fest.

'No. But she told me that she hadn't seen them for years, so she couldn't fob them off. She sounded rather tired, so I don't know if they were starting to outstay their welcome. They had brought her a big box of jellies, so I expect she didn't want to appear ungrateful.' Billie reached for her coffee, spilling it across the tabletop. Isabelle grabbed a napkin, mopped it up, in readiness to move off. Billie caught her arm.

'Can you remember *anything*, anything else at all, any names or people from that time in the nunnery?'

'Judge was called Silver, I recall that. Seemed like a genial man, to anyone who didn't know better. Regular at the convent. Wolf in sheep's clothing. If I recall rightly, he suddenly adopted a boy child around the same time. Wife too posh to push by all accounts. Who knows whether he went through the conventional channels, or if it was another lost child from God's pick-and-mix baby shop?'

20

FIVE FOR SILVER, SIX FOR GOLD

B illie raced up the crunching gravel drive at such speed that she managed to behead a whole bunch of delicate flowers. Their petals scattered wildly over the perfectly manicured lawn.

She hammered on the bespoke solid oak door, surrounded by sweet-smelling red roses. A leaded stained-glass window to one side featured the entwined family crest of the owners. It demonstrated an inherited privilege that Billie had never considered as anything special on her numerous visits here. After all, the setting was almost a replica of the home of her own parents, surroundings that she had been conditioned to expect as the norm.

Now that she knew the shocking truth of her upbringing, Billie was beginning to make sense of her recent flashbacks, panic attacks and feelings of anger and confusion. The clash of cultures suddenly forced upon her as a child had undoubtedly disturbed her to the depths of her soul. Shock had now turned to absolute fury, as she acted on Max Strong's words, urging her to confront her past.

Hearing no reply, she forcefully kicked the door, determined to get a response. The rage that Billie felt in her heart was not only for her own loss of an authentic start in life, but for all the trafficked babies. Acid rose to the back of her throat as she speculated on what truly damaging fates may have befallen the others snatched from their mothers.

During her stint with the child abuse policing team, she had seen the sickening videos, knew that child exploitation wasn't just happening to kids with different faces in some far-off country. But in her wildest dreams she could never have guessed that she had been bang in the middle of it. There was no doubt in her mind that some of the victims would not be alive today to tell any tales. She banged on the door with knuckles now, as well as heavy boots. It finally swung open.

'Billie. Why, hello dear. Come in. How lovely to see you!' Billie stepped over the threshold, aware that the demeanour that she had stupidly mistaken for graciousness, was simply a mask to cover up unspeakable truths about David's father.

David's mother appeared. Billie sensed that she was on the brink of reminding her to remove her footwear as usual, but she resorted to her default look of general disapproval instead. She was carrying a large glass of wine in her expensively manicured hands. *No change there then*, Billie couldn't avoid thinking.

'I know,' Billie announced, looking from one to the other. She was no longer their future daughter-in-law, trying eternally to keep up a show of family togetherness for David's sake, she was a senior police detective, intent on getting justice.

'About the different wedding dress that I ordered, to replace that dreadful thing David bought?' David's mother shrugged. 'I wouldn't worry about it, dear. You haven't shown any interest in the arrangements to date. Why let a little detail like a change of wedding dress cause you concern? It will go better with the hairstyle I've planned. The photographer totally agrees.'

'About the adoption and your part in it,' Billie challenged David's father.

'Your adoption, dear? Oh yes, I promised yesterday to look for the paperwork, though I'm sure it will be somewhere on public record.'

'The truth. Not the lies. That's what I'm looking for. David doesn't know about his own leading role in your dirty little family secret, does he?' She stared at David's mother, who took a step forward, agitated and angry.

'David doesn't need to know anything about that. Not that he would care,' she countered. 'He was picked out of a slum, parents who had sold their souls to drink and drugs by all accounts. They didn't want a child. We've given him everything, just as you were given everything from your parents.'

'But my mother had no choice, no knowledge of the true situation.' Billie glanced at David's father. He was looking uncomfortable now. 'Just as my birth mother had no other option. How many children have *you* fathered? How much did you get per sale?' she asked Sir James Silver. David's mother threw her drink at Billie.

'How dare you?' She gasped. 'You're talking rubbish. Tell her, James!' Billie brushed the drink from her jacket, moving forward, refusing to be silenced.

'How many half-brothers or sisters of David are walking around out there, or being used and abused, or snuffed out in films on the dark web?' Sir James Silver's face darkened.

'That's enough,' he spoke quietly, but with steel in the voice that had silenced so many people in the witness box.

'I won't keep quiet.' Billie came face to face with him.

'Do you really want to tarnish the memory of your father, disgrace your mother and probably put an end to your illustrious career? It has been, let's face it, dear, built on the back of your own lucky break. You would still be in the gutter without our interventions and there have already been rumblings that your maternal genes are showing themselves in ill-judged behaviour.'

Billie grabbed the empty glass from David's mother and flung it against the wall. It shattered into tiny pieces, along with any sense Billie had left of her rightful place in life. She moved across the room, heading for the door.

'I'll make sure that you pay for what you've done!' She was incandescent with rage.

'Then you are making a very dangerous decision,' Sir James Silver icily replied. 'Remember who I am. Understand who will be believed. It won't be the ramblings of a mad woman. I emphasise, you need to calm down, or you will be following a deathly path.' His face was white, full of menace. Billie had no doubt that he meant what he said, but she had never been one to run away from a dangerous criminal and she had absolutely no intention of being intimidated now.

'Is David around?' Billie had raced at speed to the Crown Court where her fiancé was prosecuting a major case.

'Just about to resume in Court One, dear,' Libby, the ancient court usher advised, as Billie spotted David approaching from a side office, in full court dress and short peruke. In his flying black robes and white collar with bands, contrasting with his perfectly fitting black suit, he looked like some sort of God, all golden tan and striking blue eyes.

'Billie?' He spotted her just as Libby swung the door open for him to enter and stepped to one side.

'David, we need to talk,' Billie started. Libby coughed, a signal to get a move on rather than an indicator of a chest infection. David held his finger up to indicate he would be there in a moment.

'I'm just about to go in. Is everything okay?' he asked, puzzled. It was unusual for Billie to meet him in court at lunchtime without any prior plan to do so. As he moved closer, Billie caught a hint of his intoxicating perfume. She had arranged for it to be hand-mixed herself, as a birthday gift. It was unique. The ingredients were long-lasting; beats of blackcurrant, honey and myrrh. David had joked that when he wore it at work the female clerks all fainted, such was the Herculean levels of sex appeal it channelled.

'I'm sorry about last night...' she started.

'It's fine. I had to be dragged screaming to the church myself. Goodness knows, most of us have seen a wedding already, know the drill. Up the aisle, down the aisle, eat, drink and have a very merry time...'

'In The Turret Room,' Billie teased with a smile, remembering the key she had found to the honeymoon suite. David's face fell.

'What?' he stammered. Libby coughed again. He looked across.

'Sorry, look I've got to run, darling.' Billie suddenly realised what a stupid, hot-headed and selfish idea it was to rush here and spill the beans to David about his sordid family. It wasn't the time. It certainly wasn't the place.

'Yes, of course. I'll see you tonight.' David had started to move towards the entrance to the court. He shook his head.

'Sorry, I've got to work late.' His voice was full of regret. He pulled a sweet, silly sad face. Billie smiled. He was as bad as her with his work ethic. She caught his hand, pulled him back close for a moment.

'Love you,' she said, pecking him on the cheek. It was true. It maybe wasn't the overwhelming feeling that she felt every time she set eyes on Max, but she couldn't imagine dashing David not being in her life, despite their ups and downs. After all, they had been through so much together. More than he knew, right now. Once they were married, they would start afresh, maybe even start a family of their own.

'Love you too, button nose.' David pecked Billie on the nose, using his pet nickname for her. 'Now, I *really* have got to love you and leave you.'

David waved a last goodbye, sweeping into the courtroom like a leading actor making his stage entrance, past Libby who couldn't help smiling at the exchange of the soon-to-be-married couple. The news that the dashing barrister had chosen a beautiful bride had broken more than a few admiring hearts. It had also provoked a disturbed soul, full of hate and set on revenge.

21

THE KILLER HALL OF FAME

'So, she's not dead?' Ash sounded incredulous and less than happy with Billie for leaving him stuck on a hill, surrounded by sea, in deepest Northumberland.

'That about sums up the good news, folks,' Billie surveyed her assembled MIT team, 'but there's a news blackout on that, so the info doesn't leave this room.' She looked from one to the other. 'Visiting restricted to the medical team and me, so no popping round there with flowers and chocolates.' *Or jellies*, she silently added, kicking herself for glancing at Ash as she did so, remembering that she had put that idea firmly to bed.

He was hiding something without a doubt, but Billie herself could hardly talk. Surely it was her duty to share the fact that she had uncovered extraordinarily strong personal links to Margaret Craig and Geordie Stix? The team were all well aware that Gracie-May was connected to Margaret. Billie thanked God that Joy Summers hadn't also popped up somewhere in her own damn life.

She swallowed hard. It was impossible to spill the beans yet. Not without more investigations of her own, to prove beyond any doubt whatsoever that the new information on her family background was true. The knock-on effect to her father's reputation didn't bear thinking about.

A quick reflection back to her confrontation with David's parents, proved that she was in danger of going into denial. But if she was to report how her association with the dead and gravely injured had come to pass, the Chief would whip her off the case in an instant. Such an outcome would totally disrupt the investigation and judging by the speed at which this killing spree was moving, it would also result in further innocent deaths. Billie made a final decision to focus on getting justice for the victims first. Washing her own dirty linen would have to wait until later.

'Any new intel anyone is just bursting to share?' Billie heard that breezy, confident voice that she used with the team. If only they knew the truth. Perhaps everyone else in the room was sitting here guarding personal skeletons, just like her? That thought made her feel a soupçon better about her own decision.

'Yep. Micky Flannigan's out of tonight's team,' Derek Blythe piped up. All the men in the room groaned. 'Seems that he got an injury in training. Looks like he'll be out for the season.' More mumblings of dismay.

'Anything to do with the murders then?' Billie knew that Derek Blythe was simply trying to lighten the general mood with his football comment, but they needed to keep focused on the job in hand. Nevertheless, she was saddened to hear the news. It rammed home the fact that she could easily have ended up like the Micky Flannigans of this world, never quite reaching their true potential because of a chaotic childhood. Or lack of connections. David's father had been keen to ram the benefits of those home to her earlier.

'Still trawling through the good, bad and ugly who cared for little Gracie-May,' Derek responded. 'We've taken DNA from the lot and are checking all of their movements on the night of her death.'

'Good work. I appreciate it's a mammoth job.' Billie glanced up at Gracie-May's giant photo, staring wide-eyed from the wall. She vowed silently, as she did every time that she looked at it, that she would make someone pay heavily for the damage that they had inflicted on that beautiful child.

'Anything come up on Joy Summers, Ash? You were looking into her background. The woman seems to have been an open book. Do-gooder, charity worker. How on earth can she be on a killer's shopping list?' Ash was scrolling through his phone. He glanced up, sullen and distracted.

'Nope. Nothing. We know that she taught at Sunday school sometimes. Gracie went there once. No one can remember if it was on the same day. Possible religious connection, same as Church Hill, Angel of the North and St Lucia's Nunnery have religious connections, but you've already dissed that theory.'

His attitude was unnerving Billie. It was so unlike her friend and she couldn't let it go, not when it was spilling out in front of the team. She would have to have a word, later.

'With her working at the food bank, so near the scene of crime, I still think that she encountered the killer there. Upset them somehow,' The Grass offered.

'What, like she didn't give them a big enough plateful one day?' Derek Blythe was scornful. Billie stepped in.

'Who knows? Look, this is a safe space. No idea too whacky to put forward. We're not dealing with a rational mindset here. Throw out your theories however wild they might sound.'

'Geordie Stix abused a child, years ago. Seems it was the kid of a live-in lover. Maybe that child has grown up now and is seeking revenge?' The Grass suddenly threw in, emboldened, it seemed, by Billie's defence of her. Billie caught her breath in horror, tried to cover the action by coughing.

'Unlikely. I'm aware of the case. The child was a baby. They're probably not even conscious of their background.' She hadn't been – not for all these years.

'I looked at some reports last night, ma'am. I believe the baby was a girl. I could dig a bit–'

'I said no!' Billie sharply cut The Grass off in mid-sentence, feeling her face flush. 'Let's prioritise. Geordie Stix was into drugs, fraud and theft and spent long stretches in prison, surrounded by murderers, just for starters. We have enough present-day bad guys to interrogate, before we start running off on a wild goose chase into his distant past.' Billie ran her hand through her hair in irritation. She already knew that *she* wasn't the damn killer.

'Is Margaret Craig speaking yet?' Ash questioned. To the rescue as usual, Billie thought, even though he didn't know it. She resisted the temptation to run up and hug her friend, for directing everyone's thoughts away from, well *her*.

'Not yet, but fingers crossed. I feel sure that she can give us the vital information needed to nail the perpetrators.' Billie smiled at Ash, but to her regret his attention had already waned. He was punching numbers into his mobile.

'Actually, let's not forget Ash's theory. I was given some info last night that Geordie Stix found God in prison.' Billie desperately wanted to draw Ash back to her. He quickly looked up, pushing his mobile into his pocket as she caught his eye.

'Is that where the good Lord's been all the time? I've been wondering where he was when the poor victims were being butchered,' Derek Blythe joked.

Billie rolled her eyes. That was normally an Ash-type comment, she reflected sadly. Ash's mobile rang loudly. He rummaged in his pocket and pulled it out.

'Vital info coming in from God?' Billie tried to join in the banter, chivvy Ash back to being the friend she knew and loved. Instead, he switched the mobile off and rammed it back into his pocket.

'Just a theory. I'll keep my mouth shut in future,' he answered, moodily.

'Can I say something, ma'am?' The Grass interjected. Billie nodded for the younger detective to speak. She pushed her specs up her nose, nervously.

'Joy Summers used to be a social worker. Could she have had dealings with Geordie Stix or Gracie-May? Maybe interviewed Margaret Craig when she tried to adopt her?' The Grass's fresh piece of information was news to Billie's ears. Ash was usually forensic in his investigations. If it was true, Billie couldn't believe that he would have missed the fact.

'Rubbish!' Ash exploded with annoyance. 'Nothing in her history shows she worked for social services.' His voice was defensive.

'Where did you get that intel, Green?' Billie asked.

'Permission to speak in private, ma'am?' The Grass eyed Ash up warily.

'Wait in my office.' Billie flicked her head in the direction of her tiny room. 'Okay, let's crack on.' The MIT team headed back to their tasks, raising the sound level by a few decibels. 'Ash, will you head down to the jail? I've had intel that Geordie Stix mentioned his plan to catch a big fish when he got out. Maybe he was referring to a person, rather than an animal. Could be that someone got to him first and that person has links to the others. See if anyone there got wind of something major about to kick off.'

Billie desperately wished that she had managed to get more info from Glenn Baxter. Another thing to add to her list of regrets. She had marked Geordie Stix up in her mind as a suspect, not an imminent murder victim himself. She could hardly ring up her informer this afternoon, to ask further questions.

'What, now?' Ash approached, checking his watch. It was late afternoon.

'No time like the present.' Billie was astonished that Ash should question the request, given that he'd taken time off the previous day.

'Why can't The Grass go?' Ash argued. Billie blinked.

'Because I'm telling *you* to do it.' They were face to face, staring at each other. Billie couldn't believe the conversation was happening, but she would hold her ground.

'What is it with *her* all of a sudden?' He flicked his head in The Grass's direction. She was standing to attention in Billie's office. 'One minute you hate her, next minute she's teacher's pet. Sending her presents, accepting her word over mine–'

'Don't be ridiculous,' Billie replied, but Ash was on a roll.

'Next you'll be promoting her and demoting me to your bag carrier.' He spat the words out.

'I'm simply asking you to do your job. What in the name of God has gotten into you?' Billie was cool. She had to stay in control of her team, friend or not.

'*Me?* What about you, dumping me on the top of that damn hill with a uniformed babysitter this morning?' Ash demanded. Boo looked up, raised her eyebrows, then put her head down quickly when she saw the look in Billie's eyes when Ash started pointing his finger at her.

'Chief told me when you were on gardening leave, that he was eyeing me up for the next step. Now *she's* going to be sitting in your den, sipping tea, stuffing biscuits and spinning you a line, while I'm off to the great dosshouse for the sad, bad and unhinged, lazing at Her Majesty's pleasure!' He looked at his watch again as though he had better places to go, people to see. It was clear that even if Billie forced him to follow her instructions, he wasn't going to give the job his full attention.

'I'll put Derek on the case. Go home and don't come back until you've got your head straight.' Billie folded her arms. 'You're no use to me in this state.'

'Is that an order?' Ash came close. For the first time Billie realised that he would be a formidable foe if one was facing him from the wrong side of the tracks.

'Yes, it is. I want you back to your normal self.' She hated this sudden friction between them. She squeezed his shoulder, an attempt at affection. He pulled away and without another word, picked up his jacket and stormed out of the room.

Billie was left wondering what on earth had just happened. Her world was turning upside down. Would the best man even turn up to her wedding in just a few short days, or was she going to be completely left in the lurch?

Billie returned to her room, much needed coffee in her hand. A lifeline, even if the machine stuff did taste like swill.

'Sit down, Green.' Billie took her own seat, swinging her feet up onto the corner of the table. A pile of paper clips scattered to the ground. The younger officer nervously darted to pick them up, but Billie stopped her, handing over the other disposable cup of coffee she had brought.

'How are the injuries?' She nodded to the dressing on The Grass's neck, which could be seen peeping over her starched white collar. Billie knew that the young detective really shouldn't be working a murder case today, not after her own near miss last night, but at this rate she would have no team left.

'Better, ma'am,' The Grass clearly fibbed. Billie wondered if anyone had ever told her the damn truth in her life.

'Joy Summers. What do you know that can't be told to the rest of the team?' She didn't have the energy to beat about the bush. The Grass took a deep breath.

'I know she was a social worker because she was my brother's. Seventeen years ago. She was useless.' The words sounded so incongruous coming out of The Grass's mouth that Billie took her feet off the table and sat up.

'I hated her,' The Grass added, making Billie wonder whether there was some strange character-distorting solution added to the drinks today, what with Ash kicking off and now The Grass sounding, well, totally unlike The Grass. 'I often think it was all her fault...'

The Grass removed her specs and rubbed each lens with her sleeve, wiped her eyes and put them back on again. Was she on the verge of crying? Billie took a swig of her coffee and leaned forward.

'What was all her fault?' Billie asked.

'My brother was Bobby Jenks.' The Grass lifted her chin up and stared into Billie's eyes, daring her to register shock, horror. Billie held her stare. Said nothing whilst the fact sank in.

Bobby Jenks had hit the headlines when Billie was a teenager. He wasn't much older himself, when he had entered the killer hall of fame on raping and killing half a dozen old ladies in quick succession. Not so dissimilar to the case Billie had last worked – with The Grass. The case that had ended in her own disciplinary hearing.

'Bobby did terrible, terrible things,' The Grass continued, 'but despite being a big boy, he was mentally disabled. He had the intellectual age of a ten-year-old. Easily manipulated, desperate to have friends. Some older youths got him to watch porn, egged him on. When he wasn't killing people, he was the kindest big brother you could ever wish to have.'

Billie sat back in her chair. The story for Bobby Jenks had ended in a police cell where he had met a brutal death. Officers claimed it had been self-defence.

'I overreacted when you made that arrest. I panicked,' The Grass took a swig of her coffee, 'it was the memories coming back, thinking that in the case we investigated, he could have been, the same, the same as Bobby. I now know he wasn't. He was just evil. I'm sorry, ma'am.'

Billy was sorry too. She knew in her heart that if The Grass hadn't pulled her off, she probably would have finished off the murderer of the old lady and she also accepted, though she had never admitted it even to herself, until now, that The Grass had been right to report her behaviour.

The Grass bit her lower lip. 'My mum kept begging for help from Joy Summers before it all kicked off. She desperately wanted to get Bobby placed somewhere secure, to get treatment and keep everyone safe, but half the time Miss Summers didn't turn up, or had lost his notes. People like Bobby don't come high up on the list of types to help, ma'am, that's the truth. He did the wrong thing, but he didn't deserve to die on the floor of a police cell, whatever everyone thinks.'

Billie surveyed the young detective. The oddity about The Grass had just been explained big time. She was reminded of her bitchy comments to Max Strong about the young woman in front of her now and felt sick.

'Thank you for sharing that with me, Green. It couldn't have been easy.' In fact, as the whole Bobby Jenks story made a grim dance through Billie's mind, she realised that it flung the history of her own dysfunctional family totally into the shade.

'I thought it important to the investigation, ma'am. I had hoped her job would have come to light without my input.' Billie reflected that it should have – if Ash had been doing his job correctly.

'There's another thing, ma'am,' The Grass swallowed hard, 'I didn't disclose the information when I applied to the force. I thought it would prevent me getting in, what with Mum having a bit of a vendetta against the police. You'll remember her offence with regards to PC Howe...'

The Grass tailed off, but there was no need for her to jog Billie's memory. Who could forget the tabloid papers gorging on the sensational story of the heartbroken mother, taking revenge on PC Patricia Howe, the officer who had been in the cell at the time of her killer son's death? With the female officer robbed of the chance to say goodbye to her own kids due to a lethal stroke with a carving knife, Bobby Jenk's mum had finally hung herself.

'I needed counselling and stuff afterwards. I went off the rails a bit. But I'd always wanted to be in the force, right from being a little kid and I wanted to make sure that things were done right in the future. So here I am. Anyway, just saying that it all started with Joy Summers.'

Billie was speechless for a moment.

'Would you like me to stand down?' The Grass whispered. She did look green, so much blood had drained from her already pale face. Little did she realise that Billie herself had just been experiencing similar feelings about hiding her own appalling family history. She made her decision.

'No. I want you to be responsible for looking into Joy Summer's past.' Ash had probably missed loads of other vital information if he had overlooked this. 'Somebody hated her just as much as you, it seems, so who better to find the missing link?'

The Grass let out a breath of relief. Giving a weak smile, she left the room like a puppy who had just been given a brand-new bone. Billie sighed, her head spinning with the secrets that had been revealed that day. She gathered her casework files and headed out to her car.

As she climbed behind the wheel, a file handed to Billie during the briefing fell to the floor. She picked up the scattered pictures and notes. All of Geordie Stix's previous convictions were within. Billie wondered if any early misdemeanours would reveal more about his time with Margaret Craig. One photo had landed down the side of the passenger seat. Having stretched over to retrieve it, Billie glanced at the content. The close-up autopsy study of the victim's arm caused her to gasp.

A huge black-and-white tattooed bird featured the letter M at its centre. It was a replica of the initial signature left on all four targets. Billie had trouble tearing her gaze away. A strange feeling encompassed her. Was it a memory? She felt hot and dizzy. She shook her head, willing herself to concentrate. Had he created the design during his relationship with Margaret Craig? Was that what the M denoted? The faded ink certainly looked old enough. It made her shiver.

Billie quickly stuffed the documents back into the file. As she tried to close it, a newspaper cutting caught her eye. Two tiny black-and-white photos were featured. One pictured an angry crowd, banging on the door of a prison vehicle. Another was focused on Geordie Stix, handcuffed and flanked by two prison officers, being rushed out of court. The detective felt her heart skip a beat as she read the headline.

'Paedophile Convicted of Sickening Attempted Murder of Girlfriend's Child.'

Billie felt nauseous. Fragments of moving pictures and panicked, scattered feelings sprang into her mind's eye. The tattooed arm up close, too close. A grubby shirt being removed. Scratchy hair-covered chest pressing against her tiny body.

Breathlessness. A sensation of kicking out madly in fear and fury, attempting to use her teddy bear, first as a weapon and then a shield. Searing pain as a fist hit her face, then... what? The scenario dissolved and Billie was simply sitting in a car looking at a sub headline in bold black print.

'SENTENCING JUDGE STATES THAT THE TINY VICTIM MAY NEVER RECOVER FROM HER ABUSE AT THE HANDS OF GEORGE STRACHAN.'

A tiny photo underneath the words showed a young woman who looked, even from the back shot, remarkably like Billie. Her long curly hair flying in the wind. Facing the camera was a tiny girl held tightly in the female's arms, her head nuzzled against Margaret's shoulder. Though the face was blurred out, Billie could see that she had similar curls. A one-eyed teddy bear hung from her hand. It could have been Gracie-May McGill, but it wasn't. Billie had no doubt as to the child's identity. She gasped for breath, feeling the air empty from her lungs, laid her forehead on the steering wheel, trying to centre herself.

The hard bang on the window made her jump, nerves jangling. Ash pressed his face against the glass, then wrenched the door open.

'You all right, boss?' His face was etched with worry. Billie wiped her eyes, ran her fingers through her hair.

'We need to talk,' Billie replied, pulling herself upright. She had decided to take Ash into her confidence – tell him everything. Ask for his help. Until now, they had always made a great team. The teddy bear, along with the other connections, was one coincidence too many. Ash crouched down low alongside her.

'I've just been sitting here, feeling like a total klutz. Sorry about before and missing the intel on Joy Summers... I've just been all over the place recently...' He trailed off, looking like a broken man. Could she really load him up with more troubles? Before she could make that decision, Ash spoke again.

'I'll sort it out tonight. Promise, boss. I shouldn't be taking out my issues on you.' Billie decided to shelve her own concerns, for now.

'Trouble at home?' She stroked Ash's arm. She could appreciate the stresses in a marriage to a police officer; she had it all to come, had already started experiencing the pressure. It sounded like her guess was correct, that Ash had strayed recently. Very recently, like in Northumberland last night. He nodded, rubbing his forehead, overwhelmed no doubt, with guilt.

'Hey, come on. We're in this together.' She leaned over and gave him a hug. 'I can't do without you, my best man.' Ash returned the tight squeeze of affection. They had been through a lot, at work and as long-time friends. As Max had advised, she needed to reflect on her life, move forward. One thing was for sure, she always wanted Ash and his precious little family to be close.

'Best get home. See you tomorrow.' Ash stood up, looking like he had the weight of the world on his shoulders. 'I'll be in early.' He nodded at Billie and headed for his car. Billie relaxed a little, glad that any bad feeling between the two of them had been cleared up.

Her mobile phone sprang into life. She answered. It was the replacement female police officer, whom she had arranged to be stationed outside of Margaret Craig's hospital room.

'Ma'am, news about Margaret Craig,' the officer announced. Billie's heart sank like a lump of lead.

'Has she?' she started, her tone of voice revealing her renewed feelings of stress.

'Come round. Yeah, just now.'

'On my way.' Billie turned the key in the ignition and swept out of the car park at speed, overtaking Ash's vehicle in the process. So desperate was she to clear everything in her path that she flicked on the blue flashing light and siren, failing to notice, as she navigated between the traffic, that Ash's own car was not heading in the direction of his home.

22

AN EXTREMELY DANGEROUS PATH

A s Billie sprinted along the hospital corridor, she was aware of a small commotion in the doorway to Margaret Craig's room. The pretty nurse who had been eyeing up Max when Billie had engaged in her earlier confrontation with him, was now arguing with the uniformed policewoman who had one heavily booted foot in the room and wasn't budging.

'I *insist* that you leave now, whilst the doctor is conducting his examination!' The nurse's face was inches from the officer's own.

'I have to inform you if you come one step closer, I'm booking you, despite my love for the NHS and all who sail in it,' the policewoman replied, as though the nurse's rant was like water off a duck's back to her.

Billie nodded approval at her colleague. She knew that she wouldn't be easily intimidated. A woman after her own heart.

'Good work.' Billie smiled, ignoring the nurse. 'What news?' The female officer opened the door wider for Billie to view the scene, much to the nurse's chagrin. A doctor seemed to be finishing his examination.

'Just seemed to wake up and start calling out. Wasn't making much sense, if I'm honest, ma'am. I called for Florence Nightingale here. She can possibly give you more details than she's given me. I'm on her naughty step.' The policewoman raised her eyebrows at the nurse, completely unfazed by the aggravation being directed at her.

'She didn't say anything about the stuff *you* lot are interested in, that's for sure!' The nurse's voice was clipped in annoyance. 'She just kept calling out for her daughter.'

Billie felt as though her heart was breaking. She wanted to scream out the truth, but instead she willed the doctor to finish his examination. He crossed to the door, revealing Margaret Craig, eyes shut once again.

'She needs rest,' the doctor ignored Billie, talking to the nurse, 'inform her next of kin, only one visitor at a time.' He marched off up the corridor. The nurse glanced in at Margaret.

'The sad thing is, her notes say she hasn't got a daughter, hasn't got anyone but you lot, hanging around like hyenas circling...' She folded her arms, upset now more than angry.

Billie desperately wanted to shut the door, have some time alone in the room. She caught the policewoman's eye.

'Get yourself home. I'll sit here until the late shift comes on.' The female officer smiled with relief.

'Thanks, ma'am, got three kids and a pile of ironing as big as the Eiger.' She glanced sympathetically at the nurse. 'Got some munchkins that you're missing too, love?' The nurse nodded ruefully.

'Two girls, I hardly see them, with the hours that I work here.' She shook her head. 'I'm meant to be on my tea break now.' Billie took the opportunity to make a suggestion.

'Officer, having a cuppa before you head off?' She needed some space and clearly the nurse needed a bit of tender loving care. The policewoman winked at Billie.

'Funnily enough I was thinking of just that, ma'am.' She

turned to the nurse. 'Fancy joining me? We'll get a slab of cake down our necks too. Bit of comfort food will do us the world of good.' She tucked her police cap under one arm and linked the nurse with the other, guiding her away down the corridor, looking for all the world like the two had been best friends forever.

Billie quickly crossed over to Margaret Craig's bedside and pulled up a chair. The woman looked peaceful and calm despite her horrific injuries. As Billie tentatively took her hand, the older woman's eyelids flickered. Billie smoothed her thumb over Margaret's pale skin, suddenly feeling cold fingers winding around her own.

Margaret slowly opened her eyes and stared at Billie. She returned her gaze, feeling as though she was time travelling. A familiar feeling surged deep in her heart, though she had no clear memory of holding this hand ever before. Margaret moved her lips, struggling to make words. Billie leaned forward.

'I'm here,' Billie whispered softly, 'what is it you want to say?' She moved her head nearer. Margaret reached out and ran her fingers through Billie's hair. It was a sensation that filled Billie with calm, a habit that she was aware that she resorted to at times of stress. Here it was, the feeling that she had been subconsciously trying to recreate, for all of her life.

'How can I be cool, when there's fire in those curls of yours?'

Her voice was so very faint, but the lilt and lyrics of the song that Margaret Craig was straining to sing, wrapped around Billie like a warm blanket. The tune was embedded in her soul, though she felt as though she hadn't heard it for a thousand years.

Billie immediately recalled the words, welcomed the melody like an old friend. It was the tune that had so terribly long ago, swept away tears or lulled her to sleep. A greeting that she had been crying out for, ever since that desperate moment when she had been ripped, screaming, from her birth mother's arms.

'I'm so very proud of you, my lovely baby,' Margaret whispered with difficulty, managing a weak smile of satisfaction that belied the agonising pain she must still be enduring.

Like a moth to a flame, Billie was drawn to the woman looking at her with such maternal love. Nothing could stop her yearning to climb up onto the bed and wrap her arms around Margaret Craig. Finally, she succumbed, snuggling up beside the patient, in a spoon position. Like a mother cradling her child.

～

So it was that an hour later, Max Strong opened the door to reveal Billie and Margaret lying entwined on the bed. They were both fast asleep. Max took in the view, as the pretty nurse pinned herself to his side. She peeped over his shoulder.

'Best not wake them.' The nurse was squinting at the machines all around the bed.

'Blood pressure's finally normal, heart rate down. Is that the answer, Dr Strong?' the nurse nodded at the view before them, 'take a copper into your bed and all of your troubles are over?' Max's dark eyes were transfixed on the scene. At first, he couldn't speak. Finally, he tore his gaze away.

'If only life were that simple, sister,' he answered, a hint of regret in his voice. 'For someone like me, that would be an extremely dangerous path to take.'

～

Billie woke with a start. She blinked, registering the safe sanctuary of her mother's arms, wanting desperately to close her eyes to the real world once more. However, the ring of her mobile phone was insistent, the caller clearly on a mission to be heard. Worrying that Margaret might be disturbed, Billie regretfully slid away from the sleeping patient, managing to wrestle her phone from her pocket.

'Yep?' she whispered huskily, aware that she had just awoken from the deepest sleep she could remember for months.

'Derek Blythe, ma'am. Sorry to ring you so late in the evening.' Billie checked her watch. How long had she been asleep here?

'Hang on,' Billie whispered, creeping quietly out of the door, startling the night-shift police officer stationed outside. She brushed past him.

'What is it?' Billie started to pace the corridor, sensing trouble brewing – again.

'Been on my mind a bit, ma'am. I didn't know whether to say anything or not, but I thought that you should be warned...' He trailed off as though he hadn't made a final decision on it.

'Spill,' Billie answered. It was an order. Exactly what he had been waiting for.

'It's The Grass. You know who her brother is?' Derek Blythe started.

'Yes, I do. Bobby Jenks.' Billie hoped that was the sum of the tale. She had started to reassess her feelings towards The Grass, had come to terms with her own part in the relationship breakdown with her fellow officer and found herself wanting. The wind had been taken slightly out of Derek Blythe's sails at Billie's answer.

'Then she's changed her name.' Derek Blythe sounded highly suspicious.

'I believe she uses the maiden name of her mother,' Billie responded.

'What, so people wouldn't connect her to a murderer?' He snorted back in derision. 'Her mother killed one of our own.'

'Have you got something new to tell me?' Billie wasn't in the mood to go over the grisly details twice in one day.

'Yeah. The reason I was doing some background was that she's a sneaky little character. Caught her going through files not related to the job in hand, that sort of thing. Spotted her round the car park talking to ne'er-do-wells a few times, too, and tonight, just after you left, I saw her hand over some files to a guy. Looked like police issue. I was tempted to intervene, but thought I would wait until tomorrow, check she just wasn't carrying out your orders, ma'am. That was before I dug out who she was related to...'

'Did you recognise the person she was meeting?' Billie silently reasoned that the contact could have been one of the pet informants that all detectives groomed. She had just asked The Grass to find background on Joy Summers.

'Yeah. That so-called criminal psychologist chap. The one that the Chief claims is practically God when it comes to looking into warped minds,' he answered sarcastically. 'Pile of rubbish if you ask me.'

Billie swallowed hard.

'The thing is, I also caught them together in the MIT room the other night. I nipped back when I realised that I'd forgotten my training kit. Heads together. Thick as thieves, they were. He had no right to be in there, ma'am, what with the scene-of-crime photos on the wall and other confidential information all around, not without your say so.' Billie felt anger rise through her chest. That was definitely the truth.

'Thanks, Derek. Good man.' As Billie wound up the call, she wondered what on earth The Grass and Max Strong were up to. The pretty nurse walked down the corridor. Still at work. This time she smiled wearily at Billie.

'Dr Strong around tonight?' Billie asked. She had noticed his name on the door of an office further along the corridor. She squinted at the wall clock. It was gone 11pm, so the chances were slim to zero.

'Just left five minutes ago,' the nurse nodded towards the exit, 'he had a woman with him.' By her disenchanted air, she appeared to have resigned herself to having zilch chance left with him, in the romance department.

'It was Harry Potter, ma'am,' the policeman guarding the door interjected. 'Well,' he smiled sheepishly, 'that's what we called her when she was still on the beat. Dead ringer. Can't even recall her real name,' he added with a grin.

Billie stood stock still as the information hit home. She had believed Max when he had told her that he wasn't interested in a relationship. She had sympathised when he had recounted the heartbreaking story of his wife's death. But he and The Grass appeared to be totally in each other's pockets. Had he been lying to her too?

'Bought her a wizard's hat once as a joke.' The policeman chuckled. He was obviously on a roll now. 'And a Hogwarts scarf.' He slapped his knee in amusement.

Billie checked once more on Margaret. Her heart ached for the sleeping patient, but it was time to head for home. She seriously needed to get her head straight. Sleep on this new information and then act. Why on earth was The Grass sneaking around the MIT office with Max Strong? Billie didn't know what, exactly, the two of them were up to, but she vowed to find out. If it was the last thing she ever did.

23

THE CASTLE OF DREAMS

It was one of the most horrific sights that Billie had ever seen. So long dead that she couldn't even identify the body – if it was a corpse. She bent down, took a sniff and reeled back in disgust, gingerly picking the offending item up and hurling it in the bin. It may have been midnight and she was furiously hungry, but even she couldn't eat *that*.

As Billie continued to rake in the back of the fridge, hopes fading rapidly, the front door could be heard opening. Kate popped her head around the kitchen door, her still bruised face looking eerie in the light from the icy grave for long-forgotten food.

'Having a séance?' Kate teased as she squinted into the darkness.

'Too hungry to turn on the light.' Billie reached in for another mould-raddled item and yanked it out, pulling a face as she hurled it through the air to join the rest of the freshly departed. 'Watch out. Unidentified flying object heading your way.' She slammed the fridge door shut, all hope lost, along with any further illumination on the situation.

'Good job I brought chips then.' Billie heard the soft thud of a takeaway bag being placed on the table, bumped into Kate in the darkness and then fumbled for the light switch, as her housemate pulled off her hat and gloves and headed for her room, still limping a little.

'Yay! I want to marry you and have your babies!' Billie called after her, ravenously opening the bag. Kate laughed, shouting back.

'Don't nick the lot, I'm starving too!' Billie could hear her running the shower. 'Just got to get into my comfy kit. I'm a mess – crazy day...' She trailed off.

'Hard time at work then?' Billie managed to spit the words out through a mouthful of chips as Kate padded back into the room in a fluffy pink onesie and bed socks, flinging herself down at the table. 'Join the club.' Billie dunked one of her chips in the white cup full of gooey chip-shop curry that she knew Kate was addicted to.

'Mine!' Kate grabbed the cup, pretending to be affronted. Billie felt her shoulders relax. Kate was one of the few people right now, it seemed, who wasn't lining up to stab her in the back.

'Saw that latest victim, strung up on the hill. It's all over the web today,' Kate shivered, 'still, what a way to go. Wouldn't mind my last view being seaside and sand, I can tell you.'

Billie thought back to her evening at the hospital, careful not to give away the truth that Margaret had survived, not even to the one person who kept her fed these days.

'On those murder mysteries on the telly, it's always the cop that did it,' Kate joked, pointing a chip in Billie's direction. 'So I'm keeping an eye on you.' She chuckled. 'If you go on the run, count me in for an around-the-world backpacking trip.' Kate threw the chip up in the air and caught it in her mouth. 'I'm on the lookout for new horizons.'

'Job getting to you that much?' Billie patted her friend's

hand, suddenly concerned that Kate's flippancy masked real issues.

'Just thinking that life's too short. Especially after last night. I'd give anything for the freedom to do my own thing. Not have someone else always running the show...' Kate trailed off. She gave Billie's hand a squeeze, let it go and took her takeaway debris to the bin.

Kate's words had struck a chord with Billie. She thought of David choosing her wedding dress, his mum and dad taking over absolutely everything, the Chief forcing her to seek counselling with Max Strong, her secret adoption, and her father's strong encouragement to join the police. Billie realised that she'd had no true control of her own life either, not really. Not ever.

'Think about it,' Kate called over her shoulder, 'let's run away together. You'd never have to see David's mother again.'

'Now you're talking!' Billie quipped, downing her last chip.

'I'm all done in. See you in the morning.' Kate padded off to her room, shutting her door behind her. It was only moments before the familiar strains of the children's magpie lullaby could be heard as usual, at bedtime.

Billie headed for her own room, determined now to face the task that she had been avoiding since that first night. Her father's black box of dark surprises had lain closed in the corner of the room, after she had slammed it shut on discovering her adoption photograph. It was time to uncover any other chilling secrets that might be waiting to jump out.

Billie lifted the box onto the bed, took a deep breath and opened it, hauling the top mound of paperwork out. It was the content placed under the false bottom of the box that she intended to investigate first. She forced herself to look at the photograph again, the picture which had revealed her adoption.

Her heart went out to her dear mother, who had brought

her up with such unconditional warmth and kindness, the woman who had loved roses and cooked terribly. Billie smiled, tears filling her eyes. She'd picked that trait up from her, hence the takeaway addiction. Nurture had won over nature there, unless Margaret Craig also turned out to be a useless cook.

The expectant new 'mother' in the picture, smiling with happiness, had simply considered Billie to be an orphan desperately in need of love. How that dear woman had been duped by Billie's dad. A lifetime of lies. She had gone to her grave never knowing the truth.

Billie lifted the photo, kissed the woman's image gently then ripped the picture in half, reminding herself to purchase a pretty frame. The image of her proud-looking dad landed in the wastepaper basket with a dull thud.

Another photo lay under the first. A wider view of the jolly adoption scene. An additional female could be seen now, standing next to Billie's dad. There was something about the young woman, something that rang a bell with Billie. Her clothes were smart, fashionable for the time. Billie tracked downwards, then stopped dead. It was her legs that suddenly caused ice-cold recognition to sweep through the detective's body. Although the ankles had grown stout over the years and the feet had spread, trotter-like, the strawberry birthmark had remained the same.

Billie knew that she didn't really need to turn over the photo, but she was drawn, as though by a magnet, to read her mother's carefully penned handwriting.

Billie's adoption ceremony 1990. Mum, Dad, Billie and social worker Joy Summers.

Billie's mobile suddenly sprang into tune. She reached for it, not even registering that it was now well beyond midnight. Never the time for good news to come calling.

'DSI Billie Wilde,' she answered, still staring at the photo.

'Ma'am?' It was The Grass. Billie immediately dropped the photo, her senses on high alert.

'Green?' She didn't know why she was calling at this late hour, but Billie was determined to sort out the situation involving The Grass and Max without further pussyfooting around. 'I want you in my office at eight tomorrow morning.'

'I think you need to come now, ma'am.' The Grass's voice sounded nervous, edgy.

'What?' Billie clocked the time.

'It's an emergency, ma'am. I haven't told anyone else and neither should you. You need to come alone.'

Billie's mind started racing as she recalled Derek Blythe's phone call. The Grass certainly had motive for killing Joy Summers and had been first on the murder scenes of both the social worker and Geordie Stix. What was it Josta had mentioned about Green having been a tightrope walker? The information had seemed utterly ludicrous at the time, but it meant that she would have no fear of heights, or climbing... not even the Angel of the North...

What about Max Strong? Josta had mentioned that he had taken a knife, exactly like the one the killer used, on his army missions abroad. He would certainly be capable of the crimes, with his forces training and history. He had also confessed to having gone crazy, after his wife's death. What's more, he knew Margaret Craig. As her shrink, he would be sure to have accessed some of her secrets. Billie thought the utterly unthinkable. Could they be working together? Could the two of them seriously be murderers?

'What emergency?' Billie's voice was forceful. She felt her pulse quicken. Could they be planning an attack on Billie herself? The idea seemed preposterous. It was Max who had flagged the idea that Billie could be a target, told her to take care. Had he been playing mind games? The police officer in the hospital had confirmed that they were together tonight. Was he with The Grass right now?

'I can't tell you on the phone,' the Grass answered evasively, 'but you have to come quickly, ma'am. You really must come right now. *Please!*'

Billie made her decision. If this was to be the final reckoning with the serial killers, then she wouldn't shirk from the job. Bring it on.

'Where are you?' Billie was already heading to the door. She was up for a fight.

'It's down by the docks, a side street. Boutique hotel called The Castle of Dreams.'

'Wait for me outside.' Billie raced out to her car. The place sounded more like a dosshouse than a boutique hotel. Billie took off at speed through the dark streets in the direction of the docks, engaging her car phone system as she jumped red lights. Her danger radar was on high alert. If her mad imaginings turned out to be true, she needed someone to back her up. Ash's home number picked up after several rings.

'Ash,' she started. But Jas answered. The new baby was screaming in the background.

'Christ, Billie, you've woken the baby!' Jas sounded furious, like she had just finally lulled the newborn into sleep.

'Sorry, it's an emergency. Is he there?' Billie made a mental note to send flowers to Jas in apology. The young mother was normally so sunny-natured, the rebuking had come as a shock.

'No he bloody isn't!' Jas replied. 'But then he never is here. He'll be on whatever wild goose chase you've forced on him tonight!' The baby's screams got louder. Billie had no intention of telling Jas that, in fact, Ash must still be sorting out his clandestine life. She would take the flack instead.

'Look, I've got to go!' Jas's voice changed from harsh, to soft and gentle in a heartbeat. 'It's all right, mummy's here, darling.' The phone went dead. None of the usual pleasantries to soften Billie's reprimand.

Billie cursed. She could call for alternative backup, but she wasn't ready to drag her family skeletons out of the cupboard, strip her sordid life story bare for every Tom, Dick and Harry to feast on, without a fight. With the new revelation of Joy Summers in her past, she couldn't go on denying that she must somehow be personally involved and not just as the SIO at the local MIT.

Accepting that this was going to be a one-woman mission, Billie put her foot down. Adrenaline started to surge through her veins. If her wild suspicions about Max Strong and The Grass turned out to be correct, she knew that she was going to need every ounce of strength in her body, in order to take on the coming battle and still live to tell the tale.

The treacle-dark waters of the river were caught in a dull sickly light, pooling onto the ground directly ahead, as Billie turned her car down the narrow lane. High Victorian windowless buildings loomed menacingly on either side, their brick walls ingrained with the grimy sweat and dust of years of hard labour.

Billie regretted that these once vibrant industrial hubs were now dead. She could do with some activity now. The place was eerily silent. Even allowing for the recent surge in industrial design for entertainment venues, Billie couldn't imagine there could be a boutique hotel, as The Grass had called it, in this dark and foreboding location.

It was the dim-yellow glow catching off the lenses of The Grass's specs that drew Billie's attention to her first. She was leaning heavily against a brick wall, where the lane met the dockside. Billie pulled the car in and stepped out, scanning the surrounding area as The Grass rushed up to her.

'You've got to come quickly, ma'am.' She flicked her head towards a door facing the dockside. It was open just a crack, showing the source of the ineffective illumination.

'What the hell is this, Green?' Billie's breathing was quickening. Something didn't feel right. Was this some sort of ambush?

'It's up the stairs at the top.' The Grass stepped back. Billie looked up at a sign above the anonymous-looking doorway, where tiny letters flagged up The Castle of Dreams. She swallowed hard, reached for her retractable truncheon.

'Lead the way.' Billie could see that The Grass was acting strangely even by her standards and a quick glance inside had shown a tight winding staircase leading to the top, so dimly lit that she couldn't see what lay ahead.

'I don't think…' The Grass started.

'I said get up there.' Billie's voice was firm. She nodded towards the staircase, flicked out her truncheon.

'I don't think you'll be needing that, ma'am,' The Grass replied, finishing her sentence.

'I'll be the judge of that,' Billie answered, 'now walk…' Billie glanced back as she followed The Grass up the steep staircase, hoping to God that Max Strong wasn't about to run up behind her. Being sandwiched between the two of them would put her in a vulnerable position that could prove to be deadly.

As they rounded the first stair landing, Billie heard a movement and darted around. A thin, grey-faced man peeped out of a scruffy door.

'I told you to stay inside, sir!' The Grass called to the man, glancing at Billie.

'I'm not moving from right here.' He leaned against the dingy wall of what appeared to be his personal living quarters. He shook his head at Billie in horror, eyes wide. He bent towards her, whispered, 'You don't want to go up there, dear. You'll end up dead too.'

'What is going on?' Billie barked at The Grass, who was disappearing into the darkness above. 'And can someone tell me where the damn main light is here?'

The man skulked out of the door, hit a switch and the whole staircase was suddenly illuminated in a fluorescent light, showing dirty corners and more rooms, all with names printed on the doors.

'Up here, ma'am,' The Grass called. Billie took the stairs two at a time, almost bumping into The Grass, who she vowed was going to pay for this ridiculous game of cat and mouse.

'In The Turret Room.' The Grass stepped to one side as Billie clocked the name, got a flash of memory of the keys belonging to David. The ones she thought opened the door to her honeymoon suite. She entered the room, immediately registering through the shock and horror, that there would be no honeymoon for her – or wedding either for that matter.

Billie's knees gave way and she hit the floor with a thud, her steadying hands immediately covered with thick sticky blood, the same gore that was splashed around the walls and over the vast bed. The source of the red psychedelic scenario was not one hideously mutilated body, but two.

David was hanging from the chains and cuffs already fitted into the ceiling. His ankles, one now tattooed with the letter M, were also encased in cuffs and chains, firmly welded to the bedstead. The specific S and M interior design of the room had clearly saved the murderer from the need to roll out fishing twine or hoist the body.

Billie's memory of her dashing barrister lover, making his charismatic entrance into the courtroom, had now been slashed away by the vision facing her. David was totally naked, his clothes carefully folded to one side on the velvet chaise lounge. He hadn't been dragged here, nor drugged against his will. Though he had no doubt struggled like a demon against the vicious wounds inflicted by the clearly frenzied knife attack.

Billie tore her gaze away from David's one-time stunning features, now frozen in a death mask of terror and pain. Instead, she tried to make sense of the second bloody figure slumped against David's groin, enveloped in so much blood that both bodies seemed at first to meld into one. Dressed in a strange combination of black-belted leather straps and chains, which nevertheless left little to the imagination, Ash had also been the victim of the savage attack and tattooed M on the ankle. Blood oozed from every wound and orifice.

Billie let out a silent, yet utterly harrowing scream, rocking back on her knees, her scarlet hands spread out in shock. Utter torment momentarily froze her pose there on the sticky, nylon carpet. The Grass stepped forward. Touched Billie's shoulder.

'I didn't know what to do, ma'am,' The Grass looked at Billie nervously, 'do you want me to call in the team right now, or do you need a moment?'

The question was answered before Billie could find any words, with a feeble moan, and movement of flesh within the bloody scenario on the bed.

'He's still alive.' Billie gasped. 'He's still alive!'

24

A STAB IN THE BACK?

'No. You're having a laugh, Billie?' The Chief spoke quietly, shaking his head in disbelief as he stepped out of his office. He held out his arms, either to offer solace or to prevent her from heading into the MIT room. Neither option worked for her.

'Well, it has been a funny old day already, sir.' Billie gave a grim smile. She took a step sideways, tried to bypass him. 'I'm a bit late for the breakfast meeting,' she added, hoping he would make himself scarce.

'You should be at home. It's only a few hours since...'

'My fiancé was murdered? Caught in flagrante with my wingman, who may, or most likely will not, survive to tell the tale?' She knew that she sounded harsh and uncaring, but it was the only way she could get through this hellish nightmare.

'There's a news blackout. No names of victims, or circumstances.' The Chief reached out and rubbed Billie's shoulder. She gritted her teeth. She really couldn't cope with mawkish sentiment right now. 'You need to be with David's mum,' the Chief continued.

'With respect sir, I think I've already suffered enough.' The

Chief was well aware of Billie's feelings towards her now never-to-be mother-in-law. Billie made a move to get by him. He caught her arm.

'You clearly haven't heard about David's dad then?' The Chief's voice softened as he broke the news. 'He collapsed last night when he was told what had happened. A stroke. It's looking bad for him. I'm so sorry, Billie.'

Well every cloud has a silver lining, Billie thought to herself. She sincerely hoped that he would die a painful death and rot in hell, meeting all those little children he had helped sell off to strangers, on the way.

'I really must get on,' she answered, refusing to feign sorrow at the news.

'Get yourself home. That's an order.'

'And do what?' Billie snapped. 'Cancel my damn wedding? Go on a solo honeymoon?' Kate had mentioned her backpacking plan again, when Billie had finally arrived home, shut the front door on the whole sordid scenario and fallen into her friend's arms, sobbing like a baby. Maybe she would take Kate up on the offer once this case was put to bed. Hadn't Max Strong advised her to self-reflect and then decide who and where she wanted to be in life? Well, the field was wide open now.

Billie pushed the image of Max out of her mind. He had rung first thing this morning. Despite the news blackout, he seemed to have known the score. Maybe he'd indulged in pillow talk with The Grass? After all, few people could keep schtum having witnessed that bloody scene. Billie had made it clear that she didn't want to speak to him, and dear Kate had been like a Rottweiler. Billie had heard her forcefully blocking his second and third attempts to make contact.

'I'm taking you off the case, trying to free up someone to take over.' The Chief was blocking the entrance to the MIT room with his body.

'Do that and I'll resign,' Billie answered forcefully.

'Don't be silly.'

'It's no joke. I stay on the case or I walk – out of the force for good. Do you want my dad to be turning in his grave?'

Billie didn't care if he was. She had a strong suspicion that her father's disgusting deeds in the past were coming back to haunt her. She intended to find out exactly why. Shock and grief could come later. Right now, she was in no mood to play victim.

The Chief locked stares with Billie for a beat and then stepped aside. 'You're a chip off the old block, that's for sure.' The Chief shook his head in wonder and more than a little admiration for her stance. 'I'm backing you all the way then, Billie. Anything you need...' But Billie was already on her way into the MIT room, where the team fell silent at her arrival.

'Okay, let's not beat about the bush. Turns out that Ash has been best man in more ways than one.' She grimly mimed hitting a drum kit and symbols. The MIT team were still stunned at the news, aware that Billie was putting on an act to ease their discomfort at the situation. 'Now if I can get through this, we all can. But as far as Jas is concerned, he was simply on an enquiry in connection with the case when he was attacked. Clear, everybody? She's got enough on her plate. He can tell her the truth himself, should he so choose.'

'If he ever recovers.' Derek Blythe looked shell-shocked. Boo zipped towards Billie, handing her a mug of coffee. She squeezed her hand in a show of solidarity.

'What I don't get,' said Derek Blythe, 'is how The Grass has discovered the murder scenes, all alone, three times out of five. I've been in the job twenty-five years and never been first to discover a dead body, not until a member of the public rang it in.'

The Grass entered the room only a moment later, her eyes shadowed from lack of sleep.

'Sorry I'm late, ma'am.' She nodded, taking her seat.

'Been busy sharpening up your knives?' Derek Blythe goaded.

'Chasing up the manager of the food bank that Joy Summers was helping out with, ma'am, to see if anyone suspect was hanging around there on the day of her murder.'

'Well, you were just a few steps away as usual,' Derek Blythe interjected.

'And?' Billie asked The Grass.

'Just some kids. School holidays, so they provide free meals then. Apart from that group there was no one else present. She took some photos for them, said one was mistakenly on her own phone. She's going to send it over later.'

'Our hope is that this morning Margaret Craig might have recovered enough to tell us why she was phoning Geordie on the day of his death.' Billie's no-nonsense delivery covered up a maelstrom of emotions, surging in waves through her body. 'Derek, get over to the hospital as soon as the docs give the okay. Check if Ash is in a position to give any information. Boo, go through his recent interviews with suspects. He may have ruffled some feathers.' She couldn't face him herself. Not yet. Maybe not ever.

'Let's also go over all of the DNA evidence again, with the extra staff the Chief has dragged in...' The members of the MIT team exchanged less than cheerful glances at the sight of the eager young interns drafted in to view hours of CCTV footage and man the phones. 'See if any new fingerprint matches have been dredged up, partial prints, *anything*.'

As she noticed one of the new trainees innocently pin up a huge picture of David to join the rest on the wall of the mutilated and dead, Billie was forced to speedily head for the door.

'Ma'am, you asked to see me first thing?' The Grass intercepted Billie, who bit her lip hard and nodded.

'In my office.' She swung open the door to let The Grass enter, slammed it shut behind her and leant on it for just a moment, to regain her equilibrium.

'What exactly is your relationship with Dr Max Strong?' The Grass blinked.

'He's my counsellor, ma'am. I've been seeing him ever since I refused everyone's advice and decided to join the force. People kept telling me that I must be mad. He was recommended.' The Grass rubbed her nose. Billie could tell that it wasn't the whole story.

'Bit odd, isn't it, meeting your shrink in this office, without my permission and in wino dives down dark alleyways?' Billie needled. The Grass swallowed hard.

'The Chief told me to work with Dr Strong, profiling the female who appeared to have been involved in the GBH of a particular man in the vicinity of The Dive Bar...' Billie froze. She had thought the case had been washed away in the wake of a serial murderer being on the prowl. 'He wasn't the first victim, ma'am, but the Chief wanted to make sure that particular attack wasn't, in fact, linked to a separate ongoing investigation of a serious nature.'

Billie rubbed her head, utterly ashamed once more that she had put the position and possible life of an undercover officer in jeopardy by clearly looking so out of it, that he had felt forced to protect her.

'And did he indeed profile the female?' Billie tilted her chin up, willing The Grass to reply in the negative. The younger detective reached in a bag she had slung over her shoulder, offering a file to Billie.

'I told the Chief I lost this. That's why I was late. Luckily, he was distracted with everything else kicking off. I suggest that you build a big bonfire in your back garden and pour a can of petrol over it, ma'am.' Billie swallowed hard.

'What cracked thoughts *exactly* did Dr Max Strong put into your head?' Billie challenged weakly, grabbing the file from the Grass's outstretched hand.

'He didn't stab you in the back, ma'am. One of my old informants was in the bar. Took some footage on his mobile of the female on the dance floor.' The Grass lifted a scruffy mobile phone from her bag, setting the replay in motion.

Billie mentally threw herself under her desk and hid, feeling her face burn in utter mortification. The footage showed her strutting around making an utter fool of herself, trying to beckon Glenn Baxter onto the dance floor whilst he had undoubtedly been trying to keep a low profile. On reflection, it turned out that she had been lucky not to have had full recall of the night.

The Grass pushed the device across the desk.

'Luckily, it was a police-issue phone. No internet connection. He was happy to hand it back for the price of a one-way ticket to Thailand. Fancied moving in with his mate and a few dancing girls on Pattaya Beach.' Billie leaned back in the chair.

'Why are you doing this?' she asked The Grass.

'Reckon I owe you, ma'am. To make up for reporting you before,' The Grass replied.

'Now I owe you,' Billie answered quietly, aware that every action had consequences.

'About 200 quid for a one-way economy ticket, ma'am,' The Grass got up out of her seat, 'when you've got a bit less on your plate that is.' She closed the door behind her, leaving Billie almost tearful with relief and gratitude. She had underestimated The Grass big time.

As Billie stuffed the file and phone into her bag, Boo banged on the door then burst into the room, tearing a strip of paint off the edge of the door frame.

'Sorry to barge in, ma'am, but the hospital's on the phone. They'd like you to get over there fast.'

Billie was out of her seat in a second, sprinting at full pelt out of the building. Flinging her bag on the back seat of her car, she clipped the magnetic blue light onto the bonnet. As she forced the vehicle into the traffic, embarking on a race against time, she desperately prayed that at last, she would get the answers she needed.

25

DEADLY PILLOW TALK

Billie speedily cut through streams of visitors to the hospital critical care wing. A palpable air of tension hung like thick fog, despite the vision of the colourful café serving less than healthy snacks and cheery walls encouraging all to inject with the latest vaccine.

Those who were newly out on parole, having done their time at the sickbeds of loved ones, were engulfed in an almost visible cloak of guilt for having picked up speed as the exit sign beckoned. Others were trundling slowly towards various wards, carrying hospital flowers way beyond revival, preparing to put on a happy face.

Billie took the stairs three at a time to the first floor, where Margaret Craig lay within a single room at the end of the corridor. She noticed a doctor entering the room and also, to her annoyance, the doddering copper, who she had demanded to be removed the day before, sitting outside. She reasoned that his vigilant female colleague did need to see her kids sometime.

As Billie gathered pace, she nearly collided with a body coming at speed from a side room. She swerved in avoidance, jack-knifing around as a hand whipped out and caught her by the wrist. 'Are you happy now?' Jas, Ash's wife shouted. She looked dreadful, her eyes puffed and red, face tear-stained. She was carrying the new baby in her arms. 'I told him you'd work him to death and you've damn well done it – as good as!'

Billie was stunned for a moment. She still hadn't allowed herself to explore the full implications of David's death, in The Turret Room of a sleazy S&M-themed hotel. A quick check had confirmed that he had booked in willingly, with his playmate, Ash. It had been a regular date night for months; a fact which if revealed, may have taken the venomous sting out of Jas's voice.

'Do you realise that the doctors think he might never recover?' An angry cascade of salty tears surged down her face.

Billie couldn't share another newly discovered fact with Jas, either; that David and Ash had also been visitors at the sister hotel, The Paradise. Number one choice had been the new Wild West-themed room there. Funny, Billie thought, how David had never mentioned his love of cowboys.

'The crash team had to rush in this morning... it was horrible. I had to ring his mum and dad and tell them that their son might not pull through. Can you *imagine* how that feels?' Jas was pacing the corridor, attempting to placate the infant, all the while becoming more emotional herself.

Billie recalled the conversation she'd shared with Ash in the car the day before, his feelings of having been pressured by family expectations into a life at odds with his real character. The truth was that David hadn't had a chance to explore his authentic personality either. His history, like Billie's own, had been snuffed out. Now that baby boy, snatched from the arms of an unknown mother, had lost his future too.

Billie kept silent. Jas had been told nothing of David's demise. She vowed that she would keep her own inner tears and utter devastation on lockdown, until this madness was over. Only then would she allow herself to find a dark place to hide away and lick the wounds that were threatening to tear her sanity to shreds.

'And where have you been until now? At bloody work no doubt, when your *friend*, actually the man who helped choose your *wedding dress*, because you couldn't be bothered to do it yourself, is lying at death's door!'

Billie glanced behind Jas, catching a glimpse of Ash through the slatted blinds. He looked deathly. His face was cut and bruised by the fight he had no doubt put up. There were dressings over his slashed throat, tubes and machines seemingly everywhere. Billie closed her eyes tight for a moment, willing that final scene from The Turret Room to go away.

'Jas–' Billie started, as the baby let out a high-pitched scream which quickly gathered momentum.

'Don't bloody Jas me, like you're some sort of friend! I've got to change this one,' she flicked her head back towards Ash's bed, 'just like I'll probably be changing *that* one for the rest of our lives. Surely it's your damn duty as the poster girl for the police to sit there for five minutes and hold his hand – if you can spare him the time that is.'

She stormed away, leaving Billie frozen to the spot for a beat. Along the corridor, she noticed another nurse, masked up, going into Margaret Craig's room. Billie desperately wanted to see her mother. She glanced again at Ash, her heart starting to break. Taking a deep breath, she stepped over the threshold into her old friend's sick room.

A smell of disinfectant and medicinal chemicals faintly hung in the air. Ash was slightly propped up on pillows, wearing a hospital-issue robe, rather than the leather-and-chain ensemble Billie had last seen him in. She flung the memory aside, sitting in the chair recently vacated by Jas. It was still warm.

Despite her vow only a minute before, Billie felt hot tears

roll down her cheeks, knowing in her heart that she was willing to forgive Ash's secrets and deceits, if only he could survive this.

She reached out and stroked Ash's hand. It looked sore and bruised from the line that had been put in. His eyes flickered, opened and focused on Billie's face, tears suddenly welling up and pouring down his face.

'Sorry,' he mouthed the words, the tracheostomy tube inserted into his throat making it impossible to speak, but Billie understood. 'I'm so sorry.' He started crying more forcefully. Billie grabbed a wodge of tissues from the side of the bed and patted his face with them.

'Ssh. It's okay.' Billie tried a smile. 'Hey, at least I don't have to suffer your excruciating best man's speech,' she teased. 'God knows how many of David's secrets you would have shared for a laugh. It might have put me off my wedding breakfast,' she added, desperately trying the dark humour tactics that the two shared at work, to get through hellish experiences.

Ash smiled briefly, before shaking his head and starting to cry again. He was clearly in terrible shock and pain, within his heart as well as his body.

'I love you,' he mouthed, gripping Billie's hand. She leaned forward and kissed him on the forehead.

'Love you too,' she whispered, 'and so did David. That's okay with me, sweetheart. Really, that's okay with me.'

Strangely, she realised that she was telling the absolute truth. She wondered what that said about her relationship? Perhaps exactly what she had admitted to Kate, that she had loved David like a brother. Maybe he had loved her the same way – as a sibling, unable to confess his true inclinations. Instead, they had been brainwashed into following the outwardly perfect, yet truly warped paths set by their captors. At least David had died without any knowledge of his sordid start in life. Billie nudged Ash gently.

'So, what I need now, is for you to stop lazing around here, get your bum out of bed and come back to work.'

Ash gave a sad smile and then lay back on the pillow, closing his eyes with the effort of attempting to make conversation. Billie stroked his hand.

'Who did this, Ash,' Billie whispered, 'who on earth did this to you?'

Ash flicked his eyes open again, a sense of urgency in his manner as he grabbed Billie's hand, shook it and started mouthing something Billie couldn't make out.

Billie leaned close, her heart beating. Ash lifted his arm with some effort and tried to reach for the phone in her front pocket.

'Phone? My phone?' Billie grabbed the phone as Ash nodded. He slapped her hand, struggling with the effort of movement.

'What? My phone, my hand?' Billie couldn't make out what he was trying to tell her, whilst Ash became more agitated. Jas suddenly bundled back into the room carrying the still grizzling baby.

She started with concern. 'What's wrong? What are you trying to tell me, Ash?' Billie bent over him, her voice full of desperation. Ash spotted the red scarf draped around Jas's neck, started waving his arm towards it, then grabbing Billie's hand and phone in agitation. 'Try again!'

'Leave him alone!' Jas tried to pull Billie away from Ash. 'Are you bloody mad? Get off him!' The baby started screaming. Billie's new nurse friend suddenly opened the door.

'DSI Wilde. Sorry. It's an emergency.' Billie glanced at the nurse, then back to Ash. He had slumped on the pillow, all energy spent.

'I'll be back.' Billie smoothed her hand over Ash's before heading out of the room behind the nurse.

'Don't let her back in. She's a mad woman!' Jas's final cry was ringing in her ears as she moved at speed along the corridor towards Margaret Craig's room. The nurse stopped at the door with Max Strong's name on it, checked the room was empty and waved a puzzled Billie inside. She noticed for the first time that the nurse looked visibly upset.

'I'm sorry to tell you that Margaret Craig passed away a few minutes ago,' she announced.

'What?' Billie heard the question come from her own lips, but the voice sounded far away. Her legs momentarily buckled under her. The nurse caught her before she fell, guiding her expertly to a seat. 'Just sit there for a moment,' the nurse soothed, 'I can see it's a shock. I know that you had a soft spot for her. I did too.' The nurse wiped a tear away, as it trickled down her face. 'She was a lovely woman. Seemed to be making real progress this morning. Still continuously asking for her daughter, mind you, first thing. Are you certain she didn't have one?' Billie wanted to scream out the truth, that she had two mothers and had lost them both within weeks, tell the nurse that her heart was breaking into tiny pieces, but she tried to steady her voice instead.

'How?' Billie damned herself for not having arrived earlier. 'The message that I got was that she was talking...' *If only I hadn't bumped into Jas.* The thought flitted through her mind. The nurse shook her head in puzzlement.

'Her heart just seemed to stop beating, after Dr Strong went in. I was checking her meds, and everything seemed fine. Considerably improved. She said that she felt much better, she just wanted to talk to her daughter.' Billie's heart broke.

'Max Strong was the last person to see her alive?' She got up from the chair and started pacing the room. The nurse shrugged.

'I guess so. That was when I was called to another patient.'

'I want to see her.' Billie swept out of the door and across the corridor.

'Who was the last person to enter this room?' she demanded from the policeman, who looked like a rabbit caught in headlights.

'Um, I went for a comfort break, ma'am,' he started. Billie mentally picked him up by the scruff of his neck and flung him as far away from her as possible. She pushed open the door to Margaret Craig's room and was almost physically winded by the sight of the dead woman. Her mother was lying on a pillow, looking for all the world as though she was simply sleeping. Unwilling to believe the truth, Billie approached the motionless body and checked for a pulse on her still warm skin. There was none.

Billie had to use every ounce of strength not to fling herself on the dead woman, hug her tightly, and beg her to sing the lullaby that had been buried deep in Billie's heart, for one last time. She quelled the sickness rising in her chest, rubbed her eyes and turned to scan the room. A pillow lay on the floor.

'Was that there when you left the room?' Billie questioned the nurse.

'No, of course not,' the nurse replied heading to pick it up.

'Don't touch it.' Billie's mind was racing.

'Get me Max Strong. No one goes in or out of this room until I say so.' Her voice brooked no argument. She pulled out her phone. Punched in a number. It was The Grass who answered.

'Get the team down to the hospital. Pronto. Margaret Craig is deceased. Looks like homicide.'

'Wha...?' The nurse looked panicked.

'*You,* idiot,' Billie was leaning over the policeman, still static on his seat. 'Let anyone *at all* in or out of this room before the MIT team arrive and I swear I will have your balls.'

'But, ma'am,' he stuttered as Billie swung around, on hearing footsteps approaching. Max, with his golden, tanned skin and dark-chocolate eyes, looked out of place in a location for the critically ill. He headed towards Billie, holding out his hands.

'Billie, I'm so sorry. I've just heard the news about–'

Billie sprang towards him, grabbing his arms and propelling him backwards towards the wall.

'Did you kill her?' she shouted. Thoughts whirled through her mind. He had been involved in surveillance of her, and what of the incident in the dark alleyway? Had he *really* come to her aid, or had he been involved in the assault? He was also one of the very few people who knew that Margaret Craig had survived her attack. Max clenched Billie's arms. She felt his strength. Had he been playing her for a fool for all of this time?

'Calm down.' Max's eyes seemed to look into the depths of Billie's soul. His voice was soft. He smoothed his hand down her arm. She slapped it away.

'Don't touch me.' Billie moved close into him, her voice a steely whisper. 'Did you kill my mother?' she demanded. Max frowned.

'Your fiancé? I've just found out.' His voice sounded so sincere. Billie reminded herself he was a shrink. He probably practised in a mirror when training. 'I'm so sorry. When I rang this morning, to tell you that Margaret was conscious, I had no idea about David.'

Billie remembered the phone calls earlier that morning from him. Kate had blocked him on Billie's request.

'Margaret Craig is dead. You were the last person to see her alive,' Billie emphasised. She wouldn't let him bring David into it. It was more than her body and soul could bear right now and she needed to keep it together. Max Strong looked momentarily confused.

The skirmish had brought other members of staff from

rooms around them. A doctor who looked like he should still be at school intervened.

'That's actually not the case,' he addressed Billie, 'I checked on Mrs Craig just after Dr Strong left the room and a nurse also came in as I was examining her. She was still there when I left.' Billie turned to look at the nurse, who shook her head.

'Not me,' she replied.

'If I recall rightly, she had blonde hair,' the doctor offered.

'That's right, ma'am,' the lazy policeman had finally found his voice, 'tall girl. She was wearing a mask. Said she'd be a few minutes so if I needed a comfort break...'

The nurse shrugged. 'I don't know who that would be. We don't need to wear masks on this floor and there definitely isn't anyone who fits that description on duty this morning.'

Billie ran her fingers through her hair. She had seen the blonde nurse entering Margaret Craig's room. Had she not been intercepted by Jas, she would have caught her in the act. She had let the damn killer murder her mother and just walk away! The colour visibly drained from her face.

'I need CCTV footage,' Billie demanded, turning to Max. 'There's a news blackout. How do you know about David? Where were *you* last night?' Max's dark eyes flickered momentarily, but he remained calm as he replied.

'I worked here until late and then picked Josta up from an event and stayed the night. She's just called me from work, having found out about your fiancé on arrival.' He didn't add that she was now undoubtedly conducting an autopsy on the man that Billie should be marrying in a few days, but the horrific realisation finally hit her full on.

'Can someone bring tea please?' She heard Max's calm voice and felt his strong arm around her waist gently guiding her into his room and onto a seat. The fight had gone out of her for a moment as she let herself be led, only aware of the blood beating around her head.

Max pulled up a chair alongside Billie as she bent forward in her seat, willing herself not to faint. He gently lifted her hair away from her face, running his fingers through it as he smoothed it back, whilst she fought to regain control. A cup of tea was brought to the room and taken by Max. He gently held it to Billie's lips to drink. She took a hot, sugary sip, hearing the door softly close, leaving her alone with the doctor.

A few minutes of silence passed as Billie caught her breath, aware of one emotion merging into another; horror, sickness, numbness, finally embarrassment at showing what Billie perceived to be weakness, on duty.

'I must get on,' she finally mumbled, attempting to push herself up from the chair.

'Not so quick, Billie.' Max felt the pulse in Billie's wrist. His touch was like an electric shock to her system. 'Give yourself a few minutes. I have something to show you...'

Max stood up and headed for a wall of filing cabinets on one side of his office. Taking a key from his pocket, he opened a drawer and lifted out a large folder. He placed it on his desk in front of Billie.

'You're in danger, Billie. You must know now that this is personal?'

'How long have you known that Margaret Craig was my mother?' Billie answered. How long had Max Strong been keeping information from her that could have been vital?

'Since this morning when she confessed that was the case. She told me that she wanted to talk, urgently. I explained the situation to your flatmate on the phone when I rang.'

'That Margaret was alive and talking?' Alarm bells started ringing at the back of Billie's head. Kate hadn't passed that information on, probably to protect her from having to deal with an urgent issue only hours after the death of her fiancé. Could Kate have mentioned that Margaret was still alive innocently to someone else? Billie had a mental picture of the masked nurse entering the room.

'Margaret was finally ready to tell you everything,' Max gently explained. 'During the time we had worked together, she'd chosen to share some details about her daughter. Then I met you and I had no doubts who that must be, from her descriptions. She had told me that you had become extraordinarily successful, a leader. Brave, beautiful, feisty and bright.' He smiled gently. Billie swallowed hard.

'Margaret was heartbroken when she learned of Gracie-May's fate. I suggested that she get in touch with the police to explain her connection with the little girl. On her birthday, she rang to share that she had taken my advice...'

Billy gulped down her tea, realising that Max had made a bigger impact on her life than she could ever have imagined.

'...she also confided that she had finally made contact once more, with the child that she had lost. She was joyful, full of excitement and relief that she still loved her daughter just as much as an adult as she had as a child. I believe she had an invite to your wedding. No names were mentioned at the time, of course.' Billie rubbed her eyes. She couldn't, wouldn't, break down here.

'But why would anyone want to kill her?' Billie picked up the file from the table. It had her name written on it.

'She was being blackmailed. By people threatening to reveal your background publicly.'

'What?' Billie replied. 'So why didn't she tell my father? I discovered that they were still in touch.' Max stared at Billie for a moment, as though weighing up how much more grief she could take.

'I fear that she did.' Max said the words carefully, allowing the reality to sink in.

'That can't be true.' Billie gasped. 'You're saying their deaths...'

'I'm saying that you are in serious danger, Billie. Do you really think that your father didn't attempt to stop them? Margaret revealed that the blackmailers were people from the past. Individuals who knew you as a young child and are so damaged now, that they are using psychological projection to hold *you* responsible for the murders that they are committing.'

'What do you mean?' Billie shook her head. 'This shrink-speak of yours makes no sense...'

'I think you have blocked out much of your early years, Billie, hence your PTSD incidents.'

Billie saw in her mind's eye, the newspaper article referring to her abuse by Geordie Stix. She mentally hurled it away.

'Victim blaming, is a well-known condition. I didn't make it up, Freud identified the phenomena,' Max continued. 'A blamer is a type of narcissist, with an inflated sense of self. Everything bad that happens around them, regardless of whether it is their fault or not, is immediately attributed to another person. You are the golden child who escaped and has grasped success. The ultimate target.'

'What's this?' Billie stripped off the tape sealing the file before her.

'Margaret gave it to me last week. Said it had to be given to the head of the murder squad if anything happened to her, hence your name being on it. She knew that I had guessed the truth, but I wanted her to confirm in her own time.'

Billie opened the file. A will had been laid on top. She opened it. Margaret had left everything she had owned to her. Billie surveyed the rest of the contents – birthday cards and notes lovingly written in her father's handwriting to Margaret Craig, vowing everlasting love, photos of Billie within, charting every high point in her life from the day she had left her birth mother.

'It was a true love affair...' Billie whispered the words, tears filling her eyes.

'Just because you love one person deeply, Billie,' Max said softly, 'it doesn't mean that you can never love anyone else.' Billie looked up. It appeared to be a truth that he was finally coming to terms with himself.

'We all make mistakes,' he added, 'some of us follow destructive paths, with terrible consequences. No one is perfect. Perhaps it's time to forgive, if not forget and finally move forward.'

There was a sharp knock on the door. A junior doctor popped her head around.

'Dr Strong, might I ask for urgent assistance with a psychotic patient please?' She appeared desperate for help. Max crossed the room towards the door.

'Stay right where you are, Billie. I'll be back in five minutes. Promise me you won't go anywhere.'

Billie was already lifting the heap of photos and paperwork. Suddenly she stopped dead. A photo lay near the bottom of the pile. It showed a young Margaret Craig, looking almost like Billie's twin sister. At her feet on a sandy beach, Billie had been frozen for eternity, an innocent baby, happily playing. Next to her were two other older children, a boy, head down, concentrating hard on the intricate sandcastle he was building and a girl looking directly into the camera. Billie lifted the photo close. It was a familiar sort of face...

A knock on the door heralded the arrival of The Grass.

'Ma'am, the team are here. Crime scene fully secured. Would you like me to view CCTV footage? Security have just arrived to say it's all available?'

'Yes...' Billie was distracted as she stood up and headed out into the corridor. The Grass followed her past Margaret Craig's door. Luckily, Billie's focus was elsewhere.

'That reminds me, ma'am, about your friend the other night, after the incident in the alleyway.' Billie stopped dead.

'What about her?' Billie asked as she looked at the photo once again.

'Well, we were both in A and E and she had to take her top off and well, ma'am, I'm only saying this because my brother, he used to cut himself too... I think she needs help.'

Billie stared for a beat and then dropped the photo in utter shock. Everything had suddenly become crystal clear. She headed through the door at the end of the corridor and rushed down the stairs, nearly knocking the crime scene manager, Charlie Holden, off his feet.

'Boo printed off the photo sent through from the woman running the food bank.' Charlie waved an A4 photo in his hand. Billie took it from him. Five minutes earlier it would have been a bigger shock. Now it just confirmed her worst suspicions.

26

A TERRIFYING JOURNEY

The unit was on a bleak industrial estate. No expense wasted on kids excluded from mainstream schools. Billie doubted whether those who made such lacklustre design decisions ever stopped to ponder on the terrifying journeys that many of the kids had endured, before ending up here. The Unteachables. Such a sad label to stick on them, Billie couldn't help thinking, as she entered a dingy reception area, smelling of cheap disinfectant and damp clothing. No one was around.

'Hello, Kate?' Billie called, her body tense and alert. Footsteps could be heard from an unseen area beyond an inner door, coming closer. A man, probably around sixty years old, thinning on top but showing taut, well-toned muscles and an air of being able to handle himself in a physical confrontation, appeared through the doorway. He smiled.

'Can I help?' He looked genial enough, but Billie wasn't in the mood for jolly small talk. She flashed her badge.

'I'm looking for Kate,' she announced.

'Haven't got any Kates here, love.' He shrugged. 'The kids come and go, though, so I can look and see when we had the last Kate in. Common name after all.'

Billie mentally kicked herself once again. That's why she had chosen it.

'Staff member. Not one of the kids.' Billie pulled out the photo that Charlie Holden had handed her in the hospital. It was a silly picture of her lodger, surrounded by kids, pulling a face whilst eating a plate of chips. Joy Summers could be seen in the background, cleaning tables. The last photograph of her alive. The man chuckled.

'That's Shannon and the current group, down the food bank, looks like. Loves her chips she does. She's taken the kids out climbing today,' he shook his head good-naturedly, 'eating chips and climbing. That's what our lovely Shannon does best.'

'Good climber yourself, are you...?' Billie looked at the sinewy arm muscles of the man. It had needed more than one killer to hoist Gracie-May to the top of the Angel of the North, to haul Joy Summers onto a wooden cross. She wiped away further horrific scenarios threatening to slice through her mind's eye.

'Pete Burton's the name.' He rubbed his left flank. 'No, total non-starter since I've been on the list for a hip replacement. Been waiting two years now. I leave all the daredevil stuff to Shannon. I'm more of a father figure, counsellor and law enforcer. I tell you what, outdoor pursuits are only the half of it when you're minding youngsters like these. Good for them, though, the fresh air and activities. Some of the kids have never seen a real cow, or open countryside, let alone climbed a mountain before they come to us.' He shook his head sadly.

'Been running this for thirty years now and we do get the odd happy ending out of it. Worth all the aggro.' He chuckled. 'And believe me, there's a lot of aggro with these little tykes. Mind you, Shannon has turned out all right. One of our success stories, she is.'

Pete Burton crossed over the small reception area to a wall

covered in poster-sized photos. He jabbed his finger at one of them.

'There she is, when she had just come into care and we took her on her first outdoor course.' Billie approached, looking carefully. A sullen pre-teenager stood apart from a group of children, who were grinning and pulling silly faces for the photographer.

Billie suddenly felt the room move around her. Now the sensation of being gripped, vice-like, in a stranger's arms. She could see a younger Margaret Craig, desperately crying, trying to wrestle Billie's captor. An older female child was screaming out too. The girl ran forward, attempting to place a teddy bear into Billie's outstretched chubby baby fingers. The blue fluffy toy spiralled to the floor, winking a helpless farewell with its single eye. Next, the terrifying emotion of being rushed away. The recollection faded, just as spontaneously as it had descended. Billie was left in no doubt that it was the harrowing last glimpse of the door being slammed shut on her former life, forever.

The young girl still looked as distraught in the photo as she had done during Billie's recollection, in which she was shouting for Joy Summers to bring Billie back. She steadied herself on the side of the desk, trying to stay calm and remain alert.

'She took to climbing like a duck to water, Shannon,' Pete Burton continued, totally unaware of Billie's traumatic flashback, 'would have been a world beater if she'd had the right start in life. Definitely would have gone down in the history books.' He shook his head. 'Loved free climbing. No ropes, no safety net. A right little daredevil.'

A memory of little Gracie-May McGill swinging in the early morning breeze flashed through Billie's mind's eye. Shannon, because now the detective knew the truth, she couldn't use the name Kate ever again, had played the distraught member of the public, at the murder location. She had even put on a show of trying to revive her. Billie shivered with the recollection.

'She could be a manipulative little minx, mind,' he recalled, 'so cool, she'd put a cucumber to shame. Gave the impression that butter wouldn't melt in her mouth when she was planning mischief.'

'Is that right?' Billie mumbled in encouragement, *tell me about it*, she screamed inside. Though she had felt that she had been taken for a fool on several occasions in the past few days, this revelation wiped everything else off the slate.

'I was in on some of her counselling sessions,' Pete Burton was in full flow now. 'She said her dad would hang all of the kids high up on tree branches, hooks and whatnot if they'd been naughty. Terrified the life out of her. He used to threaten her with a knife. But she trained herself not to fear heights, not to let him see she was petrified. Said it just made him worse. Amazing what some of these poor youngsters have had to put up with. No wonder so many victims become sadists themselves.'

Billie suddenly felt herself go hot. A winding sensation of being slammed up against a wall. The loop of the coat she was wearing hooked on a clothes peg in a hallway, high above a hard, broken-tiled floor. A feeling of terror that she would fall and smash her head open. The terrifying face of a young Geordie Stix, scruffy and cackling with laughter, holding a pair of scissors to her face as tears spilled down her soft baby cheeks. Billie brushed her fingers through her hair, willing herself to shut out the memories tumbling forth. A last image of Geordie Stix hanging high above the River Tyne, suffering a dose of his own cruel medicine, finally calmed her mind.

'Do you know if she free climbed in any local places, Angel of the North for instance?' Billie was relieved that her voice gave away nothing of her feelings. Pete Burton shrugged, chuckling.

'Probably. I got a grant to take the kids away one summer not long after she came into care. She scrambled halfway up The Blackpool Tower, on the outside, with no safety kit as soon as my back was turned. Took a little runt of a kid up on her back too. Strong as an ox she is. Nearly lost my job over that one, I can tell you. She always seemed to get away with laying the blame on someone else.' His voice seemed to hold admiration for Shannon's exploits rather than horror.

'Can you give me a rundown of your own whereabouts over the past week, last night for starters?' Billie wasn't about to join his one-man Shannon fan club. She would be checking out the hip replacement claim too.

'On a flight from Benidorm. All-nighter. Been away with the wife for a fortnight. Shannon said I needed a break and she knew the area. She'd lived out there for a bit. Booked it all up for us as a surprise. Said she'd hold the fort, bless her. We touched down at dawn. No doubt she'll have had her hands full with the little tearaways we've got in now.'

Or a hand-picked supply of willing accomplices, Billie reflected as her mobile rang. Josta's name flashed up. She took the call.

'My dear, I'm so sorry to hear your news,' Josta started, 'but some vital information has emerged, Boo said you are still very much on the case...'

'I'm on the way.' Billie ended the call, heading towards her car. She knew that in the circumstances, Josta would never have called unless the news was urgent.

'Tell her to return the messages I left on her mobile, as soon as she gets back,' Billie instructed. God knows she had left enough calls on the way.

'She's not in any trouble, is she?' Pete Burton followed her. 'What should I tell her?' Billie had already started the engine.

'Tell her Billie's coming to get her,' the detective replied, moving off at speed.

27

WAKE THE DEAD

The door to the morgue slammed against the wall with a crash loud enough to wake the dead, such was the speed at which Billie was moving. At first the examination room appeared empty, despite being brimful with its own distinctive atmosphere and aroma.

There was something else mixed through that fatal fragrance now. Something that she immediately recognised. It was David's expensive eau de parfum. The one that he wore to impress. Billie remembered he had been wearing it in The Turret Room.

Glancing over to the corner of the examination bay, she spotted the shape of a body on a gurney. It was covered in an evidence sheet. As she crossed over, a morgue assistant appeared from a back room. A handsome young man. The thought ran through Billie's head that David might have been attracted to him in life.

'Hey, you can't just come in here!' The young man was clearly yet another new intern. It seemed to be the season for them. Billie held up her hand, brooking no argument as she crossed over to the table. The intern rushed from the room, calling for Josta. The senior forensic pathologist burst through the door a moment later.

'Oh, my dear love. I don't think that's a good idea,' she started.

'It's okay. As you've always said, the deceased body is just an empty house that the owner has vacated. Sometimes they leave it in a mess, that's all.'

Billie ran her finger down over the shape under the sheet. She had no wish to pull it back. Beneath her was her past and the future that she had once taken for granted. Now hacked to death in so many ways. Whatever the truth of their relationship, Billie knew that David didn't deserve to be laid out on a cold, hard slab like this.

'I'll make them pay for this, sweetheart,' she whispered. 'Love you.' It wasn't a lie. She had loved him; occasionally with passion, or annoyance or exasperation, or just like someone she had expected to be around forever. She would always feel guilt that she had shared that information with Kate. There were many sorts of love, Billie reflected. But she guessed that it was Ash who had been David's true soulmate.

Billie kissed her fingertip and brushed the top of the sheet with her hand, in a poignant farewell to her fiancé.

'I've just boiled the kettle in the waiting room,' Billie felt Josta's arm link her own, 'we have some test results. But I fear you may need something stronger than tea, my dear.'

Billie followed Josta out of the examination suite and into a room across the corridor. A painting of a sandy beach fringing a deep blue ocean, hung on one wall. Across from it, a small aquarium held tropical fish. Billie felt a surge of sympathy towards them. Just like her they could only dream of a paradise that would never be theirs.

Josta poured boiling water over powdered coffee and handed

the mug to Billie. The acrid smell wiped out all memories of David's unique aroma.

'I won't beat around the bush, dear. I appreciate time is now of the essence.' Josta took a swig of her own coffee and winced.

'I have been liaising with the forensics team and they've been rushing through samples. There is a DNA link between Gracie-May McGill and Geordie Stix.'

Billie took in the information. If Kate was Shannon, the mother of Gracie-May, Geordie Stix would show up as–

'Father, as well as grandfather. A case of incest, I'm afraid.' Josta took another swig of her mug, whilst checking the notes in her hand. Billie rubbed her face as she absorbed the news.

'It also appears that one of the new interns the chief inspector has drafted in has a special interest in fingerprints. This morning he conducted a particularly in-depth search, including all the usual crime-scene exclusions. Something interesting popped up.'

Billie knew what was coming.

'The young lady who was with you when you found Gracie May; he has unearthed a partial fingerprint from Gracie-May's body that is a match with hers.'

'She was wearing gloves when we recovered Gracie-May.'

Billie pulled out her mobile and found the video footage that she had recorded at the scene. Kate's red leather gloves could be seen in shot as she jumped up to reach one of Gracie's tethers. Billie scrolled forward. She was still wearing them when she had been directed by Billie to sit away from the scene, in a misguided attempt to spare her the full horror. Now Billie understood Ash's frantic gesticulations earlier. Kate must have been wearing the same red gloves in The Turret Room.

Josta raised her eyebrows, taking another gulp of coffee.

'Then she must have touched Gracie-May before you both discovered her. I'm afraid the dead never lie, my dear.'

Billie's phone rang loudly, making her jump. She clicked on the video call. It was Shannon looking upbeat, even jolly.

'Hiya! Charlie said you called by work to pick me up?' Shannon sounded like she didn't have a care in the world.

'Where are you?'

'I'm texting you the address. My brother's just bought a place. I'm there waiting. He's dying to see you.'

Billie flicked the mobile off, taking a swig of her coffee. She had seen the location in the background, knew exactly where to go.

'Billie, surely you're calling for backup?' Josta pleaded, having witnessed the interaction. But Billie was already slamming down her mug. She headed out into the corridor, catching a hint of David's exclusive perfume for one last time. His covered body was being wheeled towards the storage bay. The sensation of pain and fury only added momentum to her movements as she broke into a sprint.

Billie hurled the exit door open, with Josta's ongoing entreaties ringing in her ears. Billie understood the warning and was in absolutely no doubt about the potentially murderous welcome that would be awaiting her. But this was family business, and she had every intention of putting an end to the orgy of murder and mayhem entirely by herself.

28

SEVEN FOR A SECRET NEVER TOLD?

S t Lucia's Nunnery loomed into view in a matter of minutes. Hardly surprising; Billie had been speeding like a scud missile fixed on a deadly target. Had the derelict building *really* been purchased by Shannon's brother? Billie doubted it. The subject had never been mentioned before. Her guess was that the story was a ploy, created to trap her alone in a secluded location. Less messy than an attempt to slaughter her at home.

Billie parked the car outside of the wooded grounds of the nunnery, taking the decision to travel the driveway on foot. As she stealthily approached the huge building, her mobile burst into life. She damned it, reaching to switch the device to silent. The name Glenn Baxter was flashing on the screen. Knowing that if she were to call back, she would be ringing the UCO's death knell, she quickly answered.

'Hi,' she whispered, hunched behind a tree, scanning the building ahead for any signs of a lively welcome awaiting her.

'Called at a bad time?' His own voice was also hushed. Billie got a sudden, crazy, nervous urge to giggle.

'Yep. This is no job for grown-ups.' She had a picture of him similarly hiding from view, risking his own life in order to make contact.

'Gotta make it quick anyway. I just got some new intel on Geordie Stix's nearest and dearest. Listen up...' The information took seconds to impart, before Glenn Baxter abruptly hung up. No request for a dinner date this time. Billie couldn't have responded anyway. She had been momentarily shocked silent at the name just passed to her. Shannon did indeed have a sibling and from her knowledge of the character, Billie knew that they would be a seriously formidable foe.

She moved forward, crossed the gravel drive and stole quickly up the stone stairs to the huge oak door. It was unlocked, the residents already there and awaiting her arrival. Billie took a deep breath. She would need all her strength and wits about her, to ensure that she would get out of the coming reunion alive. She pushed the door open.

Dust hung in the air as Billie crept into the hallway. To the left, through an empty room, she could see a large window overlooking the back garden, where discarded scene-of-crime tape fluttered in the breeze, still caught on the wooden cross where Joy Summers had taken her last bloody breath.

Flicking her head to the right, Billie blinked as she realised for the first time that the small room now in her sights had been the spot where the corrupt social worker had torn her away from Margaret Craig's arms all those years ago. The kidnapper could never have guessed for a moment then, that she too, would face her own dreadful farewell many years later, only a beat away, in that very garden.

Billie heard the smallest of sounds, coming from the floor above. She moved quickly across the hallway, creeping up the wide curving staircase, damning the creaking wooden boards beneath her feet. Suddenly, the sound of footsteps running upwards. Confirmation that her arrival had not gone unnoticed.

She took off in chase, nerves taut, mind alert, keeping close to the winding bannister. 'Shannon!' Billie could feel her heart slamming against her chest as she veered left at the first landing and raced along the corridor. She suddenly caught sight of a fragment of a shape turning at the end. More footsteps could now be heard, racing upwards and then along the floor above her head. She guessed where the chase would finish, having explored the nunnery several times during her childhood acting stint. For a split second the thought came into Billie's mind that it was strange how this location had a pattern of repeating throughout her life. She felt as though she was surrounded by ghosts.

Max Strong's voice suddenly came into her head, as though whispered in her ear, retelling the story of his own childhood drama here at the nunnery. Billie stopped. Stood still for a beat, listening. She could hear blood pounding around her head. Quietly, she turned, then doubled back along the corridor and across the top of the staircase to the opposite wing. The office that had featured in Max's tale, was halfway along.

Billie slipped inside. The old bookcase had long since been emptied and moved away. But the little door was there. Billie carefully tugged it open. A long set of ladders reached up into the darkness. Billie took them quietly but at speed, hearing the haunting children's a cappella version of the magpie counting rhyme, coming from above. '*One for sorrow, Two for joy, Three for a maiden, Four for her boy, Five for silver, Six for gold, Seven for a secret, never to be told.*'

Cautiously, she pulled herself up into the high, ancient brick room housing the bell tower. Keeping to the shadows, she turned to the left, pinning herself to the wall. Scanning around, she slowly started to edge her way along, inch by inch, trying to acclimatise to the dim, suffocating, musty space.

The dark body hit her like a missile, with incredible power, bowling Billie over into the centre of the room. She kicked out, struggling hard, but a punch made contact so forcefully with her face, that her head ricocheted against the cold hard floor. She was stunned for a moment, before opening her eyes just a fraction, enough to now see the carnage facing her.

All around the tower were huge photographs of the recent murder victims. Underneath each one, a line from the ancient magpie rhyme. Billie wanted to vomit when a photo of her parents came into focus. Their gold Mercedes car was pictured smashed to smithereens at the bottom of the cliff where they had met their agonising end. Their shattered, bloodied bodies could be seen hanging half out of the glossy vehicle. Below the terrible tableau, in large black scribbled graffiti, the words, '*six for gold*'. Billie wanted to cry out, feeling a searing pain in her head and in her heart. But instead she remained still. It was a matter of life or death.

'Come down and finish it off! Seven for a secret never to be told – you said.'

The voice wasn't Shannon's. Billie blinked into the darkness, adjusting her narrowed eyes to the dim light coming in from high above, where a platform above the bell was open on three sides. Shannon was standing upon it. Thin slivers of decorative brickwork, on the front corners of the platform, were the only fragile structures between her and the long drop to the ground below. She was still wearing the nurse's garb, without the blonde wig. Her own hair was now blowing wildly in the breeze. The famous fishing knife, just as Josta had described, was in her hand. A large rope noose adorned her neck.

'I can't do it.' She was sobbing. Billie felt a hard kick in her back. The kick of a professional.

'Don't be stupid. She's just caved her head in. Bring the bloody knife down. I've only got this.'

Billie felt the searing pain of a craft knife, sinking into the skin behind her ankle bone. She struggled with all her strength not to shriek out in agony.

'You'll just beat me up like before, when I didn't finish her off in the church.'

A vision of the statue of Christ hurtling towards her, flashed through Billie's mind, followed by the memory of Shannon, bruised and sobbing, before she had led her into that dark alley and a vicious assault.

'You deserved it! See how we nearly got caught down that alleyway? If you'd drugged up the bitch properly in the first place at The Dive Bar, you and your little mates could have snuffed her out early on,' the carver snapped back.

The penny finally dropped, the reason why Billie had felt so inebriated on the single cocktail. She fought a desperate mental battle to ride the pain and hold her position as the carver twisted the knife. She knew now exactly who was holding the weapon, thanking God that Glenn Baxter had given her the name just in time. She tried to steady the shockwaves surging through her body and focus instead on her knowledge on the weakness of the perpetrator.

'She's the whole reason we've had our lives wrecked. Blabbing off to Mummy Dearest...' The craft knife finally stopped moving.

'Well I've just finished that one off MJ,' Shannon argued.

Billie suddenly sprang into life. Lunging forward, she struck her attacker with every ounce of force she could muster. Micky Flannigan flew back against the wall, stunned. Billie jumped up and stamped hard on his bandaged leg, certain that the injury had been caused by their clash in the dark lane, rather than his lame claims about football training.

'Your bloody psycho father raped me when I was four years old!' Billie screamed out with a venom she hadn't known that she was capable of, a lifetime of pent-up emotion erupting from inside of her. It was the truth.

'So? He did that to all of us and you weren't even his kid!' Shannon yelled, turning off the crocodile tears in a beat. 'MJ's right, it was *you* who broke up the family, same as a magpie wrecks nests, swanning off to your perfect life, leaving us to suffer.'

Billie recalled the photo she had looked at in Max's office. The children alongside her on the beach, Shannon and MJ, aka Kate and Micky. Billie felt the blood trickling down her ankle. 'M for *Magpie*...' Billie inwardly gasped.

Micky smirked as he pushed himself up again, moving forward. Picking up his craft knife from the floor, he flicked the blade to full length, confident that he was more than a match for her. 'Yeah, you were never one of us. You just moved in, with that crappy mother you're named after, no matter what stuck-up title you give yourself now. You're just little Maggie Byrd, the magpie–'

'And magpies are all killers and thieves, Dad said.' Shannon joined in the chorus.

'You're right about that,' Billie whispered, taking her one-time chance to whip out the knife she had pocketed from Josta's office and catapult forward, thrusting the fishing blade straight into Mickey's heart. He immediately dropped to the floor. A clean and precise kill.

'Christ almighty! You shouldn't have done that!' Shannon cried, as Billie turned to Gracie-May's huge photo pinned to the wall. It seemed to be silently urging her to finish the job. Shannon followed her stare.

'Why your own baby?' Billie asked, her voice icily cold as she moved in Shannon's direction.

'One for sorrow?' Shannon seemed to switch off any distress over Micky's fate in a beat, turning the pity back to herself. 'That was Dad's fault. You saw how cut up I was. But I could see that she'd turned into a right handful, just like you. Took Dad to see her when he got out. Micky was minding her in the park. Dad said, "She's another magpie, you mark my words, do away with her quick". So we did. It was your Teddy that put her to sleep. She wasn't in any pain or anything. It was me that was hurting.'

Billie closed her eyes for a moment, refusing to let details of little Gracie-May's last moments cloud her focus.

'We could still go away together, backpacking.' Shannon suddenly giggled madly. 'Let's face it, we've got no one left to miss us.' She waved her hand at the huge photos. 'They were the ones that caused us to be apart in the first place. It was all their fault. Even Dad got to be a pain in the end, wouldn't stop pawing me... still he's up there now in bright lights.' Shannon nodded to the photo of Geordie Stix hanging from the crane, the words, '*Four for her Boy*' scrawled underneath.

Billie started to carefully make her way up the narrow and crumbling stone steps attached to the bell tower wall. There was a sheer drop down one side where the huge bell filled the space. One wrong move and she would be over, with nothing to soften her fall, but it was the only route to where Shannon was swaying above, humming the magpie rhyme.

'Time to stop blaming everyone else and face the truth.' Billie's voice was calm as she took each precarious step. Nothing was ever going to stop her getting her prey. Didn't magpies always eject songbirds from their nests in the end?

Shannon stopped singing and suddenly reached behind her. Billie had just a moment to register the flash of yellow, comprehend that Shannon was holding a Taser gun in her hand, when the full force of the shock hit her. She toppled like a dead weight from the steps, banging against the bell before landing on the hard stone floor. Excruciating pain overwhelmed her senses, whilst muscle contractions locked her whole body.

The open dead eyes of Micky Flannigan, only inches from her face, stared straight into hers.

'But it's all *your* fault. You were the magpie who broke up our little nest. You and all the coven up here. I kept giving you chances, but your mummy wouldn't pay and now you're telling me we can't go away together, even though I got rid of dearest David. Five for Silver,' she added, proud of her work.

Billie forced her eyes anywhere but into Micky's. Above, she could see a blown-up selfie of herself, alongside Shannon. They were pulling funny faces. Underneath were the words, *'Seven for a Secret Never Told.'*

Billie managed to twist her body around a little. The Taser crackled and flashed across the room again in response. Billie was hit by another wave of horrific agony, her heart palpitating rapidly with the torture. Shannon appeared totally unmoved by her suffering.

'Nicked this from your copper friend. Hit the jackpot when we finished off those two lover boys. Amazing what people keep in their car boot. Shame we hadn't done him in first, this would have made life a lot easier.' She giggled.

Billie realised Ash must have been so keen to make his date, that he had forgotten to check his police-issue Taser gun back in at base. She damned herself now, for wilfully choosing not to carry one herself. Shannon hit Billie a third time, clearly trigger-happy with her new toy. All claims of friendship now totally forgotten. Billie wasn't sure if she could stand much more pain.

'After getting to know you, like a sister, all over again, I didn't think I could do this. So rather than have MJ kill me, for copping out, I was going to do away with myself.' Shannon waved the noose tied loosely around her neck, chattering away, like she was simply passing time. Billie found it more chilling than the coldest of threats.

'But as you're not going to play ball, it's time to drop that idea, go travelling alone. Perhaps Spain, again. Time to say adios, amigo.' Shannon pointed the fishing knife, still tightly clenched in her other hand, at Billie.

'Police! Drop the Taser or I'll fire!' The Grass emerged through the hatch into the room. Shannon looked startled. 'I mean it. Drop the Taser. Right now.' Shannon moved nervously across the platform. She had nowhere to hide. Finally, she loosened her grip on the taser and let it spin to the floor below, ricocheting off the bell before it landed.

'Okay, ma'am? Josta was worried about you.' The Grass glanced at Billie, all the while keeping her weapon trained on Shannon. Billie nodded, as she attempted to pull herself up to a sitting position.

'Time to face the music, Shannon.' Billie's voice was hoarse, almost a whisper.

'No. Stay back or I'll do it, I'll jump!' Shannon was panicked now. She tightened the noose around her neck and started pacing back and forth like a caged animal.

'No don't!' Billie pleaded. Despite the truth of the situation, her mind was full of conflict as well as pain. Recent memories of the fun times she had shared with her housemate skipped through her head. 'You've been abused too. You can get help,' she begged, though her happy recollections were now interlaced with newly accessed images of Micky and Kate, way back, when they had answered to the names of MJ and Shannon, the quasi-siblings that she had spent her early years with. A momentary wave of terror engulfed her as she recalled the older children taunting her with sharp twigs, whilst Geordie Stix laughed cruelly, having hung her by her coat hood treacherously high on a tree branch.

'Go for it,' The Grass spoke evenly, her weapon still pointing at Shannon. 'The hell you're going to face in the slammer is going to be even worse than the one heading your way if you take the leap of faith. A female who kills her own child, her dad, three old women... don't go planning to take any showers alone...' The Grass shook her head, as though in dismay.

'Tell her to shut her face!' Shannon pleaded with Billie.

'Come down, Shannon.' Billie shook her still-addled head. Was The Grass coercing her to jump?

'...that's if you make it to prison. Soon as we take you in, the nightmare begins. Police don't take kindly to anyone who kills one of their own...' Billie thought of her dad, '...you know it's true, ma'am.' The Grass was undoubtedly thinking of her brother.

Billie never really knew whether Shannon slipped or jumped in that instant, though in her heart, she guessed the truth. All that she was suddenly aware of was her former housemate's body taking flight from her high platform, jerking madly through the air in a terrible murderous jig before finally slowing down, swaying back and forth on the rope, banging against the huge bell in a solemn final death toll.

The Grass crouched on the floor, dropping her weapon next to Billie as she checked Micky's pulse. Billie already knew he wouldn't have one. She blinked hard. Was she imagining things?

'That's not a real gun.' Billie finally found her voice. She looked from the weapon to The Grass.

'Confiscated it from a kid down the street,' The Grass replied. 'It had me worried for a minute. No wonder sprogs grow into killers when parents give them toys like this.' Billie didn't know whether to laugh or cry. The Grass glanced up at the horrific image of Shannon, still softly banging against the bell.

'You'll have to write up a report. Explain what happened.' Billie couldn't even contemplate the idea. She didn't know how on earth she would begin or end it.

'I know I didn't follow correct procedure, ma'am. I'll quite understand if you take the decision to grass me up.'

29

SEX AND DRUGS AND ROCK AND ROLL

It was a crazy day right from the start, the day that Billie Wilde finally reclaimed her history and laid the past to rest. Margaret Craig's tragically premature burial place was bedecked in a sea of magnificent white lilies, hugged by stems of rosemary, in a fragrant vow of remembrance. Billie would never forget, but she had finally learned to forgive, to free herself to live in the present. Not that it had been an easy journey.

The daylight was dying, the sky now streaked with the rose-pink hue of a healing wound. *Red sky at night, sailors' delight.* The rhyme skipped through Billie's head. Memories of Max Strong having turned up at her door unexpectedly, made her heart rock, as though caught on a wave.

'Beautiful.' Billie thought he was talking about the view from the garden, though his eyes never left hers. She had moved into Margaret Craig's former home that morning. It was now her own, complete with a stunning view over the Alnmouth estuary. It felt good to have finally escaped from the houses of deception she had always inhabited.

The Chief had visited first thing, further lifting her spirits by confirming that she could return to work. He'd also given in to her pleas to stay as SIO on the MIT team, conceding that with Billie's record, she would definitely have created merry havoc with the IT system if she had taken the responsibility that came with the current deputy chief's vacancy.

'It's a beautiful headstone.' Max had accompanied Billie here to the churchyard to see the new addition to Margaret Craig's grave, cut in purest white Carrara marble. A photo of Billie as a baby on her mother's knee adorned the centre. An engraving lay below.

Margaret, beloved mother of Maggie (Billie)
Keeping you close, in my heart, forever.

Max's mobile suddenly rang. He quickly reached for it, mouthing the word 'sorry' as he stepped away. Billie smiled. He was a busy man. She was looking forward to being busy herself once again, with all the ups and downs that her job entailed, including taking urgent calls at awkward moments.

She reached for a tiny posy of daisies, making her way to the very edge of the churchyard. Here another memorial stood, a sculpture of two small children holding hands. The boy had a ball tucked under his arm, the girl a teddy bear. They appeared to be skipping through a sea of wild blue forget-me-nots. Billie laid down her posy at their tiny feet.

Perhaps incongruously, to a random passer-by, the children were facing away from the rest of the graves. Billie had chosen this spot especially. It overlooked a playground, lapped by toe-tickling waves, golden sand and bright bobbing boats.

The body of Gracie-May McGill was buried here. Billie hoped that in spirit at least, the tiny angel could at last access the simple pleasures that all children dream of. The sculpture was also an act of remembrance, to the many other tiny souls lost.

Their futures destroyed because of the actions of mad, bad or sad adults.

After much soul-searching, Billie had purposely alluded to Micky and Shannon in her tribute. She had arrived at the conclusion that no child was born harbouring a dream of becoming a failure, a jailbird or a killer. Their chances of winning or losing in this crazy game of life, largely fell to the family that they had been dealt at the start. In truth, she had picked up a hand luckier than so many. As Billie moved away, she noticed another funeral cortège approaching. The large gathering followed an elaborate glass carriage pulled by magnificent black horses, plumes bedecking their proud heads. A funeral director, dapper in top hat and tails, holding a cane in his hand, headed up the procession.

Billie stepped to one side, bowing her head in a show of respect as the group came alongside her. Glancing up, she now noticed the name '*Jesus*' created in bright flowers flanking the coffin within the carriage. Billie tucked her head down further, grateful that she had her hoodie pulled up and was dressed-down in jeans.

She was in no doubt that this was the funeral of the recently deceased gangland leader Jesus O'Brian. Gossipy visits from Boo during Billie's leave of absence, had revealed that this Godfather had probably been taken out by a rival. He hadn't operated on her patch luckily, but she still didn't want any overlapping lowlifes spotting her off duty.

Head still down, Billie started to move away as the cortège finally passed, almost colliding with one of the stragglers bringing up the rear of the procession. With a start, she found herself looking straight into the eyes of Glenn Baxter.

'You trying to tap me up, love?' He said the words loudly. The two men alongside him laughed.

'Think she fancies you, Glenn,' one wag joined in.

'That right? Whisper your number, Princess,' he invited, bending close to her ear, 'and I'll give you a call.' He stepped back, holding her gaze for a split second before she pushed on by. She had to admire his sheer bloody bravery.

'I'd better watch out; she looks like a boyfriend basher that one!' He played to the crowd as they continued towards the graveside. She concealed a smile of her own. She still hadn't had a chance to thank him for his heads up on Micky Flannigan. That bit of info had probably been a lifesaver.

Max joined her. 'Everything okay?' He frowned in the direction of the cortège, now stopping at a family vault in the most scenic side of the cemetery.

'Fine.' Billie smiled. She realised that for once everything did feel bright in her life. He touched her shoulder as they walked out of the gates to the churchyard. She shivered as they came to a halt beside their cars.

'So, if you need anything...' Max caught her hand for a moment.

'Yep, call the old battleaxe,' Billie joked. In truth Dr Jill Adams had turned out to be a guiding light, as Billie had fought to put the fragments of her darkly shattered soul back together again. 'Good job you dumped me.' She mock-punched his arm.

Max's eyes flashed, as though he had been about to offer a different solution. Billie knew that she wanted to move forward too. She returned his gentle grip on her hand.

'Max...' she started, before his phone rang once more. He looked as though he was going to ignore it for a moment before he finally broke free and answered.

'Yes...' His dark eyes suddenly looked troubled. 'Okay. I'll be there in ten.' He sighed, glancing at Billie.

'Blues and twos?' Billie asked, her heart sinking.

''Fraid so,' he answered, taking a step backwards.

'Okay. Bye then. See you around.' Billie fumbled for her car keys, rushing away up the street, suddenly flustered. *She'd almost made a fool of herself again, about to ask him... what? To come back and see her scene-of-crime etchings?* She jumped into her car, head down, pretending to busy herself with her bag on the passenger seat.

'Billie?' Max had stopped, taken a few steps forward, but Billie, engulfed in embarrassment, hadn't heard him call her name. Her own mobile was now ringing loud and clear. It was her work theme tune. She fumbled in her bag, hurling items out in her search for the device. She'd never been more pleased to hear it.

'Boo?' Billie pushed her hoodie back, running her fingers through her hair.

'News hot off the press. Our friendly neighbourhood criminal kingpin Christy Callaghan has just been parted from his wallet,' Boo exclaimed.

'Funny, I'm just watching Jesus O'Brian's final goodbye.' Billie could see the coffin being interned across the graveyard as she spoke.

'Sorry you can't make the last supper then, ma'am. Chief said you're back on the job.'

'On my way. Where's the body?' Billie hurled the car key in the ignition.

'Good question. So far, we've just got his head, surrounded by a nice array of crudities sitting on one of those sharing platters at his strip club. Better get ready for sex and drugs and rock and roll.'

'With an offer like that, how could I refuse?' Billie slammed the car into gear and raced off like a bat out of hell, not even looking into her back mirror. If she had, she would have caught Max Strong heading at pace towards her. Instead, she was hurtling towards arguably the greatest passion of her life, the true love branded deeply and darkly inside her DNA – murder.

THE END

ACKNOWLEDGEMENTS

It was while I was attending a live rendition of The Unthanks' haunting *Magpie* song, that the idea for this story came to me. Listen to it here and feel shivers run down your spine: https://www.youtube.com/watch?v=_fPbWEaɪcyg. I played this endlessly throughout the writing process, so a huge thank you to The Unthanks for giving me such inspiration.

Another thanks to big sis Denise Howe, who was sitting next to me at the time and whispered, 'You'll have to have seven murders, in that case.' There have been a few Paddington-style hard stares in her direction since, as I set off on a crazy writing journey to bring her observation to life – or as it turned out, many deaths.

The resulting story was shortlisted for the Lindisfarne Prize for Outstanding Debut Crime Fiction, sponsored by best-selling author L J Ross. Without her backing of the prize and encouragement of new writers, then you wouldn't be reading this today, so a big round of applause to her.

Bloodhound Books, my publishers, have turned out to be the dream team, with Fred and Betsy Reavley at the helm. They have created a hugely professional business whilst being enormously kind and absolutely calm throughout the publishing process. A special thanks to my editor Ian Skewis, for his attention to detail and ability to make me laugh at his insights and Tara Lyons, always patient in the face of so many questions!

A special thank you to my good friends Maggie and Craig Weir who loaned me their names, and my hero Daryn Robinson, for showing me that challenges are simply there to be overcome. Also, to Russell who forced me to read to him so often as a child that when I ran out of books, I had no choice but to start creating new stories of my own.

Last but very much not least, my biggest thanks to my husband, Bob Whittaker, who has heard me talk about this story so many times he probably knows the characters as well as I do. As a result, his thoughts may have turned to murder nearly as often as mine have. His endless patience, support and encouragement mean absolutely everything and have allowed me to finally follow my dream.

If you'd like to contact me, I would love to hear from readers.
Facebook: Marrisse Whittaker Author
Twitter: @MarrisseWhitt
Instagram: MarrisseWhittakerAuthor

A NOTE FROM THE PUBLISHER

Thank you for reading this book. If you enjoyed it please do consider leaving a review on Amazon to help others find it too.

We hate typos. All of our books have been rigorously edited and proofread, but sometimes mistakes do slip through. If you have spotted a typo, please do let us know and we can get it amended within hours.

info@bloodhoundbooks.com

Made in the USA
Las Vegas, NV
29 May 2021

23849178R00163